C000081427

1952 Eliz

67
877
7
1586–1647
1824–81
1817–

30
)
55–

723

THEODORE ODRACH

THE VILLAGE TEACHER AND OTHER STORIES

Translated from the Ukrainian by Erma Odrach

GLAGOSLAV PUBLICATIONS

CONTENTS

A FEW WORDS
FROM THE TRANSLATOR

My father died when I was nine years old. I never really knew him and most of what I remember is observational. I recall him hugging me, taking me to the park but I don't recall exchanging words with him, though of course I did. He was an enigmatic figure, always in the shadows, always with his head in the clouds. I never understood him, and he seemed so unfamiliar, so distant. He was a complicated man, too complicated for a young child's mind. As irrational as it all was, in many ways he frightened me. My father agonized over my view of him, and no matter how hard he tried to fix it, there was no fixing it. And yet, in spite of it all, I came to learn later into my adult life he somehow knew I would one day translate his work.

Born in the heart of the Pinsk Marshes in Belarus, one of the largest marshlands in Europe, my father was a true fisherman – it was in his blood. From our Toronto home, at every opportunity, he would disappear to a lake somewhere, or a river, or his favorite spot on the Toronto Islands. At the Islands he would often stay all night. On many occasions, with my mother and sister, we would take the streetcar to the docks and catch the early morning ferry to meet him. My father's love of fishing went beyond fishing and one day he announced to us he wanted to start a worm farm. Thanks to my mother, that never happened.

When I began translating my father's work, it was then I came to realize how inextricably connected his fishing was to his writing. To be out in a peaceful and quiet setting, in the open with nature, was the perfect way for him to escape reality and focus on his stories. Fishing allowed for reflection and meditation and gave him much-needed piece of mind. But that's not to say he didn't catch fish. Quite the contrary, our fridge and freezer were always stocked with trout, carp, bass, perch – every freshwater fish imaginable.

In the evenings, when my father came home from work, which was at a local printing shop, the most prominent sound in our house was that of his typewriter. It was a thirty-five-pound cast iron Olympia, which he brought with him after living in England for five years. The tapping of the keys often put me to sleep. I was always keen to know if his stories had happy endings. I don't know if I ever got an answer but there always came a smile.

When my father died it was a horrible day and I thought I was dreaming. But I wasn't dreaming, it was all very real. His office stood empty, there was no one at his desk, and the sound of the typewriter was gone. On a bookshelf by the window on the top was a line of books written in Cyrillic, published in such places as Buenos Aires, Toronto and New York. Some were hard-cover, some were soft and they all had my father's name on them. So many books. I wondered what was in them. I had only a vague idea.

THEODORE ODRACH

Years passed, almost twenty. I kept thinking about my father's books still up on the shelf of our bookcase. Though I was familiar with the Cyrillic alphabet and knew the Ukrainian language, reading and understanding Ukrainian on a literary level was a completely different matter. My father's books were virtually incomprehensible to me. Then one day I became determined to learn about his world. Armed with a Ukrainian-English dictionary, I started the laborious task of decoding my father's words. When I got stuck, I reverted to my mother, who, luckily for me, knew my father's work well, as he had read her all his manuscripts. But my mother was German and could sometimes explain only in German. So, in many instances the common route for us was from Ukrainian to German to English.

Once the transcribing was finished, I found myself completely absorbed. A turbulent time in history was laid out before me – the Second World War. There were real people living in the pages, there was conflict, and bombs were going off from all sides. My father was as much an eyewitness as he was an author.

But the question remained, would I be able to put it all into English and honor the original? I wasn't a translator and I'd never translated anything before. Then I began to play around with words. I paid attention to style, I listened for tone, for cadence, I kept an eye on pace. And suddenly it occurred to me: if I could capture my father's voice and keep myself invisible, I could do it.

Soon came another question: was there an audience out there for a deceased Ukrainian author from Belarus, immigrant to Canada, whose work was now in translation? In all honesty, I had my doubts. Nevertheless, I continued to translate. As a sort of test-run, I started sending stories and novel excerpts out to literary magazines. Happily, before long, these pieces began getting accepted in both Canada and the U.S. *Connecticut Review, Antigonish Review, The New Quarterly* to name a few. Later came a story in *The Penguin Book of Christmas Stories*, then the publication of *Wave of Terror,* Chicago Review Press, and now *The Village Teacher* by Glagoslav Publications, and not to forget, an honorable mention from the Translation Center at Columbia University.

In translating my father, I've worked closely with his published work as well as with his original corresponding drafts and manuscripts, which, for the most part, contained multiple corrections and revisions. Sometimes my father had several versions of one story. I chose to use certain versions and passages I felt would provide a broader and more comprehensive representation of his work.

I learned a lot about my father – that he had a humorous side, that he was thoughtful, insightful, that he had a sense of civility and humaneness. Had it not been for translation, I would never have known.

ACKNOWLEDGEMENTS

I would like to express a heartfelt thanks to the people who helped me in the translation of these stories. My mother, Klara, who was the voice of my father and my savior; my husband, Michael, who displayed unwavering devotion to my father's work, whose discerning observations and impressions were very much appreciated, whose tech help was indispensable; Jane Wilson who spent long hours reading my drafts and offering me her clear and insightful criticisms and comments; Claire who gave invaluable support and last-minute advice; Tanya who challenged me and shared her unique perspectives.

*This translation is in memory
of my mother and father*

WITNESS

They were walking along a green path up into the blue horizon and day in and day out Grandfather Korny watched
after them; he could not seem to get enough. His grandchildren were up front: Prohor, Danilo, Anna, and behind them
his son Yevhen with his wife. The path was narrow and like
a scroll of cotton, it meandered upward, then disappeared
into the blue sky. They continued to walk along the path that
seemed to have no end.

Grandfather Korny shouted out to them.

"Stop! Please stop! Let me get a better look at you. You're
so frail, and why are you in such a hurry? Is the way to
Heaven so far?"

But the drifters did not stop; they remained unrespon-
sive. The old man began to call them out by name: "Yevhen,
my son, Sonia, my daughter-in-law, my grandchildren,
Anna, Prohor, Danilo, stop!"

Still, the drifters did not respond. They walked in a zig-
zag between the faint clouds that floated across the sky, toward a large bend. And every time the old man saw them in
his fantasy they were always hurrying upon the same path.

"What an endless road before you, my dear children," the
old man clasped his chest.

Fifteen years had already passed since they had left Grandfather Korny, and for all that time he carried their faces in his heart. They had swollen, cracked mouths with open red sores on their cheeks. Death peered through their sunken eyes. At first, their coughing was dry and faint, later it intensified and they began to choke, then the blood started, and finally death. One after the other, within a year, they all left Grandfather Korny, except Orest, the youngest.

At times Grandfather Korny cursed his health, "If only I could have a heart attack and be freed. It's time for me to catch up to my children."

But the old man's heart was strong. As he watched his family walk along the green path, suddenly he realized they were dead. They no longer had faces, only silhouettes. He recognized them by the way they walked. Yevhen held Sonia's hand, Anna was up front, and behind Anna shoulder to shoulder, walked the boys, Prohor and Danilo. The old man watched them for a long time and wept.

"They're so quiet. The boys were always very playful and Anna was such a chatterbox. Now they're just walking and they don't say a word."

When their image disappeared from the old man's mind, he made the sign of the cross and stepped up to a slender aspen that grew in his backyard behind the well.

"I planted this tree," he began to himself, "in my yard as witness to my grief. One day I walked to the edge of the village, to the coppice, and thought to myself, which tree should I transplant? An alder is much too ordinary and a birch too hefty. Then I noticed a slender aspen leaning up against a cranberry bush. The leaves rustled magically and seemed to whisper, 'Old man, take me to your yard.' So, I took the aspen and now look what a beauty it's become, it's blossomed like a young girl. It keeps soaring upward and I keep digging my feet deeper into the ground."

From next door a couple of men hopped over the fence and entered the yard; one was in army uniform, the other, dressed like a peasant. Catching sight of the old man, they made toward him.

Ignoring them, Korny started talking to his aspen, "Two years have barely passed, and look what's already happened. Like worms, they bore into your flesh and there's no escape."

"Hello, old man!" a pair of steely blue eyes peered from under a helmet. It was Deputy Julikov of the Pinsk Division. He asked impatiently, "Well, old man, when do you plan to pay your taxes?"

Korny looked up, "There's nothing to pay them with, Comrade. There's hardly enough to eat." Then back to his aspen, "Hah, isn't that the truth? And you are my witness."

The man in peasant clothes, whose name was Sopun and who also happened to be the village chairman, hastened to apologize on the old man's behalf.

"Comrade Julikov, as you can see, the old man's not quite right in the head. There's no point in talking to him."

Julikov laughed, "Don't worry, I've seen his kind before!" Then to the old man, "Tell me, why didn't your grandson go out into the woods and haul logs with the rest of them?"

Ignoring the question, looking up at the shimmering young leaves of his aspen, Korny said:

"You see how they torment the aged, my little aspen? And when the Reds were fleeing from Warsaw, I saved the life of one of their soldiers. I covered him with hay in a barn. The Poles poked around with their bayonets but couldn't find him anywhere. And when they threw me up against the wall and threatened to shoot me, I didn't care, because I was happy to have saved a human life."

"We know all your little tricks, old man," said Julikov with a rush of anger. "Where's your grandson?"

"I don't know; I don't follow him around. He's young and always on the go; he has his own roads."

At once, Korny turned to look up at the sky. He shouted, "You're off again my dead ones! But Anna, your feet must hurt. You're so little. Yevhen, take her in your arms! Our Father who art in Heaven ... Dear God, give them eternal shelter."

"Idiot!" Julikov spat between his feet. "We're not through with you yet, old man – not by a long shot."

"He's senile, comrade," Sopun tried to explain. "He always babbles like that to his son and grandchildren. They all died of consumption years ago."

Julikov hardly listened. He signaled with his head for Sopun to follow him into the old man's house. Once inside they searched for the grandson. They looked in closets, under the beds, behind the stove, but he was nowhere to be found.

"The son-of-a-bitch!" yelled Julikov. "He thinks he can fool us!"

"But the old man's confused, Comrade," Sopun pointed out again. Following Julikov out into the yard, he couldn't help but say to himself but in such a way Julikov couldn't hear, "Confused, yes, just like the rest of us."

THEODORE ODRACH

Julikov swung round and drilled his eyes into Sopun. "I heard what you just said. You may be village chairman but you're a complete idiot."

Later that day a car appeared from the direction of Pinsk. It let out a series of honks. For some reason, it turned toward Grandfather Korny's house and stopped before the gates of his yard. Two officials in black leather jackets and steel helmets stepped out. Julikov and Sopun, who happened to be there, rushed to greet them. They stood at attention and saluted.

"Does Kornelius Pavlovich Kovb live here?" asked the shorter of the two.

"Over there, Comrade," pointed Julikov. "He's sitting under that tree."

Without another word, the officials turned toward the aspen. Julikov and Sopun followed close behind.

"Hello, old man," the officials called out.

Korny ignored them and proceeded to talk to the aspen, "How the boys liked to swing from your branches. And little Anna would lift her pretty little head and laugh and laugh."

"Er, excuse me, Comrades," Sopun took it upon himself to address the officials. "You must understand, the old man has hallucinations. He's not quite right in the head."

"Not quite right in the head? Well, we'll see about that! And who are you?"

"My name is Sopun, I'm the village chairman."

The shorter official glimpsed quickly at his watch. He said in a matter-of-fact tone, "Very well, Sopun. Call a meeting in front of the gates of Kornelius Pavlovich Kovb's house. In half an hour. We have a very urgent matter to address."

Sopun jumped at the command, and as fast as his legs could carry him, made for the village.

"And why are you still here?" the officials turned irritably to Julikov. "Don't you have work to do?"

Julikov wrung his hands and for some reason he looked excited and his face was all red. As it turned out, he had just seen something behind Korny's house, and it looked like a young man. He believed it might be Korny's grandson. He needed to tell the officials.

"Sirs, I have to tell you something. Over there, just right now, behind the house, I saw old man Korny's grandson, the one you've been ..."

But the officials were preoccupied with their own matters and hardly listened to what Julikov had to say. They cut him off abruptly.

"Enough of your empty talk. There's no time to waste. The meeting's in half an hour. You can tell us later."

Under Sopun's orders, ten peasants scattered throughout the village. They banged on doors and windows and shouted out to passersby, "Listen up, people! There's an important meeting out in the pasture! Officials from Pinsk have arrived!"

The bells from the little Orthodox church began to chime and drums started to beat. From all ends of the village people emerged and streamed toward the pasture. A table decked with a white embroidered cloth was set under the open sky and around the table were benches and chairs. Red banners with hammers and sickles were suspended from high wooden poles on either side and everywhere were picture-posters of Stalin. In the middle of the table sat the two

THEODORE ODRACH

officials and between them, to everyone's amazement, was Grandfather Korny. But Grandfather Korny looked numb and dazed as if he didn't understand what was going on. A crowd of people elbowed forward to get a better look; those who were at the back stood on tiptoe. All were eager to find out why an emergency meeting had been called.

"Why on earth did they sit that poor old man between those two wolves in helmets?" The people wanted to know.

"Comrades!" the shorter official rose from the table and pierced his gaze into the crowd. "Be proud. Your village will go down in the history of the Soviet Union – and in gold letters. This old man here, Kornelius Pavlovich Kovb, has become the first to be honored in the western region of the U.S.S.R. His name will become the symbol of the endless devotion to our socialist Fatherland. Allow me to explain: when our glorious Red Army was cold and hungry and forced out of Warsaw, this old man did not lose faith. At a most critical moment, he risked sacrificing himself to save the life of one of our soldiers."

Turning to Korny, he smiled warmly and courteously, "Comrades, do you realize whose life he saved? Korny Pavlovich Kovb saved the life of our national hero, General Pipigin!"

Pulling a crumpled piece of paper from his jacket pocket, he proceeded to read out loud: "Eternal gratitude to Kornelius Pavlovich Kovb, signed, I.C. Pipigin, General of the Western Division."

"Bravo, Korny, bravo!" Julikov's voice suddenly surged throughout the crowd.

"Bravo!" the villagers joined in. Then barely a minute passed and their voices began to wane. Many started scratching their heads and shrugging. They didn't quite understand what was going on.

The official then poked his head inside his satchel and pulled out a gold medal tied to a silk ribbon. It was a Vladimir Lenin medal, beloved founder of the Russian Communist Party. Grandfather Korny was asked to stand up. Staring out into the crowd, the medal was pinned to his chest. After a short while, both officials shook his hand. The taller of the two spoke to the crowd:

"What an honor for Kornelius Kovb! Our dear Comrade Joseph Vissarionovich Stalin, leader of the greatest proletarian movement the world has ever seen, gave us a strict order, 'Bring Kornelius Pavlovich Kovb to Moscow. I want to meet him.'" Then with his face filling with emotion, looking as if about to tear up, he ended, "Yes, the Supreme Soviet wants to honor you, Korny Pavlovich, personally in the Kremlin."

"Bravo!" shouted Julikov again.

"Bravo!" repeated the crowd.

A big black car parked by the gates gave a loud honk. Somewhere from the crowd, a drum began to beat and soon after it was joined by the sound of mandolins. The officials took the old man by the arm, escorted him to the car, and placed him in the back seat by the window. The motor started up and made in the direction of Pinsk. The musicians accompanied them a short distance. Villagers waved their hands until the car disappeared from sight.

* * *

Grandfather Korny dressed in his Sunday best sat quietly in the big black car. Lenin's medal shone brilliantly on his chest. In the front seat next to the driver sat a superior officer by the name of Shelugin. Shelugin hardly moved a muscle and his eyes were cold as ice.

"Tomorrow morning, old man," Shelugin smiled, "you will take the train to Moscow, first class, of course. In the Kremlin, you will have the honor of meeting Stalin. And Pipigin is flying in from Siberia just to see you."

There was mockery on Shelugin's voice but the old man didn't notice.

"What are you going to tell Stalin, old man?"

"What is there to say?" Korny shrugged then looked straight at Shelugin. "You know, you have evil eyes."

Shelugin winced slightly; he continued to badger the old man, "I want to know what you plan to tell Stalin?"

Korny became restless in his movements. He said quietly but with conviction, "Comrade Stalin probably doesn't know what an evil man Julikov is. He forces people to sign up for the *kolkhoz* and sends my grandson to labor in the woods for hours on end. Many of our men have dropped dead from overwork. Innocent villagers – men, women, and children – are being loaded up into boxcars like cattle and sent to the ends of the earth, to forced labor camps in Archangel by the White Sea. And the priest, what do you think Julikov did with him? He took possession of his house and turned it into government offices. The priest is now dead. And why are we being tormented with such high taxes?"

Shelugin pursed his lips. He didn't even try to hide his agitation. After a moment he offered the old man a Makhorka cigarette.

"What you say is very smart, old man. In fact, it all makes perfect sense. Don't forget to tell Stalin everything. He is a very kind and understanding man and will punish all those who do evil. Is there anything else on your mind?"

Grandfather Korny thought a moment, then leaning toward the window, shouted up at the sky: "There you are, my dear ones, you're already at the bend! Yevhen, can't you see little Anna is exhausted? Carry her in your arms, please!"

At once the open fields spread out as far as the eye could see and the air became full of buzzing insects. The car came to a screeching halt and the back door was flung open. But the car was still only halfway to Pinsk. A stout and balding man in NKVD uniform was standing by the roadside as if expecting them. With a Tokarev pistol in hand, he made toward the car. Grabbing Korny by the arm, he shouted:

"Get out, old man."

Grandfather Korny did not resist.

Pushing Korny toward a ditch, he then rammed his pistol into the old man's head. He pulled the trigger. The old man fell to the ground, dead.

Shelugin watched and he couldn't stop laughing. "Hey, Korny," he shouted, "don't forget to tell Comrade Stalin everything. Hah, hah, hah!"

The car started up and didn't stop until it reached Pinsk.

* * *

THEODORE ODRACH

German warplanes roared over Pinsk and the surrounding villages. From time to time, gunfire sounded and bomb explosions shook the earth. The entire region was under German attack and Russian soldiers started to panic and flee along the main road. Shooting intensified and huge balls of light shot up into the sky.

On a little hill in a nearby village not far from Pinsk stood a young man quietly looking down to where his grandfather's farmstead used to be. His feet were fixed to the ground, and for the longest time, he stared at something hanging from the aspen tree. He released a barely discernable smile, then swung around and disappeared behind a wall of trees.

The villagers stormed out of their houses to watch the German planes fly at high speeds across the sky. In order to get a better look at the road where the Bolshevik troops were fleeing, a young woman ran all the way to Grandfather Korny's yard. She quickly scanned the spot where his house used to stand: his land, a couple of months ago had been appropriated by the state and turned into a *kolkhoz*. Heaving a bitter sigh, swinging around, her eye caught sight of the little aspen tree. Suddenly her face turned a ghost white. Racing back to the village, she screamed:

"A hanged man, a hanged man! Help!"

It was not long before a group of villagers appeared before the slender aspen that grew behind the well. They shook their heads curiously as they watched the hanged man swing on the largest of the limbs. They recognized the insignia and uniform almost instantly. It was Deputy Julikov.

"Would you look at that," someone remarked, "such a small tree and the limb held out just fine."

WHISTLE STOP

A shack built from narrow, unpeeled logs, a storage building from old wooden planks, to the left a cowshed, and beyond the cowshed vast fields of mud. An old weather-beaten sign hung over the shack door: STEBLY STATION. Before the war, this little train station had been abandoned and would have made the ideal hermitage but now everything was changed. Tracks shot in a straight line eastward, past Sarny, to Kyiv. The front had already extended beyond Kharkiv and trainloads of German troops pushed endlessly in this direction.

Kurt Kleist, a potbellied man of late middle age, was stationed in Stebly but had little to do to pass the time of day. The trains never stopped here and when they passed by, his assistant, the local peasant, Kirilo Borozn, attended to the semaphores. So, day in and day out Kurt Kleist sat in his office and yawned from boredom. The solitary life in a foreign land did not appeal to him. When he became nostalgic, he phoned his good friend, Heinz Ziggy, a construction worker stationed in Kovel.

"Hello, Heinz, is that you?"

"It's me. Are you thinking about Berlin again?"

"I miss it terribly and I'm bored to death."

"You are an odd one, Kurt," Heinz reproached his friend. "You have nothing to fear from silence. Remember how every Saturday we used to drive out of Siemensstadt, past Potsdam, out to the country? The woods, the lakes – remember how quiet it was? You don't know how good you have it out there, my friend."

"It was different then and it's different now."

After this short discussion, they joked and kidded each other.

"Hey, you haven't forgotten about your garden and your barn, have you? And what about Gretchen?"

"Leave Gretchen out of this, will you, Kurt? Poor Gretchen, who's looking after her now? She really liked all that juicy grass I used to bring down from Hazelhorst. My wife's too lazy to chop it up for her; she never really cared for Gretchen much."

"Heinz, I've got an idea. Try to get a transfer and come here; we could keep each other company. There's a cowshed out back and you could even keep a couple of goats. I know how crazy you are for those goats of yours." Kleist began to imitate the sound of a goat, and then let out a loud laugh, "You get transferred here and you can keep a thousand goats!"

"*Herr Gott!*" Heinz was impressed.

And on this note, the conversation ended.

The front continued to push into the USSR. Day in and day out trains filled with soldiers headed east. They passed the little station carrying powerful cannons and zenithals, their muzzles directed toward the sky. Young German men, under the sign of the Swastika, were determined to conquer the boundless regions of the Soviet Union.

One day, quite unexpectedly, a train stopped at Stebly Station; a few army officials stepped down from the last car. They barely acknowledged Kleist and began to examine the surroundings. They carefully looked through their binoculars and measured the vast mudlands, now partially frozen over, that stretched north of the tracks.

"There are going to be changes," thought Kleist restlessly, as the army officials set off in the direction of Sarny. "If Stebly is going to become an army base, then they'll probably find a commander and chase me off."

Walking up to a peasant, who was repairing something behind the cowshed, he uttered in a worried tone, "There are going to be changes, Kirilo."

But the peasant looked confused; he shrugged his broad shoulders and said, "*Nicht verstehe.*"

He didn't understand German.

"They're going to chase me off," grumbled Kleist angrily to himself, "they're going to chase me off and he *nicht verstehe!*"

And he didn't realize that in his tone there was a touch of regret. Was it possible he had got used to this silence after all? Perhaps Heinz was right, perhaps silence was a man's best friend, especially in these troubled times of warplanes and bloodshed. Most people would give anything to be in his place.

One evening another train stopped at the station, at the end of which was a trailer filled with bricks. Aided by some peasants sent over by the Stebly village chairman, Kleist began to unload. They were piled up on a cleared stretch of land to the right of the cowshed. Within three

THEODORE ODRACH

days another four trailers appeared carrying more bricks and other building materials such as flat crates of glass, tightly wrapped parcels of aluminum, and sacks of cement, all of which were piled up and covered with canvas.

"I bet this is going to be an army post," Kleist repeated to himself for the hundredth time.

Every day he nervously awaited the arrival of some new commander and construction workers. But no one appeared. The trains no longer stopped. Three weeks had gone by and he was anxious. He phoned his superiors in Kovel to inquire about their plans for Stebly but their answer was abrupt; they pointed out that they were well aware of the situation, that this was strictly a military affair, and that Kurt Kleist ought not to question the authority of the army.

Kleist remained on the alert and expected the worst.

One morning a motor car approached the little station from the direction of Kovel. Kleist waited anxiously on the platform and thought to himself, "Maybe now they will tell me what's going on."

In the distance, he could already see the vague outline of four men, and when the motor just barely came to a halt before the office door, among them, he recognized his old friend, Heinz Ziggy, who was waving. Heinz was the first to disembark, pulling out an overstuffed rucksack behind him.

"Well, well, here we are, my good friend, we're together after all," Heinz laughed and then punched his friend playfully in the arm. "It seems you've gotten fat, heh, Kurt? This Ukrainian grub is pushing you out in all directions."

One of the soldiers rolled down the window of the car, pulled out a sealed envelope from his jacket pocket, and handed it to Kleist.

"A letter!" exclaimed Kleist and tore it open. It was from his wife. She wrote nonchalantly about her domestic affairs and then began to complain about the shortage of food supplies. She asked her husband why he didn't send her parcels; her acquaintances received at least three a week from their husbands, who also happened to be stationed in Ukraine. Then she made a list of all their names. "They're all bathing in butter and sausages and I have to spread my bread with margarine! Have you forgotten about your Veronica?"

"It's true, it's true," thought Kleist with a touch of guilt, "I have been somewhat neglectful. I'll have to send a little something her way."

As he read the last lines his face lit up with excitement and his hands began to tremble.

"Willy! Willy! My son! Look, Heinz, look! Willy got a medal for heroism and now he's a lieutenant! The first in the Kleist family to reach lieutenant. Imagine, my son, Willy!"

Heinz looked at his friend with little enthusiasm. Shaking his head, he said in a grave tone, "Those Russians are a sly bunch, what good will rank do your Willy out on the battlefield? Who knows what will happen in Stalingrad, the Russians might ..."

"The Russians? They don't stand a chance!" Kleist snapped. "We'll chase those bastards back over the Urals. My Willy will see to that!"

Swinging around he motioned to Kirilo, "Kirilo, where can I get a little schnapps around here? I want to celebrate."

THEODORE ODRACH

"*Nicht verstehe.*" The big peasant slouched forward and shook his head.

"Schnapps! Schnapps!" Kleist gesticulated wildly.

"Oh, schnapps, you mean homebrew. Homebrew?" A big fleshy grin stretched across his face. "Go to Stebly, to Nastia, the one without children, she's got plenty to eat and drink."

Kleist only vaguely understood what the peasant said but the words Nastia and without children were clear enough.

He and Heinz momentarily set out along the tracks toward Stebly. The village was not far, and just as they were beginning to pass the outlying houses, Kleist turned seriously to his friend. He appeared impatient. He said haughtily, "You know, Heinz, we're going to have to teach these peasants a thing or two. After all, isn't that why we're here, to enlighten them?"

"Leave it be, Kurt, they can't understand you anyway."

"They'd better understand me!" Kleist punched his fist angrily in the air.

Half an hour later Kleist stood on the steps of the village square and called out to the passing people. They gathered round and he began his speech. But the people were baffled, they looked at each other and shrugged their shoulders – they didn't understand a word of German. Kleist was becoming irritated, he raised his voice and shouted at them as loud as he could: "*Führer! Reich! Deutsche Wehrmacht!*" Barely having uttered these words, suddenly his voice began to scratch and he fell in a fit of coughing. He paused for several seconds. Finally, he began again, "People, not to worry, we'll put an end to the Bolsheviks. My son, Lieutenant Willy Kleist, will personally fight them off at Stalingrad!"

He had more to say but his throat ran dry. It was at this moment that he remembered Heinz.

"Heinz! Where are you?" he called out into the crowd.

But Heinz was nowhere to be found. He decided to walk over to the village clubhouse and ask the deputy for directions to Nastia's house. As it turned out, there were several Nastias in the village.

Kleist lost his temper, "Nastia, Nastia, damn it! The one with schnapps!"

At last, he was directed to her house which was on the village's edge. After banging on the door several times, a woman answered, somewhere in her forties with small round eyes, a full mouth, and disheveled hair. She snarled under her breath in Ukrainian.

"May his stomach rot in hell! That filthy Kirilo must have sent him here."

"Calm down, Nastia, calm down," this was her husband, Prohor, from somewhere inside the house. "If the German wants to drink, let him come in and drink, as long as he leaves us in peace."

In Nastia's house, Kleist behaved civilly. He drank his vodka slowly and was in high spirits. He boasted about his son, Willy, how he was promoted to lieutenant, and how he was serving on the front. The hosts listened politely, but not being able to understand, they kept nodding their heads as if in agreement and excusing themselves.

Suddenly from outside came the sound of voices. Some young people had gathered round Nastia's house, and they were laughing and shouting, and over their voices came the bleating of a goat.

"My God, not a goat already!" laughed Kleist, running to look out the window.

The door of the house swung open and there on the threshold stood the happy Heinz. He held onto the reins firmly as his goat kicked and tugged in all directions.

"Good people here, Kurt," began Heinz. "They wanted to give it to me for nothing but I traded it for a piece of cloth. Let's go home, Kurt, I don't want any drink."

This kind gesture sobered Kleist.

The two men bade Nastia and her husband goodbye, and after shaking their hands, assured them no harm would come their way.

* * *

Life at Stebly station was quiet, maybe too quiet. For several weeks there had been very little traffic. But this soon changed. Somewhere past Horin, Ukrainian partisans had torn up the tracks, and in retaliation, the Gestapo started destroying surrounding villages. Stebly was attacked and burned to the ground. Heinz turned to Kleist with alarm.

"Our soldiers were good soldiers once, now they're nothing more than bandits. I'm ashamed Kurt."

Kleist remained silent. Heinz continued:

"They beat the man who I got my goat Mimi from until he was half dead, and then they confiscated everything. They destroyed Nastia's house. It's not right, Kurt."

Kleist swung around to face his friend; he was beside himself with anger, "What about those bastards who are tearing up the tracks – you don't consider them bandits?"

"Of course, they're bandits but why make innocent people pay when it's the Bolsheviks behind it all?"

"How do you know?"

"I just know, that's all. I know these peasants well. I walk from village to village looking for feed for my Mimi; they give me feed but refuse money. They like to be asked."

Heinz rose quietly from his seat, went outside, and made for the barn out back to look in on Mimi.

Kurt stood by the window and stared blankly outside; the white snow sparkled in the moonlight and the tall stand of trees cast long shadows across the tracks. He didn't altogether approve of what had happened in Stebly but at the same time, he was not particularly concerned. The vast wasteland with its thick winter covering looked mysterious. For some reason, he began to think about Berlin, about his wife, Veronica, and about his little boy, Willy, of how he used to run up and down the walkway in his diapers. Now he was a soldier, a lieutenant. For a moment this thought disconcerted him and he became filled with worry. He dropped his head and closed his eyes. The shack was silent and he dozed off. Within seconds he was awakened by a peculiar sound. Someone was scratching on the window. Assuming it was Heinz, he didn't bother to raise his head. But the scratching continued, it strengthened. When Kleist peered outside, he came face-to-face with a stranger in uniform, and this stranger was pressing his nose flat against the pane. He had a pale complexion, and his big, round blue eyes were staring straight at him. A cold chill rushed up his spine and his heart began to pound.

"Willy, Willy, is that you?"

THEODORE ODRACH

He ran frantically out the door, through the snow, to the front window, yelling: "Willy! Willy! Where are you? Come inside; you'll catch your death out here!"

But as he stood there, he became dumbfounded. His son was not there and the snow underfoot had not been touched. He took out his flashlight and carefully surveyed the ground; there were no tracks. Running over to the storage area and searching through the bricks, he found no one. He then walked over to the shack porch and scanned the snow by the door. Again, he came up empty. Peering inside through an opening in the curtain, he noticed Heinz was already warming his hands over the cast iron stove. As he entered, he heard him mumbling to himself.

"I'm going to have to fix that barn tomorrow; the frost is getting in through the cracks. Mimi is shivering from the cold."

Kleist ignored Heinz. After a moment he began quietly, "You were outside, Heinz, was someone out there? Maybe prowling around, trying to steal some supplies?"

Falling silent a moment, when he started up again, it was as if he had given it all some thought. Waving his hand, he said with resignation, "Oh, maybe it's for the best. Everything is coming to a bad end anyway. The Russians are advancing, the Germans are retreating, things have gotten so mixed up. At Uhovetsk, the Bolsheviks bombarded the tracks, where one car was derailed and rolled into a ditch. Our people blame it on the Ukrainians, then burn their villages and kill the inhabitants. The Bolsheviks are destroying the local people with the German hand."

Kleist and Heinz sat in silence. Finally, Kleist raised his head and smiled strangely. He began, "I saw my Willy, Heinz, outside the window."

"Willy? What the devil are you talking about? If he was here, well, where is he now? Why didn't he come in to warm up?"

"You really are an old goat, Heinz!" Kleist became exasperated.

"What on earth are you talking about? You're not making any sense."

"I saw my Willy, and he was wearing a helmet, the one he wore to the front."

"I don't understand, Kurt. Why didn't he ..."

"Stop it, will you, Heinz! It was Willy, I tell you. I saw him clearly. He was there, outside the window; he was there, and then he wasn't there. He didn't even leave any tracks in the snow."

A sharp wind howled outside, the window rattled, and the logs crackled in the stove. Heinz's face showed confusion, "How odd. You mean you really saw him?"

"I'm positive it was my Willy. It's like he was trying to tell me something." Submerging his head between his shoulders, he sat there for several minutes.

Then he decided he was thirsty. He asked Heinz, "Is there any vodka?"

"Yes."

"Give me a shot, will you?"

"Wait a minute, let's pray first."

"Pray? What for?"

"For Willy, and, well, for you too."

THEODORE ODRACH

"Fine, if you want you go ahead and pray. Leave me out of it."

Heinz knelt beside the stove, folded his hands over his chest, and then lowered his head. He didn't utter a word, not even a whisper; he prayed fervently to himself.

Kleist lifted a glass of vodka and gulped it down and then he filled it up again. Praying was nothing but nonsense, it was for the weak and Germans had to be strong, they had to conquer the weak.

The next day before noon a car drove up unexpectedly from Kovel and Kleist went out to meet it. There was a telegram for him. He began to read it slowly; there was only one sentence typed out on an elongated piece of paper: *Wilhelm Kleist died a hero's death, December 1942, Stalingrad.*

Kleist's hand stiffened, he couldn't move. The telegram fell out of his grip. A strong wind scooped it up and chased it off along the snow-covered tracks toward Stebly…

Pressing his eyes closed to conceal the tears, his shoulders heaved. He was broken up, then he became angry. Flinging himself around, back to the shack, he stormed up to the wall and pulled down his rifle that hung on a nail. He took it apart, cleaned and oiled it, then strapped it over his shoulder. He filled his belt with bullets.

"I'm going to get those bastards!"

"What are you talking about?" Heinz came at him.

"They killed my Willy!"

"Have you lost your mind? Put away the rifle, my friend, and let's pray."

"To hell with your praying!" Kleist's outburst was so violent that Heinz almost fell back. "Praying is for the weak and to survive in this miserable world you've got to be strong. Everything is built on bloodshed."

"You're talking like a lunatic, Kurt. What good is revenge? Do you want to go around killing innocent people who never even knew your Willy? Do you want innocent blood on your hands?"

"To hell with your moralizing!"

"Kurt, let me tell you a little story," Heinz kept his voice steady. "You agree? All right then. In Kovel, I used to run into an SS man by the name of Oksenmeyer. Like all murderers, he was a despicable man and each encounter with him cost me my nerve. Sometimes his eyes gleamed with a phosphorescent-like light and that's how I knew he craved human blood. He would ravage the streets and kill anyone who crossed his way. His favorite method was to punch his victim in the stomach, kick him in the chest, then in the head, and when he or she lost consciousness, put a bullet between the eyes. This always put him in a good mood, and later he joked around with his buddies and told anecdotes.

"One day his hunting backfired; Oksenmeyer attacked a man who was physically swifter and stronger than he was. The man punched Oksenmeyer so viciously in the face that he fell backward and banged his head on a rock. He squirmed around on the ground for about half an hour and when he finally came to the street was empty. A demonic anger had developed inside him and all he needed was someone to attack; he was so desperate to kill he almost pounced on a fellow SS man. As he was coming out of a side laneway leading to Monopoleva Street, a five-year-old Jewish girl skipped across his way. She wore a ripped skirt and black braids hung down her back. Oksenmeyer became delirious. He grabbed her by the arms, turned her upside down, and clasped his big hands around her tiny ankles. He swung her back and forth, then rammed her head into a telephone pole. The little girl didn't even wince."

"Why are you telling me this?"

"Just listen to what happened to him."

"What could possibly have happened?" Kleist threw back his head. "He probably got a medal."

"This war has made a monster out of you. You used to be a different man."

"Well then, what happened to this Oksenmeyer?"

"He hanged himself on the gates of the Gestapo offices."

"I bet the bandits hanged him."

"No, Kurt, he hanged himself; he couldn't stand it anymore. He killed himself."

* * *

The next morning Kleist signed up with the soon-to-arrive execution squad that was to raid Skulin, a village on the forest's edge. Since Kleist was most familiar with the area, he was appointed leader. Four army trucks filled with ammunition charged into Skulin and soldiers with their machine guns chased the people into the main square. The outlying houses were already set on fire and thick black smoke spread over the forest like a storm cloud.

Heinz stood on the platform of the little station and watched through his binoculars. He had always liked Skulin. The villagers treated him well. They often filled up his rucksack with potatoes, cabbage, even salt pork, and Mimi always had enough feed. Now they were being attacked, murdered. The smoke thickened and spread across the sky. The village rooftops were no longer visible. Heinz dropped his head and the binoculars fell to the ground. The shooting started and soon after the sound of bombardment filled the air.

"Oh, my God! They're finishing off the peasants!" Heinz ran inside. He fell on his cot, curled up in the fetal position, and trembled. A gruesome vision entered his mind, of Kleist, his potbelly thrust forward, his rifle aimed at the forehead of some screaming woman.

The shots took over the shack. Heinz threw a pillow over his head and plugged his ears with his fingers. "Why is this happening? Why is this happening? *Alles kaput.* Germany has gone to the Devil."

In time the gunfire began to die off and finally everything became still. Heinz could not get up from the cot. Suddenly the door flew open and he could hear panting and puffing on the threshold. He peered out from under his pillow and then jumped to his feet. It was Kleist. He was standing in the doorway but in his underwear, without a helmet, without boots. His feet were wrapped in rags and his face was blue. He stood shivering and gnashing his teeth.

"Those bastard partisans. They jumped us from behind, shot almost all our men in cold blood."

"Did they take your rifle?" Heinz asked, privately feeling relieved.

"They took all our rifles, yes, and they almost killed me too because they thought I was a Gestapo."

"You idiot," Heinz shook his head. "Was all this worth it? How are your feet?"

"They feel numb. I would never have made it without these rags, but then again, my fat protected me too. When I got away, I ran across the field as fast as I could. I was so exhausted but kept on going, because I knew if I didn't I would have frozen to death. Those who ran toward Kovel probably didn't make it. They're bandits, Heinz, nothing but bandits."

Kleist spat and swore, then made threats, but Heinz persuaded him to lie down and rest. He gave his friend half a glass of vodka, then brought in a bucket of snow and began to rub his legs and chest. Kleist lay still. The white spots on his skin gradually turned pink and he was soon able to move the toes on his left foot.

"You're lucky to be alive, Kurt," Heinz said to him later.

But Kleist was fuming, "Those bandits, how dare they disarm a German soldier! Don't they know what a German soldier means?"

"What a fool you are, Kurt. I never realized you could be such a fool."

Three days later Kleist had regained his strength. After the raid on Skulin, the grief for his son somehow dissipated. Though the fighting in the region continued, he made a point of staying as far away as possible from any battle. He drank vodka instead. Heinz continued to walk from village to village asking for feed for his Mimi. But the villagers were now on guard and no longer friendly.

One day Heinz landed in a distant village and his appearance caused quite the stir. A group of armed partisans jumped out from between two houses and motioned Heinz in the direction of headquarters, which was really just a tumbledown cottage made of wood and with a thatched roof. He was put before the commander and interrogated. The commander, who happened to speak fluent German, asked.

"Who are you?"

"Heinz Ziggy."

"Who sent you?"

"I came on my own. I'm looking for feed for my goat, Mimi."

"Where did you come from?"

"From Stebly Station."

The commander looked at him askance. His face crimsoned.

"Don't play stupid with me. Are you an informer?"

"No, I'm just an ordinary man."

Suddenly a young partisan with cropped yellow hair and a thick red neck entered. He was carrying a message for his superior. When he caught sight of Heinz, a smile stretched across his face, and he became so enthusiastic he even forgot to stand at attention.

"Heinz Ziggy!" he exclaimed, "What the devil brought you all this way?"

Leaning over to the commander, the young partisan whispered something into his ear. The commander raised his brows with interest and then sternly looked at Heinz. He said, "We will let you go this time. Tell your friend, Kurt Kleist, if he joins up with an execution squad again, we will get him personally. You may go."

When Heinz returned to the station, he told his friend what the commander had said.

Kleist became furious, and yelling something barely comprehensible, grabbed hold of his rifle, "I'm going to shoot those bastards. They threaten me!"

"You're a fool, Kurt; nothing but a fool."

At that moment someone tapped on the door. It slowly creaked open. The vague outline of a man appeared in the dark. Kleist stood on guard and aimed his rifle.

"Hey, what are you doing?" a voice said, "I'm unarmed. I come in peace. Don't shoot, don't shoot."

"*Heraus!*" yelled Kleist, signaling with his rifle, motioning for the intruder to step into the light.

"Prohor, is that you?" Heinz called out.

Prohor entered slowly, his eyes darting about the room.

"What do you want, Prohor?" asked Kleist.

"I ... I ... was walking along and thought to myself ... to come and visit you." He anxiously rubbed his hands together. "Your people burned down my house and now I'm no more than a beggar, and my wife too, the whole village, as a matter of fact."

"What are you getting at, Prohor?" Kleist gave an impatient look.

Gathering up his courage, Prohor got to the point, "Well, I was just looking at your material over there. What is it for, anyway? It's just going to rot with all this bad weather we've been having. War is war, but a man can't live without a roof over his head. And so, I thought to myself ... if you could maybe sell me something; for example, some glass, some roofing. I could throw together a shack come spring."

Heinz opened his eyes wide. He was utterly shocked by the proposition. Not only was it forbidden to tamper with Reich property but to do so was highly dangerous. He turned to Kleist. At first, Kleist was outraged by the presumptuousness of it all but after a few moments he waved his hand and said almost indifferently:

"Oh, to hell with it all. The end is coming anyway."

Grabbing a pad and pencil, he began to jot down some numbers, adding and subtracting them. He said matter-of-factly, "This is what it will cost you: one sheet of roofing for one chicken or a bottle of schnapps; two sheets of glass for a kilogram of bacon or two bottles of schnapps."

Prohor rubbed the nape of his neck; he seemed unsure about the offer. He became bold and began to gesticulate with his hands, improvising a slab of bacon, a piece of sausage as if trying to get a better deal.

Kleist stomped his foot angrily to the ground, "Get the hell out of here. This isn't some common marketplace, don't try and bargain with me!"

Prohor tensed up and wiped his forehead. He had indeed gone too far. He smiled fawningly and pulled out a bottle of vodka from under his coat. And on this note, the business transactions began.

That evening Prohor and his brother-in-law appeared at the station with a sleigh. His brother-in-law lived on a well-camouflaged farmstead on the edge of the forest, where he kept chickens and pigs; this was why they came with considerable offerings.

The exchange of goods was swift and business-like. The bacon, the sausages, and the bottles of vodka made Kleist happy: the vodka blunted the grief he felt for his son and the food he was able to send to Veronica on a regular basis.

He drank day and night and no longer concerned himself with possible changes to come at Stebly Station, or for that matter, with the outcome of the war. His desire for revenge transformed itself into apathy. He ate and drank without limit.

At first, business at the station was carried out at night or in the late evening hours, but later Prohor began to arrive in broad daylight. Before long other villagers showed up. The big piles of roofing gradually started to diminish, crates of glass disappeared, and the supply of bricks and cement got smaller and smaller. Heinz no longer needed to walk from village to village in search of feed for Mimi. Trade at the little station was very good.

"What's going to happen when the authorities find out about our little set-up?" Heinz turned concernedly to his friend one day.

"Nothing's going to happen," laughed Kleist. Sitting in silence for several minutes, suddenly his eyes welled with tears, "I lost my Willy; I don't give a damn about anything anymore."

Meanwhile, the fighting continued – the Germans, the Ukrainians, the Poles, and the Russians. The ground trembled from bomb explosions and bullets perforated the air. But Stebly Station was like a tranquil island surrounded by a turbulent sea. No one seemed interested in it. The two friends spent their time peacefully eating, drinking and playing cards. But that's not to say, they weren't without their worries.

One afternoon a group of soldiers appeared in several armored cars. They stopped just beyond the tracks, assembled themselves into three rows, and standing at attention, awaited instruction from their commander.

When the commander zoomed up to the platform in his Volkswagen, the two friends approached with caution.

"Kleist!" shouted the commander. "You're coming with us. I have orders that you join our division."

Kleist's head was throbbing, he had a hangover. He blurted out:

"No, no, I can't go with you, sir, I'm very sick. *Ich bin ganz kaput.*"

"Quiet! Go and get ready!"

"But it's my head, it's been pounding ever since I got news of the death of my son, Willy – Lieutenant Willy Kleist. The doctor over in Kovel told me to take it easy. 'You must rest,' he said, 'and not think of anything because you might get a heart attack.'"

"Is this true?" the commander narrowed his eyes.

"The honest truth."

"Well, we'll let it go for now. This looks like it's a matter for the higher-ups. You'll be hearing from them." The commander waved his hand, got back into his car, and drove away.

Heinz turned to his friend. He let out a sigh of relief, "That was a close call, Kurt. You might not be so lucky next time."

Kleist shrugged and then buried his head deep between his shoulders.

Barely a moment passed when suddenly Heinz called out with panic in his voice, "*Herr Gott*! The supplies! The commander probably noticed some of the supplies were missing!"

Kleist shook his head, "No, I'm sure he didn't."

Both men became uneasy and they began to worry.

* * *

"They came and took Kurt, Mimi," Heinz stroked his goat and wept. "They took him to Kovel. They will probably shoot him there for treason. Why didn't they arrest me? Will they shoot him, Mimi; what do you think?"

Mimi stood unmoving; she didn't even give a snort. She gazed into her master's eyes.

"Maybe they took him to Dachau," he thought, becoming somewhat relieved. "At least there he will have a chance. Better to suffer a bit than to die."

From outside the snow gave a sudden creak. An old peasant in a sheepskin coat hobbled down from a sleigh, and with a big sack flung over his shoulder, approached the platform. He shouted out, "*Guten Tag!* Bricks, I need bricks, *Herr.*"

"*Schloos!* No more business," Heinz motioned with his hand. "He's gone, Kleist is gone. *Aufwiedersehen.*"

A few days later two or three more peasants appeared but Heinz shooed them off in the same way: "*Schloos!*"

Alone at the little station, Heinz became extremely restless. He couldn't find a spot for himself. He spent his days staring out the window or roaming about aimlessly in the snow. One day he received a letter from Volodimir. It was from Kleist. It turned out he had been placed in a concentration camp outside of town and he was even being treated well.

"They were going to put me in Dachau," he wrote, "but my dead Willy saved me. The father of a hero, they said, can't sit in Dachau!"

Heinz gave a sigh of relief.

It was not long before another letter arrived. It was from Berlin, from his sister-in-law, Gertrude. His wife was dead. The Americans had bombed a building and she was crushed by the debris. This news devastated him and he became delirious. He laughed out loud, but it was a hysterical laugh. Then dropping to the ground, he extended his arms high over his head. He tried to understand. Tears poured down his cheeks and his body trembled. Stumbling outside and into the supply area, he screamed at the top of his voice, and he couldn't stop:

"Matilda! Matilda!"

A week later some local peasants saw Heinz wandering about on the frozen mudland, heading for the woods. He was never seen again. In early spring when Prohor was hauling firewood back to his house, he caught sight of a body in German uniform, already well-decomposed. On the breast of his jacket was a faded stamp in Russian print:

Death to Hitler, Kalpaka Regiment

BENNY'S STORY

Through the windows of our compartment, the landscape passed by quickly; the train was coming from Augsburg and approached Nuremberg at high speed. Opposite me sat a young man with a tired Semitic face, slumping deep into his seat, snoring intermittently to the purring sound of the engine. Up on the ledge, directly above his head, lay an overstuffed suitcase and I assumed he was some sort of salesman. He began to toss and turn, then, slowly opening his eyes, asked in a loose German jargon how far we were from Nuremberg.

"About another half hour," I replied.

"Are you perhaps Polish?" he asked me drowsily

"No, I'm from Czechoslovakia."

A warm smile appeared on his face, "Ah, Czechoslovakia, Prague, Prague, not in all my life have I seen as lovely a city as your Prague."

At that moment the train came to a stop, numerous passengers boarded, and we continued on again.

"I'm Benny Blumenkrantz," he extended his hand. Then, sinking back in his seat, he threw out his legs before him.

"Pleased to meet you. I'm Igichek Dufek."

As it turned out my fellow-traveler was a Jew from Lodz and talked to me in Polish while I spoke Czech.

"I really can't believe this war is over. What a nightmare it's been."

"It's been hell, that's for sure," I agreed. "And the Jews got the worst end of it."

"We've suffered all right. If you don't mind, Mr. Dufek, we Jews have a southern temperament; we like to talk, a bit too much sometimes, but we like to talk. Do you mind if I tell you a story, a most incredible story? You'll never believe it."

"Yes, by all means, go ahead."

"I want to tell you about what happened to me when I was placed in a concentration camp outside of Bogatynia. This was in the summer of 1944 and each day, under the guard of SS men, we prisoners were sent off to labor at a nearby train station. There were carts filled with all sorts of parcels, mostly from soldiers posted in Poland to their families in the Reich. We were made to unload all the un-damaged parcels and pack them into separate carts that were to be transported out. Those Germans, what they didn't send – fabrics, bacon, butter. As I worked, a certain parcel caught my eye. It was large and carelessly wrapped in brown paper tied with jute."

Leaning forward, Blumenkrantz lowered his voice and said in a confidential tone, "And it was severely torn. I could see a slab of bacon inside. Can you imagine what the smell of meat meant to a starving man? I became delirious. I could think of nothing else. It invaded my nostrils, every pore of my body. I ripped the parcel open, snatched out the bacon and slipped it into the bosom of my coat. It didn't even occur to me that an SS man could be watching. I quickly composed myself and resumed working.

"'Well, well, Benny,' a voice suddenly erupted from behind. 'I saw what you did. Now the question remains, what are we to do with you now?'

"An SS man stepped toward me twirling a rubber whip. A chill rushed up my spine.

"'You're a stupid Jew,' he went on. 'Who goes and hides bacon like that? Why a blind fool can see there's something stuffed inside your coat. Aren't you scared of eating pig meat?'

"'No. Still before the war I ate bacon, in fact, all kinds of pork.'

"The SS man glimpsed at his watch and burst into a loud and derisive laugh. 'I want you to take that slab of bacon,' he began, 'and stash it in your barracks. Make it back here in two minutes. *Ein*, *zwei*, oh, too bad, Benny, you're half a second late.' And with his whip, he flogged me across the spine. 'You know, it's really a shame to waste such fine rubber on a good-for-nothing like you.'

"He spat between his feet and walked away.

"The SS man's name was Kurt Wilde, one of the most brutal and feared men. He always appeared during inspection time clenching his fists. And that's what I found most baffling. There I was, caught stealing bacon, and all he did was strike me across the back. I couldn't figure it out. Perhaps he wanted to toy with me, then in the dead of night creep into my barracks, grab me by the hair, and shove me into a burning oven. I was prepared to die for that slab of bacon!

"Nightfall came, we were ordered back to our barracks and nothing happened. I climbed into my cot and fell asleep. The next day again, nothing. Finally, on the third day, Wilde called me before him.

"'Did you eat up that bacon, Benny?'

"'Yes, *Herr*,' I replied.

"'And you didn't think of sharing some with me?'

"'I didn't know ...'

"This time he whipped me mercilessly.

"'This is for your thievery! This is for your unsociability! And this is for your egotism! Now march, back to your barracks!'

"He was a tyrant, but somehow there was something different about him. One day he called all the prisoners together and commanded we sit in the cross-legged fashion. He turned to one of the men and snapped:

"'What do you think of me?'

"'I think you're a very fine man, *Herr*.'

"'Liar! You think I'm a swine. No lies here or I'll chop you up into little pieces!'

He then flung himself around, and looking straight into my eyes, demanded to know, 'Benny, did you ever love a woman?'

"'Yes, *Herr*.'

"'And did you propose to her?'

"'Yes.'

"'Benny, do you see that pole over there?'

"'Yes, *Herr*, I see it.'

"'You idiot, you! That's not a pole. Don't you recognize her? That's your sweetheart. Go and make love to her! Give us some entertainment!'

THEODORE ODRACH

"'Oh, Lily, I love you. I will always love you for ever and ever.'

"And so, I went on humiliating myself but, truth be told, survival was the only thing on my mind.

"'Not like that!' Wilde walloped me over the head. 'Be more theatrical, add romance to your voice!'

"'I love you, Lily.' I embraced the pole and even tried to show emotion. What I really wanted was to spit in Wilde's face.

"But I could see Wilde growing impatient with me. Then I watched as he flung himself around and begin to search among the prisoners. Before long, he fixed his eyes on Shmuel, a former shopkeeper with a hunched back and a face that was all pock-marked.

"'Shmuel, you can do better, entertain us!'

"Shmuel threw himself on the pole, and then fell to his knees.

"'Dobo, I love you. Come into my arms. Let's get married. I have a beautiful house with large windows. Together we can sit and look out into the yard at the chickens, ducks, geese, hens, even pigeons. You see, my love, I'm in the poultry business.'

"'Enough! Enough!' Wilde couldn't listen anymore; he'd had enough. He clapped his hands, 'March, back to your barracks!'

"That was Wilde. He had an authoritative walk, his boots were always immaculately polished and his uniform pressed. True, he was despicable and loathsome, yet still, there was something that set him apart from the others. For some reason, every time he caught sight of a fence, no matter how rickety, he would climb to the top; first, he would balance on one foot, then on the other, and then he would walk with arms outstretched, dipping here and there making fantastic spins. Quite the show he put on! Later we learned he had been a tightrope walker with the Berlin circus. In Berlin, he would walk from roof to roof of the buildings there and without even a net to catch him; passers-by would gather below and watch in fascination. Tightrope walking was his greatest passion.'"

The train slowed down as we passed through a small village with crisscrossing cobblestone streets and white stuccoed houses. Blumenkrantz looked out the window, gave a little stretch, and then continued on.

"When our work at the train station ended, rumor had it we would either be transported to Dachau or worse yet butchered alive and thrown into a pit in the woods outside of Bogatynia.

"Finally, the time came. There were thirteen of us, all Jews: Shmuel and I were from Lodz, two from Ukraine, some from Warsaw, and the rest from Byelorussia. One day Wilde called us together and said:

"'If any of you try to escape, you'll get it right between the eyes. Understand?'

"That same day, under the guard of four SS men, we were packed into a cattle car, headed eastbound. Shmuel was convinced of our imminent death.

"'Benny, they'll probably do away with you first because you have such a big mouth. But I've got hope; all my life I've depended on it. I'm sure they'll let me go free. Perhaps you'd like for me to pass a little something on to your family.

I will tell your mother – over there, in the woods, beyond Bogatynia is your son's grave.'

"'You're a fool, Shmuel. If the bullets don't get you the first time, the bayonets will.'

"'Why should they kill me? I never harmed anyone.' Shmuel blinked. 'Benny, why do you talk like that, anyway? Humor me instead.'

"After four long hours of traveling, we were shoved out of the boxcar and assembled in single file a few meters from the tracks. We were deep in the woods, an abandoned little farmhouse peered out from behind a stand of tall conifers, and a powerful range of mountains obstructed the blue sky. There was an ominous calm and it seemed before long we would be digging our own graves. That day we were handed axes and told to chop down trees and with the logs build parapets for German soldiers who were to be stationed on the eastern front. Surprisingly, our food ration improved and with it our dispositions; even Shmuel managed to slip in the occasional anecdote. We worked nonstop. Wilde watched over us with the butt end of his rifle pressed against his shoulder. Next to him stood Herbst, his ruthless cohort.

"They locked us up in a chicken coop. In the mornings we were fed morsels of dried food and then chased off to work. The nights were undisturbed and we were coming to believe that perhaps our lives would be spared. Then one night came the sinister clicking of heels, later, muffled voices. Somebody was fumbling with the latch of the chicken coop. We sat motionless, our backs pinned to the wall. We listened. The door banged open. There stood Wilde and Herbst, unmoving, their faces stone-cold.

"'Get up, Jews!' they shouted.

"Under gunpoint, we stumbled into the darkness toward a huge pit we had dug the day before. I could hear Shmuel moaning under his breath. I poked him in the ribs to keep quiet.

"'Attention!' shouted Herbst.

"We stood at attention. A second more, I thought, and our bullet-riddled bodies will go tumbling into the pit one after the other. I quickly said a prayer. Then at that very moment there was an unexpected turn of events. The incredible happened and we all stood there watching in disbelief. Wilde had jumped Herbst from behind and began choking him with his hands. He called out to me:

"'Benny, quick, take off your pants!'

"Realizing what was going on, I ripped off a piece of fabric from my pant leg, formed it into a ball, and shoved it down Herbst's throat so that he couldn't scream. After a few minutes, Herbst was all tied up.

"'Benny, quick, help me throw him into the pit!'

"After we threw him over the edge, Wilde shouted out to us, 'Jews, get over there by that tree! Schnell!'

"We obeyed immediately and to our astonishment, under a pile of conifer twigs, lay rifles and SS uniforms. Wilde gave us five minutes to change and before long we had rifles flung over our shoulders and an ample supply of ammunition in our belts.

"Wilde yelled, 'Forward march!' and we followed after him.

"'Halt!' yelled Wilde when we were deep in the woods. 'From this moment on I am your commander. I'll shoot anyone who disobeys my orders. If any of you are fool enough, then kill me now, but that won't save you. The Gestapo will track you down in no time. Do you want me as your commander?'

"'Yes!' we shouted in unison.

"'This is my plan: we'll go traveling about and we'll try our best to stay out of harm's way. We will call ourselves the Jewish Brigade.'

"Then pausing a moment as if contemplating something, 'You know, Jews, yesterday I received orders from headquarters to have you all executed. But I thought to myself, to destroy a bunch of fine fellows like yourselves that would truly be a shame.'

"'Excuse me, *Herr*,' the hunchback boldly stepped forward, 'but we don't appreciate your sarcastic tone.'

"'Shmuel, come here!' Wilde was enraged.

"Blood drained from the hunchback's face and he refused to budge. A few of us kicked him toward Wilde. We knew we had no choice if we wanted to survive.

"'I'll shoot you!' Wilde pointed the spout of his rifle into Shmuel's chest. 'I don't need the likes of you in my brigade.'

"'*Herr*, I'm sorry. I don't know what came over me. I have this bad habit of talking too much sometimes.' He waved his arms in the air and tossed his head about. 'It must be this horrible heat; it's getting to me.'

"Shmuel was an annoyance and I was the first to suggest, '*Herr Offizier*, why don't we tie him up for a while. Maybe that'll shut him up.'

"'I'm not an *offizier* anymore, Benny. Right now, I'm merely a commander, or if you prefer, a commander of Jews.'

"On this day we stripped Shmuel of his clothes, tied him to a tree, and watched his body become swarmed by mosquitoes and black flies. He swelled up like a ripe tomato. Incredibly, thanks to Wilde, we had beaten death and we couldn't have Shmuel jeopardize our good fortune in any way.

"With no particular destination in mind, we pushed eastward. As far as provisions went, we had little trouble; we would slip into remote villages on the edge of the woods and stock up. Outside of Krakow, when asked by peasants what sort of brigade we were, I was chosen to act as spokesman.

"'We are the Jewish Brigade, a sector of the national Polish army. We're fighting for an independent Poland, and are now on our way to the eastern front to fight the Germans and the Russians.'

"When we reached Rzeszow we inadvertently landed in a Polish military camp. There was a minor shoot-out and within minutes we were surrounded. On the end of a twig, up went our capitulation flag. We were disarmed and cross-examined. After a short deliberation, Polish headquarters decided to release us, but the general, an older man with gray hair and bushy white brows, informed us that he would not return Wilde, due to his obviously being German. We had a brief conference and then announced:

"'General, if you don't return our commander and our weapons, you might as well kill us all. He's our leader and without him we're as good as dead.'

"'Lieutenant,' suddenly Shmuel burst in, for some reason addressing the old man as a lieutenant, 'Wilde, though he's a German, somehow, he's not a bad sort and protects us like Moses the people of Israel. Believe it or not but it's true.

He freed us from death because he could no longer bear the atrocities committed against our people. What can you possibly gain by his death?'

"Then Aaron Goldberg, a good-natured, burly tailor from Bialystock threw in, speaking distinct Polish, 'We both feel the same way about the Germans, but as you can see for yourself, Wilde is different. He once was an SS man, that's true, but his real passion has always been with the Berlin circus.'

"Our pleading finally touched the old man's heart and it was not long before he conceded. But before letting him go, raising his finger he warned us, 'Make sure your Wilde doesn't lead you to Buchenwald!'

"We made our way toward the woods and before long we spotted Ukrainian villages. They were up in smoke. The peasants were terrified of strangers, especially those who spoke German. Within our brigade, there was no predominant language. Shmuel, Goldberg, a few others and I spoke Polish, but to Wilde only in German, and our comrades from Ukraine spoke mostly Ukrainian and Russian. Creeping along the forest's edge, we slipped into a small village and to our surprise, we were momentarily surrounded by a group of armed partisans. We jumped into an empty hut and took refuge

"'Surrender!' charged a voice from outside. 'You're surrounded!'

"'Hey, we're one of you!' called out Jordan Bergman in distinct Ukrainian. 'I'm from Sheptivka myself. Born and raised there. Put forward your commander and we'll get to the bottom of this misunderstanding.'

"'Come out, one of you!' the order came pouring into the hut.

"We shoved Bergman forward. He was grabbed instantly and a gun was put to his head.

"'Give yourselves up, Red paratroopers!' another voice roared from behind the storage barn.

"The partisans had mistaken us for Bolsheviks so Wilde yelled out: '*Meine Lieben, wir sind unabgehörige Kämpfer!*'

"His impeccable Berlin accent caught them off guard and a confused silence followed. We started to make demands for the return of Bergman, but they refused. We then requested that one of them come forward to negotiate. From behind the storage barn, two partisans emerged, cautiously approaching the hut with Bergman between them. We told them our story, that we were thirteen Jews traveling with a German commander. Ironically, they didn't believe a word we said and took Wilde to be the only Jew among us.

"'What's your mission?'

"'We're not on a mission. We only want to protect our own lives. The war will end and we'll go off somewhere, probably to Palestine.'

"'To Palestine? And are you going to take your Nazi friend along with you?'

"'If he wants to come, we will take him. But I have a feeling the idea will not appeal to him.'

"Throughout the village word had spread that Jewish men were blockaded in a hut. Soon peasants arrived. Outside the door they began to haggle. Old women with big, loose bundles, hollered through the windows:

"'Hey, we've got something to trade with you. Maybe you have some nice fabric, maybe a little footwear?'

"But when they peered inside their eyes popped open in disbelief. One, two, seven, twelve SS uniforms! They froze.

"'My dear women,' called out Bratsky, a former Byelorussian teacher of mathematics, 'you've got it all wrong. You see, we're not really Germans; we're only wearing German uniforms. This man' (he pointed to Wilde) 'has been kind enough to escort us out of a prison camp and now we're simply traveling about. We call ourselves the Jewish Brigade, we're friendly, I assure you.'

"This speech made little impression on the villagers. Then Isaak Zimmerman, a native of Kyiv, took the stand. Though his tone was somewhat upbraiding, he knew how to capture the female heart.

"'We were prisoners. The Germans beat us with their rubber whips, starved us, gassed us in their ovens. The tortures we've endured!'

"He spoke with such a deep fervency, happily, we noticed that not only on the faces of the women but on the partisans as well gleamed a sense of compassion.

"'And Baba, those who tortured us are Godless. And believe you me, they don't just torment the Jews, but Ukrainians too! A Ukrainian friend of mine, Sirod Anderchishin, they tortured to death.'

"Another old woman, standing against the wall of the hut, clasped her chest.

"Zimmerman went on, 'Sirod was my very best friend, a fine human being. He shared his last morsel of bread with me. How he grieved for his wife Ludmila and his little daughter Annochka. They were killed by the Reds somewhere by the Bug River. He even...'

"But before he had a chance to finish, an ear-piercing scream resounded throughout the village. 'Eek! Danger! Take cover!'

"Gunshots erupted from the outskirts, then came the explosion of cannons. A young man, running up to the commanding partisan, shouted but one word: 'Poles!'

"By way of the meadow, a band of Polish soldiers had crept up to the village's edge and had already set fire to several farmsteads. The shooting was cause for great alarm for the commanding partisan. He turned to us and said, 'We can't trust you fellows just yet. Give up your weapons. After we chase out the Poles, then we'll deal with you.'

"We translated this for Wilde, but we noticed by his expression he was very displeased – he was not about to miss out on a good fight. Disregarding the orders, he waved his hand in the air and shouted to us:

"'Never mind what the partisan says, my chosen ones, we'll fight anyway. We'll fight the Poles. If the Poles seize the village, they probably won't harm us; at worst, they will strip us of our arms and clothes. If we help the Ukrainians, they won't detain us any longer. Actually, men, it's all the same to us who we fight, we're independent soldiers after all, no one tells us what to do. Get ready to attack!'

"'Er, Commander,' the hunchback edged forward slowly, rubbing his hands, 'if you permit, my conscience does not allow for this. I am an honest citizen of Poland and I refuse to fight the Poles. I was born in Lodz, I grew up there, and I had my shop there. I cannot and will not fight the Poles.'

THEODORE ODRACH

German forest-guard by the name of Koch, stationed by the railway tracks. And so, we became Bolsheviks on the German trail!

"'Well, my knights of Solomon,' Wilde turned to us, 'shall we murder this Koch character or not?'

"'If we must, we must,' said Aaron.

"'Let's forget about it,' Wilde waved his hand in the air. 'Why should we care about any commands from the Bolsheviks? After all, we're independent soldiers, we're the Jewish Brigade. No one orders us around.'

"Instead of killing Koch, we decided to head west because the front was already retreating. Upon reaching Pilsen, we traded our uniforms and weapons for food and civilian clothing and then headed for Bavaria. The war was over."

As the train approached Nuremberg, the passengers began to take down their luggage. When the train entered a large, dilapidated station, Blumenkrantz pulled his overstuffed suitcase down off the rack above his head.

"Are you selling food?" I finally asked him.

"No. I'm taking food to Wilde. He's in prison right now. At his trial, we plan to tell our story."

"We?"

"The Jews about whom I've been telling you. Only we don't know where the hunchback is. Well, Mr. Dufek, I must be on my way. Your Prague is truly a lovely city, a lovely city."

Blumenkrantz walked briskly down the platform and then disappeared beyond the exit gates.

THE POMERANIAN

At precisely eight o'clock every morning, Mumik, a one-year-old Pomeranian, came running out of his house to the far end of the yard, where there stood a maple tree, to relieve himself. Mumik was a compact, thickset little dog of no more than eight pounds with an impressive white coat, pointed ears, and eyes the color of beer. He would sniff the grass, bark at passersby, and chase after garden wildlife. Then he would sit and wait for Patricia, his mistress, to come out. He was fiercely loyal and protective of her.

The two would set out along the sidewalk. Patricia was elderly, somewhere in her seventies, and supported by her cane, she took small, mincing steps. Every day she and Mumik made for Zvirovy Street, then after reaching the town hall, would turn right and continue along Mist Prospect until they came to the cemetery. Day in and day out Patricia dressed in the same long black overcoat belted at the waist and the same felt hat tilted stylishly to the left. On her feet, she wore well-trodden laced leather shoes of an imported variety and her hands were always carefully gloved. As the two would approach the first intersection, looking both ways, they would stop and wait for the traffic to go by. Mumik would bark at the passing vehicles and wag his bushy tail.

Several months before, when Patricia adopted Mumik from the city pound, neighbors were considerably disturbed by the noise he made. They even threatened to call the police. But over time, everyone became accustomed to the little dog and accepted his rambunctiousness as part of their everyday lives – everyone, that is, except for Turski.

Turski was an old army veteran in his sixties, who rented a room on the second floor of Patricia's house. He almost never shaved or combed his hair and he hardly bathed or changed his clothes. He lived alone and seldom had visitors. Although he had never taken to the idea of marriage, he had always managed to chance upon a female companion. But now that he was getting on in years, he found he was entering a time of regrets; he regretted never finding a woman to share his life with, of never having children, of never accomplishing anything. He spent his days sad and blue, finding consolation only in drink. And as far as Mumik went, Turski was not particularly fond of dogs, especially little ones, and he certainly didn't appreciate being woken up day after day at the crack of dawn.

One morning, upon hearing Mumik's barking, Turski went to the window to see what was going on. Seeing the little dog and his mistress, he was struck with a most interesting thought.

"Simply amazing! Every morning the old lady walks half a kilometer to the cemetery and another half a kilometer back. That makes one kilometer a day and she's been doing it for the past ten years. Let's see..." He quickly did some mental math, "In one year that makes 365 kilometers and in ten years that makes 3,650! My God, that's almost the way to America!"

He went on to calculate further:

"If the old girl lives another ten years, then she will have walked a total of 7,300 kilometers!"

He simply couldn't wrap his head around it.

The veteran, despite his habitual drinking, was in relatively good health, although he did have a wooden right leg. While serving in the war, a landmine had ripped apart his knee, and after having laid in the ashes in an open field for several hours, he had been picked up by friendly forces and taken to a nearby camp hospital. To offset the spread of gangrene, the doctors found it necessary to amputate his leg up to the hip. Though he was assigned light clerical work at army regional headquarters for several months thereafter, any future prospects in the army were ruined. But he was never in pain, and even though he used a cane, he hardly limped.

Turski, for the most part, had a great deal of time on his hands and, therefore, much time to think. A scenario came to mind, one which happened to involve Patricia. He was now very much aware of her presence, but in a way that was new to him, a way that was even measured and calculated. He was somehow beginning to see her not only as his elderly landlady but as someone who could offer him considerable financial stability. He began toying with the idea of a union between them, a marriage of sorts. The way he saw it, plain circumstance provided enough cause to bring them together: he was old and lonely and lived from his pension, and she, having lost her husband, was old and lonely and also lived from her pension, though considerably larger than his. This is how he rationalized it: not only would life be fuller and more meaningful for them both, but they could comfort one another in times of need. And since he, Turski, was almost always broke, he saw this arrangement as the perfect opportunity.

But the problem was, he and Patricia, personality-wise, were complete opposites, they could not see eye to eye on anything. She was a pious woman, thrifty and serious, and though she possessed a genuine goodness, if there was one thing she could not tolerate it was a drunk. And Turski was just that, a drunk. Not only was he irreverent and careless, but he was always neglectful and inclined to laziness. Within the first week of every month, he squandered his money on drink, and then lived from hand to mouth; he paid rent for his room whenever he could. Although Patricia found him objectionable, she tolerated his devil-may-care ways only because he had served on the front and was a decorated army veteran.

One day after a drinking binge, Turski went downstairs to Patricia's apartment and knocked on her door. He came upon her sitting on the sofa with Mumik at her feet. Speaking in a low tone, he tried to appear sober.

"You disapprove of me, I know. Allow me to explain a few things. After I was injured on the front there was nothing left for me to live for, so I began to drink. It helped ease my pain. I drank and drank. Now I'm nothing more than a useless old drunk, and the solitariness in my life only gets worse by the day. I'm well into my sixties, and I feel ready to settle down, to start things anew. Life would be so much more bearable if you and I could somehow come to an understanding. I know you're a good few years older than I am but we could make it work. Consider it."

On another occasion, again he tried to get her to see things his way. Catching her unawares in the kitchen, coming up from behind, he thrust his arms about her and tried to kiss her on the cheek. She shooed him off by elbowing him in the ribs, "Get away from me, you drunken fool."

When one-time Turski approached Patricia in the garden, Mumik decided to take matters into his own hands. Growling and showing his teeth, completely unafraid, he threw himself on the old veteran and sank his teeth into his good leg. The bite was so deep Turski let out a scream. He tried to kick Mumik away but the little dog continued to come at him, howling and snarling.

After this incident, Turski avoided the old woman whenever he could; however, from time to time, depending on how much drink he had in him, he would try to win her over with flattery. He would call out to her in different ways but usually from afar: "Patricia, the flowers in your garden are lovely this time of year," or "Don't you look fine on such a warm, sunny afternoon," or "Mumik is so lively today."

Only when he was short of cash did he muster the courage to approach her directly. One morning as she was setting out along the walkway, he said to her:

"A good morning to you, Madame! What a lovely day it's going to be! If you don't mind, I realize it's still early in the month but, somehow, I've run out of money. Would you be able to front me a few *zlotys*?"

Almost always she would fly back at him, as she did on this very fine summer day.

"Where do you get the nerve to ask me for money when you still owe me two months' rent?"

The widow's blunt reproaches always caused Turski great grief. He knew he must watch his step and not come on bad terms with her because, as good-hearted as she was, she could readily evict him and without notice. Where would he go then? Life on this small residential street was peaceful and uneventful, and it suited him just fine. And most importantly, he was able to easily connect with all his favorite watering holes without even having to hire a cab or take the tram. Yes, he had to proceed with caution, because as bad as things were, they could easily get worse.

Somehow the years passed. Nothing of consequence happened between Turski and the old woman. They went on to live under the same roof and under the same arrangement: he occupied a room on the second floor of her house, while she lived in the apartment below. Turski continued with his drinking and carousing, and Patricia went on to maintain her staid and simple life, though it was becoming obvious she was turning more and more into a recluse. She now almost never spoke with Turski or hardly uttered a word to her neighbors. It was as if she were starting to shut herself down. Nonetheless, she continued to walk in the mornings with her dog to the cemetery but at a slower pace.

* * *

One summer morning as Patricia and Mumik started along the street, Mumik, running up ahead, upon hearing his mistress call his name, stopped suddenly and stood up on his hind legs. He waited for her to catch up. When the two came to a crossroads, making their way over to the other side, they turned down a narrow laneway that led straight to the cemetery. As they passed through the gates, which were tall and arched and made of brick, though they could still hear the sounds of the town, they felt quite at peace.

Continuing, finally they came to a largish tombstone with an engraved cross down the middle. Gold letters were carved into the fake black marble and read as follow: *In loving memory, Anton Vovk.*

Patricia looked at Mumik and gave a mournful sigh.

"Yes, my dear Anton is buried here, Mumik. And what about you? You just sit there and give me silly looks; you're lucky, you have no idea what it's like to be human. You don't feel the anguish, the despair, the pain. Your life is simple. You run around, bark, and wag your tail, and then one day you die. And nobody bats an eyelash; you're only a dog, after all. 'Mumik was here and now Mumik's gone,' people will say. But for a human death is so complicated. There's a will to consider, a funeral, a coffin, the afterlife ... What does a dog care about an afterlife?"

Mumik came toward the old widow, who had since sat down on a nearby bench. He pressed his head up against her leg. Petting him, her voice quavered and broke.

"I'm alive, Mumik, but I'm not really alive – I stopped living a long time ago when my Anton died. He was a handsome redhead with deep blue eyes and a swaggering mustache. He loved to go dancing and to the cinema. When illness consumed him, he shriveled up like a prune and lost his color, but the goodness never left him."

Mumik, with his keen sense of alertness, it was as if he understood his mistress' every word. The old woman went on.

"My Anton worked for the railroad. He would travel hundreds of kilometers at a time, and sometimes I wouldn't see him for days. He worked more than he had to because we were planning to have a big family, and he wanted to make sure we had enough for our children. But we never had children, and still today I don't know whether it was because of him or me. It would have been nice to have had a son with deep blue eyes like his, or a daughter with corn-yellow hair. But nothing ever came of it and now here I am a lonely old woman with nobody. Turski thinks that in our old age we should get married and start a new life together, but it's not that simple. All he ever wants to do is get drunk, and all I ever do is sit in front of my husband's grave. There was no man like my Anton. If the dishes needed to be washed, he'd roll up his sleeves, he would scrub the floor and dust the furniture. Oh, to live with a man like that for a hundred years!"

* * *

The years came and went and time had no mercy. Both Patricia and Turski aged considerably; however, they still managed to carry on with their lives in much the same way, going about their usual everyday business.

Turski continued to sit by the window and watch Patricia hobble along the walkway with her little dog, Mumik, who was now well into his twilight years. He had estimated the two must have already walked over seven thousand kilometers. As he watched them, he couldn't help notice how Patricia had grown old. Her thin, veined legs had weakened considerably and life had taken her strength; she was hunched over and could no longer walk without the support of her cane. The little dog had developed arthritis in his hind legs and his hair had turned gray, mostly around his eyes and mouth. Nevertheless, they continued to walk to the cemetery as always, still never missing a day.

Then came Patricia's eightieth birthday. As she rested on her sofa in the living room with the radio on, at once there was a knock on the door. It was Turski. The old woman was surprised to see him dressed not in his usual soiled and tattered garb, but, rather, in a woolen suit, freshly brushed, and with his face clean-shaven. In his hand, he carried a bouquet of red carnations. He said to her: "Please accept this humble gift from me on your birthday."

He walked up to the sofa and extended his hand. At the same time, a peculiar smile contorted his face, as though he had something else on his mind.

"If I were a wealthy man, I would never have brought you these carnations, but, rather, I would have brought you Japanese lotuses, and in a glass vase. But I wouldn't have brought the Japanese lotuses so much for your birthday, instead, I would have brought them in celebration of another occasion. What occasion you ask? By walking back and forth to the cemetery year in and year out, according to my calculations, you have accomplished the remarkable feat of having walked a total of seven thousand kilometers. Congratulations! Seven thousand kilometers, that's nothing to scoff at!"

The old woman raised her brows. She was taken aback by his remarks, though she managed to keep a civil air.

"You're a very clever man. I had no idea you were so interested in my daily routine. Have you nothing better to do with your time? And since you're so good at arithmetic, maybe you could tell me how much rent you owe me?"

The old veteran stood back.

The widow went on; she even became a little combative.

"In the beginning, you used to forget your rent by a month, but now it's going back by three. According to your estimations, I've walked a total of seven thousand kilometers, but you haven't paid me rent in three months. As we had agreed, you're supposed to pay me twenty *zlotys* a week or eighty *zlotys* a month. If you're so good with numbers, tell me, how much is eighty times three?"

Turski flushed with embarrassment.

"Go on, tell me."

"Two hundred and forty,"

"Two hundred and forty! Two hundred and forty *zlotys* is worth about one month of your pension! Where's the one hundred and sixty you should have left over each month after paying me rent? Where's it gone?"

Turski tried to process all that she had said. Thinking of a response, in the end, he uttered:

"That's the fate of an old army veteran. The Germans blew off my leg on the front. Then I was made into a war hero, and all the hero got in the end was a wooden leg, plus two hundred and forty *zlotys* a month in pension. Does that seem fair?"

"You're one to talk about being fair!" the widow shot back. "A man who doesn't pay his rent to a poor widow has no right to talk about what's fair. Why you should be ashamed of yourself! You live recklessly; you take whatever you can get – a crust of bread, a glass of milk, a chunk of cheese ..."

"You're right, you're right," the old veteran was in no position to argue.

"According to my calculations, you need to spend no more than a hundred and twenty *zlotys* on living expenses a month, including rent. So, you're still left with another hundred and twenty *zlotys* at the end of each month. If you had saved all this money for the past twelve years, how much would you have saved? Go on; multiply a hundred and twenty times twelve months, and then that by twelve years because that's how long you've been living in my house."

"You're being too harsh. What do you want from me?"

"I don't want anything from you. I just want you to know I'm pretty good with numbers too. If you had saved your one hundred and sixty *zlotys* in those twelve years, you'd have 23,040 *zlotys* in your pocket today. My God, 23,040 *zlotys*. I've walked seven thousand kilometers and you've frittered away 23,040 *zlotys*!"

Turski's face blanched; the sum astonished him. He had never thought of it that way. He quickly began to recall all the taverns he had frequented throughout the years. His drinking buddies came to mind: Komoda, Lopushinsky, and Sport. He found it unbelievable that he had squandered 23,040 *zlotys*. Sport was now the only one in the group left alive; the other two had died – Lopushinsky five years earlier of a stroke, and a couple of years after that, Komoda, in his hotel room, of a heart attack.

Turski stood looking at Patricia as though struck by the reality of it all. Then quite a different expression came to his face and he didn't hold back.

"23,040 *zlotys*, that certainly is capital, I agree. But what do I need money for? Life's not worth living. I drank every bit of it, it's true, and now I'm alone. But you lived piously and respectably, and you're old and just as alone as I am. At least Sport calls me up every now and then, but no one ever calls you. All I can say is that I had a good time in life when I was young and in the army. I traveled around the world, met different people, and saw different things. My life was filled with intrigue and excitement. But what about your life? After your husband died, all you ever did was walk half a kilometer to the cemetery and half a kilometer back, and now you're eighty years old!"

"What are you getting at?" the old widow narrowed her eyes.

"I don't need money. What on earth do I need money for when my life's already over?"

"What about your soul?"

"Hah, hah, hah! Even the Devil himself doesn't want the soul of a drunk. He'd take one of you over a million of my kind any day."

"My God, the things you say!"

"Well, that's my fate. Some people were born to lead happy, productive lives; others were born to be drunks. I'm just an aged handicap, whose only joy in life is to drink."

The old woman shook her head and turned away, "That's enough; I don't want to hear anymore. I think you had better go."

When Turski was already behind the door, Patricia picked Mumik up and placed him on her lap. Stroking his backside, she said to him:

"Just look what drink does to a man."

* * *

One morning setting out on her usual daily trek when Patricia had passed the cemetery gates she noticed for some reason, instead of running up ahead, Mumik stayed close by her feet. When she nearly tripped over him, she said crossly, "You silly little dog, what's the matter with you today? Go on, the grave is just beyond the bend."

As the old woman continued along the path at once she felt weak, as if her legs were about to give way beneath her. Cold shivers started down her spine. She looked round as if disoriented, not sure which way to go. She became exceptionally faint and there came a tightness in her chest. She could hardly go on the pain in her chest was so great. Stopping a moment, she leaned heavily on her cane.

Mumik sensed something was wrong. Barking and nudging her with his snout, he prodded her toward a bench in the shade. Patricia sat down and loosening her coat collar, took several breaths. After a few minutes, she seemed to revive herself. Mumik nestled beside her and the two sat there a very long while, hardly moving.

In the meantime, the sun had crawled up large and round, and puffy white clouds, one bulkier than the other, floated across the sky. The long rows of tombstones running off in either direction threw off a stifling heat and there seemed no air to breathe.

Mumik and the old woman got up and started back to the cemetery gates. She fell short of breath again, "Oh, how weary I am today. Old age is my curse. My joints creak like a rusted old cart."

The two made their way onto the street, and pausing now and then, found their way back home.

They never made it to Anton's grave.

* * *

For some reason, the following morning Turski did not see or hear Mumik out in the yard. Looking at his clock on the night table, he noticed it was already ten after eight. Was it possible the old widow had got an early start and had already left for the cemetery? Could he have slept in and missed her? He recalled waking up a few minutes past seven and thinking to himself as he got out of bed that Patricia had probably already passed his window. He then decided to wait in his room until nine o'clock because that was the time she usually returned home. But she didn't appear and this troubled him. As he was about to go downstairs and knock on her door, at that moment his old friend Sport came to mind – he had agreed to meet with him at a tavern on the other side of town, and he was already running late. Glimpsing at his watch, he decided the old lady would just have to wait. Grabbing his coat and hat, and stepping out onto the street, he then boarded a tram at the first crossroads. He drank with Sport for the good part of the day.

Returning home, as Turski came onto Zvirovy Street, the sun had already slipped behind the rooftops of the small wooden houses and the streetlights were on. He was surprised to find a group of people gathered in front of Patricia's house. They were shouting to one another, gesticulating, nodding their heads, and making a fuss about something. One corpulent woman somewhere in her forties was in hysterics and kept pointing at Mumik, who was sitting on the veranda.

"That little thief! He stole my ham! I went to Kruk's shop to pick up a few items – several Kaisers, a bottle of cream, and some ham. After paying and placing my purchases in my basket, Mr. Kruk, it seemed, was in for a bit of a chitchat. He asked me, 'How are things?' I answered, 'Same as usual, thank you very much, and how are things with you?' When I was ready to leave and went to pick up my basket, I noticed the ham was gone. Gone! I rushed outside and saw that little dog over there running down the street, with the ham in his mouth. I chased after him as fast as I could but was unable to catch up. I yelled out to people passing by, 'Stop that dog! Thief!'"

As Turski elbowed his way through the crowd, he noticed Mumik was panting and yelping and his ears were down. The ham lay in front of him and he snarled at anyone who tried to get near it.

"Two *zlotys* down the drain," the woman continued with her lament. "That dog's a menace, he should be euthanized!"

The old veteran tried to appease her, "That's Patricia's dog. Patricia's a fine human being and one of the most respectable people I know."

THEODORE ODRACH

The woman didn't buy it. She raised her arms, "Respectable? How respectable can she be when she's trained her dog to steal?"

"You say the ham cost you two *zlotys*?" The old veteran slipped his hand into his pocket to try and find some loose change but he was dismayed to find he had spent it all in the tavern.

"Madame," he felt awkward and embarrassed, "I'm an army invalid, I fought in the war, and I left my leg on the front. I'm an honest man and I promise that on the first of next month you will get your two *zlotys*, and with interest."

He then pushed his way onto the veranda. Mumik sat tense and showed his teeth.

"Mumik, it's me, it's all right. Where's your mistress? Is something wrong? Come on now, be a good dog. I want to help."

The veteran then turned to the people. He pointed to Mumik and said seriously, "This little dog here is no ordinary dog. He has the intelligence of a human being. He's trying to tell us something, maybe about his mistress. He took that ham for a reason."

Without a moment to lose, Turski started banging on the front door, "Open up, Patricia, open up! It's me, Turski. Are you all right in there?"

But only silence followed. Turski gave the door another bang, but again silence. He then said:

"There's another door out back. I can get in through there."

Making down the stairs, passing the storage shed, the crowd followed close behind. The door was unlatched and he hurried inside. Poking his head into the living room, then the kitchen, he called out Patricia's name. When there came no answer, he made for her bedroom.

With the curtains partially drawn, the room was filled with damp and shadows. Against the far wall upon a heavy oaken bed beneath quilted covers lay Patricia. She was staring up at the ceiling, unblinking, and not a muscle on her face moved. Turski stepped up to the side of her bed and leaned forward to get a better look. She appeared so calm and peaceful, but she looked dead to him. The old veteran ran his fingers along her cheeks, then up across the top of her forehead. He wept. He remained frozen for the longest time. At last, he turned to the crowd.

"Patricia is dead. She was one of the most generous and kindest people I've ever known. May her soul rest in peace."

The spectators looked on with hushed, sorrowful faces, then bowing their heads started in on the Lord's Prayer.

Mumik ran under the bed with his tail between his legs and let out little groaning sounds.

The next morning Turski sat by his window and looked out into the yard. It was precisely the time Patricia should have been walking down the road with Mumik on her way to the cemetery. But today there was no Patricia, and nor would there be a Patricia tomorrow, nor the day after that. She was gone and the emptiness so saddened Turski he could hardly move; he couldn't even bring himself to pour a drink. When suddenly there came a scratching at his door, getting up and opening it, he found Mumik standing there, panting, with his tongue hanging out. Picking the little dog up in his arms, he tried to console him by petting him behind the ears.

THEODORE ODRACH

"Well, Mumik, she's left us; your mistress has up and left us. It looks like it's just you and me now. What are we going to do? And how am I supposed to feed you? Maybe Sport could put us up for a while until I figure things out. I normally don't take to dogs, especially small ones, but you don't seem like such a bad sort after all."

Turski sat with Mumik for the longest time, stroking his backside, trying to get a handle on things. The situation that had developed round his life was one he had never considered. The thought of having to pack his bags and find other lodgings and with a dog completely overwhelmed him; and all together, he felt he didn't have the strength of will to deal with it all. He became dull and gloomy.

Sometime later that afternoon a message arrived for Turski. It was a summons asking that he come to the law office of Reka and Wolski at his first opportunity and to bring with him the little dog, Mumik. Turski scratched his head; he didn't know what to make of it. What could these lawyers want with him, and more so, what could they possibly want with a dog? But it made no sense. In any case, taking hold of his hat and cane and calling for Mumik, the two set out for the city center. After passing several rows of small wooden houses and later a block of buildings made of stone, coming to an intersection, Turski looked down to Mumik and said:

"Well, why do you suppose this lawyer wants to meet with us? One thing you can bet on, we'll be handed an eviction notice. It seems to me our days are numbered."

It was not long before they came upon the offices of Reka and Wolski. A paunchy, middle-aged man with brown thinning hair sat at his desk, flipping through a stack of papers. His face was round and red and he wore an extremely serious expression. Upon hearing the door open, looking up from under horned-rimmed glasses, he said at once:

"Good morning, you must be Mr. Turski." Then with his eyes wandering to the floor, "And this, I presume, is Mumik. My name is Jan Reka. Please, have a seat. I'll be with you in a moment."

As Turski settled into a rather plush armchair by the door, Mumik jumped up on the chair next to him. There was a constrained silence. The two watched Mr. Reka's every move, waiting for him to at last say what it was he had to say. Mr. Reka's tone was official.

"I have summoned you here today regarding Patricia Sadowska's last will and testament.

She has bequeathed to you, Mr. Turski, her house, personal belongings, and the total sum of 30,000 *zlotys*. But there are two stipulations: one, that you quit drink and, two, that you care for Mumik until his last remaining days. Should you fail to adhere to her two final wishes, the inheritance will automatically become forfeited and the balance of the property will be turned over to a charity and a trust will be set up for Mumik."

As Mr. Reka went on with a few other minor details, Turski could no longer hear what he was saying. He sat as though dumbstruck. He would never have expected such an outcome. He tried to absorb all that he had just heard.

The room became very still.

Then Turski turned to the little dog. The two exchanged glances. Turski's voice cracked with emotion.

"So, Mumik, it looks like the old girl had something up her sleeve all along. Who would've thought? Yes, it's just you and me now. Just you and me."

Mumik jumped on Turski's lap and Turski stroked his backside.

INTERROGATION

Three men were stationed in an old, camouflaged house somewhere in the heart of the forest. Together they formed a military tribunal and one afternoon they sat around the kitchen table, arguing. Boris, a prudent dark-haired man of the law, had before him files on paratroopers who were to be shot the next day. As he flipped through the stack of papers, he said warily, "We should start looking into these shootings more carefully. A bullet gets us nowhere. It's outright murder."

"Treat Bolsheviks Bolshevik style!" exclaimed Omelko, who was the executioner. He was short in stature with beady blue eyes and a red-hot temper. For him to shoot a human being was the same as to spit. He twisted up his mouth. "I know those bastards from the blood of my family. They'll grab you from behind and say: 'You son-of-a-bitch, today I'll shoot you in the toe, tomorrow you'll get it up the ass!'" He took a shot of whiskey. He turned on Boris sarcastically, "So, what do you suggest we do, stroke their heads?"

Boris rose gravely to his feet. He paced the room. "Revolution is no joke."

Omelko hawked the phlegm from the back of his throat and his face turned red with rage. "That's why we've got to be cold-blooded. If we hesitate, we can't shoot, if we can't shoot, we'll be shot."

"What a mad world this has become," this was Vadim. He was the judge of the tribunal, a dark-haired Poltavian in his late thirties. He listened quietly to his colleagues, but at the same time, something seemed to be troubling him.

Omelko pounced on Vadim at once, "Is that all you have to say? The world's become mad? Well, what do you propose we do about it then? I've never seen you handle a gun."

"I'm a judge not a murderer. Sometimes I've had the urge to shoot, but, unlike yourself, I have self-control. But then again, I've never had to kill my way to freedom."

The room fell silent.

After several minutes, Vadim, looking at the men, gave a wry smile, "Today it seems one of us will be questioning a rather pretty girl."

"I'll do that," volunteered Omelko.

"You're an executioner, not an interrogator," objected Vadim.

Omelko stormed to his feet, "Well, at least I get results. You two have no gumption. You'll probably melt at the very sight of her."

Vadim disregarded Omelko's comments but eyed him suspiciously. Rising from the table, putting his hands behind his back, he began to pace the room. There was something on his mind. After a moment, looking Omelko in the face, he came out with it.

"Last night the military training camp was attacked. You had been instructed specifically by headquarters to protect it with twenty of our soldiers. But there was no protection and the camp was destroyed. What happened to our soldiers?"

Omelko laughed, "Those idiots probably got drunk and passed out somewhere. We'll never win this bloody war with the likes of them."

Boris, hearing Omelko talk in such a way, wanted only to take a swing at him, but he refrained. The matter would be settled later.

Adjusting his shirt collar and straightening his jacket, Vadim walked over to the door and stepped out into the corridor. Two guards stood by the main entrance with rifles strapped over their shoulders. A blindfolded girl sat on a bench just outside the vestibule with her back against the wall. She was slight in build with a long nose that turned slightly upward and a lovely full mouth the color of raspberries. Going up to her, Vadim took her by the arm and led her into a largish room that had once been someone's living room. Vadim untied her blindfold and politely asked her to sit down. The girl obeyed. She had pastel blue eyes with soft brown lashes and her cheekbones were high and prominent in the Slavic tradition. Her beauty was staggering.

Vadim sat opposite her on a stool and jotted something down on a piece of paper. He asked without looking up.

"Your name?"

"Yanina Kenzinska."

"Where were you born?"

"In Krakow."

"Your nationality?"

"Polish."

He paused a moment, and noticing her uneasiness, grimaced ironically.

"I thought your superiors would have been more clever than that. You should have stayed home with your mother. How old are you?"

"Nineteen."

"Why are you wearing peasant clothes? Obviously, you're not a farm girl."

"I wanted to visit my sister who lives in Kolki. I thought I would be less conspicuous dressed like this."

"Where are your parents?"

"They were shot by the Germans."

Vadim threw back his head and gave a wry smile, "Well, you're putting on quite a good show."

Tapping his fingers on the side of his leg, he got up and walked over to the window. He looked outside. It was a brisk early autumn morning and the sun was just beginning to rise up over the treetops. There was a sheen of frost on the ground, and a cold and vigorous wind blew in from the north. With his back to the girl, he cautioned severely.

"I advise you to speak the truth. Don't bother with any fabrications. We know all about you."

Making his way to a filing cabinet that stood in the corner, from the top drawer he pulled out a folder and laid it on top of his desk. He looked directly at her as if he already knew it all.

"Nina Lusina, you're not going to fool us."

A tremor passed over the girl's face and she wrung her hands. "That's not my name. You probably have my real identification in your files. I'm from Krakow; my mother was Ukrainian, my father Polish. My parents left Krakow when I was twelve. My older sister married a teacher called Novak, and they live in Kolki. If you don't believe me, it can easily be verified. Kolki is not too far away."

Vadim stared at her fixedly and his stare unsettled her. She sat back in her seat, and fidgeting with her hands, lowered her eyes to the ground. Her petite shoulders heaved and all at once she began to sob. She struggled with her words.

"Your people captured me, blindfolded me, and then brought me here. Stop tormenting me with questions. Let me go! I'm just an ordinary girl."

Her helplessness and desperation had a touching, child-like charm that attracted Vadim. She wiped her eyes and nose with a handkerchief and looked pleadingly at him. Her loveliness made him uncomfortable. He almost broke down and said something to soothe her, but quickly regained himself.

"Don't cry, Nina," he said finally.

"I'm Yanina! Yanina!"

"Why are you being so stubborn? I suggest you cooperate. You may be clever, but you're in an extremely dangerous position." He glanced at his file and did not look up. He continued. "Let me see ... You parachuted into the Zumansky Forest and your mission was to reach Dolina, a Polish outpost. There you were to pass on some important documents or perhaps memorized information. It's all too obvious."

"That's not true! All you're doing is trying to confuse me! You're making it all up! You're wrong about me! You're wrong about everything!"

The blood rushed to the girl's face and she shook as if from fever. Tears poured down her cheeks and she gasped for breath. Not knowing what to do, jumping to her feet, she made her way to the window, where she tried to calm herself. She looked out into the yard.

Vadim watched her closely; he couldn't take his eyes off her. She was stunning. Her legs were long and graceful and stirred his masculinity. Though he had been hardened by revolution, he longed for the warmth of a woman.

Vadim walked toward the girl, "I have one more question to ask you. Do you know Stenka Halahin? Apparently, he flew out of Moscow a week before you. You were supposed to make contact with him."

The girl flung herself around and yelled almost hysterically, "You want to convict me at all costs, don't you!"

Vadim tried to corner her, "Stenka is in our hands. Would you like to see him?"

Her tears suddenly stopped and there came a fire to her eyes. She even became angry. She lashed out at him, "You have nothing to pin on me and you know it. You're doing this deliberately. I don't know any Stenka *Galagin*."

"Hah, just as I thought!" Vadim slapped the side of his leg and shouted triumphantly. "Now everything is clear to me. I said Halahin, and like a true Muscovite you said *Galagin*."

As Vadim stepped toward the door and called for the guards to take the girl away, at once the thought of the ruthless Omelko popped into his mind. He said to himself, "Halahin – shot dead brutally like all the others."

The girl was escorted back to her cell.

The tribunal often met at main headquarters, which for the time being was located in a well-concealed, fenced-in farmhouse protected by armed guards under the command of Lieutenant Virovy. Lieutenant Virovy, Vadim, Boris, and Omelko had just been notified by one of their informers that the Bolsheviks had discovered their location and were planning an attack in a few nights. They believed that someone within their division was leaking information to the Reds. For this reason, the headquarters had to be relocated every few weeks. A week before, when it had been based in a neighboring farmstead, it was unexpectedly attacked in the middle of the night. Virovy, Boris, and Vadim privately suspected one another. Omelko, on the other hand, because of his ruthlessness in dealing with the enemy, was beyond reproach; however, Virovy, Vadim, and Boris secretly thought him untrustworthy.

Late into the night, Vadim conferred with Boris. They studied the files on Halahin and Nina time and time again and then labored over several messages written in code. They could not decipher a word of it.

Boris questioned Vadim thoroughly about his meeting with Nina, and the next day before noon, he went to cross-examine her himself. This time the interrogation took place by the river, in a small wooden shack, which at one time had been occupied by Polish soldiers.

Boris started off by asking her how she had slept; he then offered her food. The girl stood watching him with wide open eyes.

"Nina, I want to go over a few things with you. I understand you're from Krakow."

"Yes, I lived there with my parents until I was twelve."

"What street did you live on?"

She paused a moment, then taking a deep breath, said boldly, "On Lesny Street."

"Hm ... That's odd. I don't remember any such street in Krakow. I was a student there at the university."

The girl shifted uncomfortably and tugged at her shirt collar. She fanned her face. "Um, it's a small street, more of a lane, really." Then, "It's a bit stuffy in here. Would you mind if I took off my jacket?"

"No, by all means, go ahead."

Slipping off her jacket, she instantly revealed the contours of her finely sculpted neck. Unbuttoning the top of her blouse, she leaned over slightly, exposing the gentle cleavage between her perfectly rounded breasts. Boris continued with his questioning.

"Now, Nina, let's start from the beginning."

"I already told your friend, my name is Yanina."

"Did you attend school while in Krakow?"

"Yes."

"Which one?"

"St. Vavzinsa."

Boris put the butt end of his pen to his mouth and eyed her suspiciously. He then proceeded to ask her detailed questions about Krakow, and from her answers, just as he had suspected, it was obvious this lovely creature had never been to that city.

"So, Nina," said Boris now almost unsparingly, "you've done nothing but take me on a wild goose chase. You're full of lies. You've never lived in Krakow, and I bet you never even visited there. Now I can see everything: you're not an agent but a victim of circumstance and I feel sorry for you. Yes, your superiors in Moscow sit comfortably in the Kremlin and sip fine wine while you're out here among murderers, thieves, and rapists doing their dirty work. You're still a child. Such a pity."

"I've told you a hundred times already, I'm not an agent. I've never been to Moscow and nobody sent me on any mission. Can't I get that through to you?"

"So, they've given you a good scare, have they? They say the Bolshevik hand is far-reaching and can get you anywhere."

"Why are you trying to corner me and make me into something I'm not? I'm simply a girl who was on her way to visit her sister in Kolki. And that's the truth."

"If that's the way you want to play it, that's fine by me."

Boris collected his files, and stuffing them into his satchel, walked to the door. But he ended in a threatening way, "Tomorrow we'll talk to you in another language!"

He called for the guards.

* * *

The girl was locked in a warm, tidy shack near headquarters, guarded by an armed soldier. It was late at night and big stars hung over the woods like large diamonds. In the distance, a cold eastern wind rocked the trunks of trees and rustled the leaves. A weak gas lamp on Nina's night table cast a dim light, and as she stood by the window, her shadow fell on the opposite wall. Preparing for bed, as she was about to turn out the light, she heard a sound coming from behind the door. A human form suddenly appeared on the threshold, and as it approached, she discerned the outline of Lieutenant Virovy. She threw her jacket over her shoulders and said crossly, "If you don't mind, I was just getting ready for bed."

Virovy was stirred by her impulsive movements and gazed at her curiously. He parted his lips and released a tender smile.

"I didn't come here to interrogate you," he said. "If you like, I'll go."

As he turned toward the door, the girl called after him.

"No, wait, please, stay. The truth is I'm so miserable. I noticed something about you before. You seem different from the others."

Her jacket slipped off her left shoulder and fell to her elbow; her firm little breasts stood out from under her nightgown. Virovy, absorbed by her glowing fragility, at once fell victim to his desires. Up until now, his hard and simple military life had been an exercise in self-denial and celibacy. He had not made love to a woman for months. His whole body ached, but he was determined not to allow her to win him over.

"You seem like an honest man," she remarked carefully and quietly, all the while scrutinizing him.

Virovy tried not to lose his self-control. His rugged face was tanned from the wind and his deep black eyes projected strength.

The girl looked him over almost provocatively. She said:

"I never imagined I would ever meet up with someone like you in the middle of nowhere."

Then smoothening her silky brown hair with the tips of her fingers, suddenly her face changed and she burst out crying. "Oh, you interrogators are all alike. You think I'm here with evil intentions."

Virovy looked steadfastly at her, "All the facts point against you."

Nina rubbed the nape of her neck. Slowly edging her way toward him, she released a faint smile but did not speak.

"Don't bother turning on the charm for me," he began, "even if you were a water nymph, I wouldn't get wet. Besides, I'm stronger than you are."

The girl laughed.

"I may be just a plain soldier, but I know more than you think."

"Like what?"

"Well, for one thing, you're not Polish. You're not Russian either. Something about you doesn't quite make sense."

The girl gave a twinge.

"As a matter of fact, I don't think you know who you are. The Russians obviously trained and educated you and then sent you here."

In the dim light the girl didn't notice Virovy edge toward her. And before she knew it, he grabbed her by both arms and with such violence that he ripped her nightgown. Her bare shoulders gleamed in the dark. Lifting her up in the air, pressing upon her neck, she tried to break free by screaming and punching at his chest. But he only tightened his hold over her. He shouted through his teeth, "I'll show you who you are."

She tugged at his thick black hair and tried to dig her nails into his neck.

"So, you want to tackle with me, do you? You think the school of espionage has made you invincible?"

When she started to cough and choke, he gradually released his grip until her feet touched the ground. She looked up at his red face, and the two stared at one another for the longest time.

The girl made the first move. With her eyes glittering, touching his shoulders with the tips of her fingers, she slipped her hands around his neck. When he slightly parted his mouth, she pressed her lips against his. Her breathlessness aroused him to such an extent, he kissed her again and again. He cupped her small breasts with his rugged hands. They fell to the floor, and he lowered his hard, muscular body over hers.

"It looks like the enemies have united," he whispered in her ear. "The blood rises and the devil does his work. The spirit of the Cossack is dead."

When dawn broke, Virovy got out of bed and put on his trousers. He said to the girl sternly, "Nothing has changed because of last night. You're still our prisoner."

When Virovy entered office headquarters there was a message on his desk. It was an update on recent activities in the area: Bolshevik troops had been spotted heading in the direction of Peretok; Germans had burned a few villages along the Styr River; and a band of Poles was spotted outside of Rozhyshche.

Stepping outside, he examined the surroundings. Everything seemed in order. He looked toward the shack, toward

Nina's room, and noticed her curtains were drawn. A guard sat sleeping by the door with his rifle leaning against the wall. Virovy had the urge to go to see her but his weakness suddenly enraged him.

"The hussy! She deserves to die! Women are so soft and tender, but they have all the power!"

The next day the girl was not interrogated. After the cook had taken her a tray of food, Virovy couldn't help but ask him how she was doing.

"She seems rather quiet."

Virovy sat at his desk and placed his head on his fist. He was restless and couldn't find peace of mind. A hungry passion was overtaking him and he could feel the blood boiling within him. He wanted the girl. He jumped to his feet and began to pace the room.

"Well, my blue-eyed lovely," he muttered to himself, "I'm not going to let you get away with it."

In terrible excitement, he stormed into her shack.

"I've come to a decision," he said.

The girl looked at him anxiously as she pressed herself up against the wall.

"Choose right now, one or the other. Let me warn you, if you side with the enemy, you're as good as dead."

Her face turned pale and she did not dare stir. The whites of her eyes bulged as she watched his every move.

"What will it be?" he shouted. "My colleagues are less sympathetic than I am."

She began to tremble.

"You were sent to spy on us, weren't you!"

"What do you want from me?" The girl moved to the corner of the room. "You're horrible! You're heartless and you frighten me."

"Answer me! There was a man called Halahin. Wasn't there!"

"No!"

"Yes!"

"No!"

He raised his hand as if to strike her.

"No! No! Yes!" she screamed. "Yes! Yes!"

"Were you supposed to make contact with him?"

"Yes, but he was killed. Oh, what am I saying? They'll find me and torture me. I'm as good as dead."

"Don't worry; no one is going to harm you." Virovy lowered his tone, he tried to calm her down. "Tell me, Nina, who killed Halahin?"

"A secret agent. He operates among your people and he's very dangerous." Shaking, after a moment she went on, "You were right about me. As far as I know, my parents died of starvation, but I don't know where they were from or where they are buried. I was just a baby. I was brought up and educated in Moscow, and then the Red Army sent me to spy among the Poles. That's why I speak fluent Polish."

She raised her head and Virovy wiped her tears dry with a handkerchief. Stroking her hair, he whispered, "Settle down, Nina. It's going to be all right. I promise."

"That's not my name. It was given to me in Moscow. I don't know my real name."

Folding her hands on her lap, she looked Virovy earnestly in the face. "And there's more. Maybe today, maybe tomorrow, a Soviet agent will parachute into the forest near Bereziw. He's supposed to replace the current agent, who deliberately left your military training camp unprotected. He has a radio hidden away somewhere and uses it to intercept and confuse messages. He even has special authorization to murder his own people in order to gain your trust."

* * *

The area surrounding Bereziw was swarming with partisans; they hid behind trees and in dugouts, and with their rifles loaded and ready, watched the clouded sky. German warplanes, made invisible by the overhanging gray, roared nonstop toward the Front. Late in the evening, when a thick fog settled over the forest, the buzzing sound of a plane in descent could be heard directly overhead. The partisans remained on alert and in position. A vague flickering of metal broke above a stand of pines, and soon an aircraft came into full view. It appeared as if a light wind were directing it toward a small clearing. Suddenly a body jumped out and a parachute opened and hovered above the treetops. As it glided toward the ground, somehow it became snagged by a tree limb, causing the limb to bend and crack. The paratrooper quickly unfastened the harness, and after setting himself free, clinging to the limb, proceeded to untangle the ropes from the branches. After throwing the parachute to the ground, he began to descend, swinging from branch to branch, not unlike an ape. Vigilant eyes watched his every move and rifles were aimed and ready. When he had barely touched the ground, the partisans pounced on him, grabbed

THEODORE ODRACH

his gun, and tied up his hands with rope. He was taken back to headquarters and shoved before the tribunal.

"Another Soviet bastard!" barked Omelko upon seeing him; he looked him up and down. "We'll chop you up into little pieces before the day is through!" With his anger only mounting, red in the face, he kicked him in the shins and then in the stomach.

The paratrooper moaned from pain. Looking very confused and frightened, he made a face and signaled with his head as if trying to convey some kind of message to Omelko.

"How dare you gape at me like that!" Omelko flew at him.

The paratrooper looked completely at a loss. Sweat formed on his brow and his face contorted.

"You think you recognize me, do you?" Omelko went on. "We'll get to know each other soon enough!" Raising his fist, he punched him in the jaw until blood streamed out. The paratrooper reeled but did not fall. Omelko pulled out his revolver and aimed it at his head.

At that moment, quite unexpectedly, Vadim jumped in from behind and twisted the revolver out of his hands.

Omelko was enraged. "What in devil's name are you doing?"

"Omelko, you're under arrest."

"What, have you gone mad? All of you?" He drilled his eyes into Boris, then into Vadim. He hissed like a snake. "You sons-of-bitches, you'll hang for this!"

Vadim only grimaced then turned to the paratrooper. He said to him ironically, "If it weren't for us, your comrade would have shot you dead."

The door of the courtroom opened wide. Virovy and Nina entered. Nina was dressed neatly in a white cotton blouse and gray trousers and her hair was tied back in a single braid. She stood opposite Omelko but did not utter a word.

Omelko screwed up his mouth, "You little bitch, you traitor, this is all your fault. You'll be in our hands before you know it!"

Boris signaled to the guards and the two men were taken away.

DEATH PITS

In the heart of Kovel stood a large red brick building. For a small provincial town, the building was of some architectural significance: it had broad oak doors with massive pillars, a pediment over the portico, and several stories of high arched windows. During Polish occupation, the red brick building had been a very busy place, housing government offices, and also acting as the local police station with holding cells in the basement. When in 1939, after the signing of the Molotov Ribbentrop Pact and when Bolshevik troops seized Kovel, it was in this building that the NKVD set up its regional headquarters.

As if overnight unspeakable atrocities began to occur. No one really knew precisely what went on inside the brick building, but those who dared pass by felt their bodies gripped by a dead sudden fear. The grounds were surrounded by a high wooden fence with the palings nailed so closely together it was almost impossible to see inside. The windows on the lower level were boarded with planks of scrap wood and various poster papers, and from the basement there came a cold, foul smell.

Inside the building were long, narrow corridors, branching off to the left and to the right. The endless line of doors remained closed, but from time to time the sound of type-writers or the ringing of telephones could be heard coming from the rooms. The floors were gray and made of stone, and from the cells in the dungeon, those held prisoner could hear the clicking heels of the NKVD men quickly making their way from one end to the other. During all hours of the day, with the tips of their rifles, NKVD men pushed hand-bound captives into small interrogation rooms and then banged shut the door. These captives knew they were damned, that their time had run out. In the dungeon, hope for rescue still existed, but now in the interrogation room, everything became a pitch black. Some were then taken into sealed-off chambers and tortured, while others were dragged out into the courtyard, blindfolded, and shot in the nape of the neck.

The NKVD men brought with them a new world, a world without a God. Dressed in loose-fitting shirts belted over their trousers in the typical Russian fashion with revolvers at their waists, they were lord and master.

What occurred in the red brick building between 1939 and 1941, residents of this small provincial town could not really say in any detail. They knew only that atrocities were being committed, that innocent people were tortured and murdered daily. Those who lived near the compound said that almost every night they were kept awake by the idling of trucks and that behind the idling they could hear the sound of muffled screams and then gunfire.

When in 1941 the massive forces of the German army started moving in the direction of Kovel, the NKVD men, outnumbered, fled east. Capturing Kovel, the Germans set up headquarters on the opposite end of town; the NKVD compound they boarded up and posted no trespassing signs on the front gates. For the longest time afterward, the citizens of Kovel swore they could hear unearthly sounds coming from there. They claimed that it breathed as if possessed.

One day, Yuri Lada, a local doctor, was pushed out by the residents of Kovel to approach German headquarters regarding the matter of the red brick building. Boldly entering the *Gebietskommissar's* office, he fumbled to take off his cap. He began uneasily:

"Excuse me, *Herr Gebietskommissar*, but I'm here on behalf of the people of Kovel. We're seeking permission to enter the NKVD compound. We would like to dig up our dead and give them a proper burial. We want to lay them to rest."

Clearing his throat, he had more to say, "And also, there's the matter of sanitation. The odor is getting stronger by the day and ..."

But before Lada had a chance to finish the *Gebietskommissar* cut him off abruptly.

"Enough already! Now is not the time to search for corpses when our German men on the front are dropping dead like flies! Now, get out of here before I do away with you right here and now!"

The next day the doctor again approached the *Gebietskommissar,* but this time the *Gebietskommissar* only found amusement in his request and dismissed him with a display of laughter.

"You and your corpses! Hah! Hah! Hah! A corpse is nothing but a corpse, after all. Stop wasting my time! Get out!"

But the citizens of Kovel continued to press for entry. Finally, to prevent unrest and a possible health outbreak, the *Gebietskommissar* gave in and issued a written authorization.

* * *

It was at the start of October when the gates of the NKVD compound were finally opened up. The leaves had long since fallen from the trees and a thin layer of frost covered the ground. A cold and bitter wind blew in from the north and shook the high wooden fence. The sky, dark and gray, hung heavily over the rooftops of Kovel.

The first to enter the grounds were young men. Armed with shovels and picks, they wore high leather boots and damp cloths masked the lower part or their faces. For several days the gates remained closed to the general public. The young men labored late into the night opening up enormous pits with people remains in them. They extracted body after body and laid them down in rows alongside the fence; some were already unrecognizable from decay others still had an expression of terror etched on their faces. News of the death pits quickly spread throughout the region. From every corner of Volyna people searching for family members rushed to Kovel: mothers whose sons or daughters went missing, young women looking for their husbands, men looking for their wives, children for their parents. All were white with despair as if they themselves were in the final throws of death.

The first morning the gates opened up to the general public, Alexander Didenko banged on the door of his good

THEODORE ODRACH

friend Maxim Shimko. The two had been childhood friends and had studied together at the university in Lviv. When Alexander had barely entered Maxim's house, he said quickly, unable to catch his breath.

"Maxim, you must come with me to the compound to help me find my parents. With the two of us searching things will go faster. Please, I beg you."

A shudder passed through Maxim and his heart throbbed, he could feel nausea in the pit of his stomach. He could not bear the thought of turning over corpses and looking into decomposing faces, particularly of those he might recognize. But upon seeing the distressed look on his friend's face, he quickly pulled himself together.

"Yes, Alexa; yes, of course, I will go with you."

The friends walked across town in silence. The streets were empty and not a sound came from within the rows of wooden houses they passed. As they neared the gates of the red brick building, a strong smell of chlorine and calc filled the air. The courtyard, immense and rectangular in shape, from one side was sealed off by the brick building, from the other by a high wooden fence. The pits were now all opened up. They were not wide but very deep, and inside lay bodies of men, women, children, even infants. In typical NKVD style, the victims had been brought up from their cells in the dungeon in small groups and lined up on the edge of a pit. They were then shot from the back in such a way that their bodies would drop to the bottom, forming a layer. Soon after, the next group would be brought up and another layer formed. The majority were gagged and had their arms tied behind their backs with barbed wire, the remainder were severely maimed, some with missing body parts. Those closest to the top had been buried alive, and as the dirt was shoveled down upon them, out of desperation to breathe, they had submerged their nails deep into their flesh and ripped apart their faces.

Many townspeople were crowded into the courtyard, searching the long line of corpses already laid up against the fence.

When Alexander and Maxim noticed a bloodstained pole with a metal hook lying on the ground, they concluded it had been used by the NKVD men to jiggle the corpses around to best make use of the limited space. Each pit held approximately a hundred bodies.

The two friends searched for Alexander's parents but with no luck.

Then a man's voice came tearing out from the garage that had an earthen floor:

"May God help us, there are more pits in here!"

Standing over the death pits, the citizens of Kovel became completely paralyzed. The thought of those responsible did not come to mind, at least not right away; they felt only the triumph of Hell.

In the cemetery on the outskirts of town, along the highway connecting Kovel to Lutsk, men started to dig communal graves. The carpenters of Kovel, with grim determination, set out to build coffins. Peasants from surrounding villages brought in their carts and horse-drawn wagons, and loading up with the newly-built coffins, took them to the NKVD compound to get them filled. Each coffin held two to three bodies, and once they were laid in the cemetery, the wagons returned for more.

A small Orthodox church with onion-shaped domes and stained-glass windows stood in the center of town. In the entranceway was a spectacular fresco representing Ukraine throughout the ages. Father Huba and Father Ihor were in the midst of performing a Requiem service. Father Huba, still a young man, not more than forty, with deep-set brown eyes and a kind, intelligent face, had traveled all the way from Rivne for this tragic event. Chanting in a low, mesmerizing tenor, for a brief moment, he set the people free from their grief.

Before the altar, which was elaborately carved and decked with a hemstitched cloth, stood a black symbolic coffin. With a flood of emotion, a choir of soprano and bass voices rose from the back aisles. The sweet smell of incense filled the air. The little church overflowed with people. They had come from far and wide and there were over a thousand of them. They filled the churchyard and spilled out onto the broad pot-holed street beyond.

Toward the end of the service, Father Huba and Father Ihor together began the Lord's prayer: "Our Father who art in Heaven ..." Their loud voices trailed deep into the crowd and then came back in a resounding echo.

After the service, the people assembled before the church and in a line made for the cemetery. At the head, side by side, walked the priests, bearing heavy wooden crosses and casting cedar-filled brass censers. Behind them supporting the symbolic coffin were six pallbearers. Rows of young girls dressed in traditional costume followed, carrying broad wreaths of wildflowers and signs reading Victims of Communism, In Eternal Memory and so forth. Boys walked in step with the girls. Some waved forbidden flags of yellow and blue, while others held icons framed in colorfully cross-stitched cloths. Everyone else followed – peasants, merchants, teachers, doctors, office workers, factory workers. All had come to honor the dead.

The procession slowly made its way along the road that led to Lutsk. Passing a line of tumble-down houses and small wooden shops, finally, it wound its way to the outskirts of town. When the head finally crossed the fast-moving Turya Rive and turned into the cemetery, the tail end could still be found somewhere on the other side of the Stary Bridge.

It was not long before all arrived in the cemetery. The trees stood bare and the branches snapped in the cold northerly wind. The sky had darkened and a gray impenetrable mist settled on the ground. There was no place for the sun.

The priests walked solemnly around the freshly dug graves and sprinkled them with holy water. They then began the final Requiem prayer. Soon the choir joined in, and the crowd, with their heads bent, made the sign of the cross. Then came several moments of silence.

Of great power and magnitude was the funeral in Kovel during that grave autumn in 1941.

In 1945 after four years of brutal German occupation, in Kovel things once again became as they were. Though the West had won the war, Kovel had lost; it had lost everything. The NKVD men returned, only to re-open the red brick building and once again set in motion the wheels of their apparatus.

THEODORE ODRACH

CRANE DANCE

A stream of birds fly across the bright blue sky; they flap their wings in rhythm and caw. Stefan looks up and, shading his eyes with the palm of his hand, watches as they weave in between the faint white clouds.

He calls out to them: "Where are you flying to?"

But the birds soar higher into the sky and disappear over the horizon. A wind picks up and children's singing carries across the field:

> "Happy sun so high
> Shine again on the Dunai."

Stefan lays down in a field of millet, and with the warm rays upon him, drifts into a dream world. He thinks of Grandmother Klimova's words and he repeats them to himself.

"You will see a crane dance, and when you see this dance, it will be an omen. You will be the happiest boy on earth. It will bring you good luck and you will grow up healthy and rich."

Suddenly an ear-splitting voice comes ripping across the field. It is Lida Hominkova. Her disheveled gray hair hangs loosely over her face and she waves her spade angrily in the air.

"Stefan, you lazy little brat!" she shouts. "Why aren't you tending to your herd? Take a look at what your cows are doing! How many times do I have to tell you?"

The boy jumps to his feet and in the distance sees Hominkova's potato patch being trampled.

"What you need is a good whipping," Hominkova goes on, "that'll put you straight! Your poor mama, having to put up with the likes of you! And your poor papa dead in the war. All my potatoes are ruined. Hurry up, what are you waiting for? Grab a stick and chase off your cows."

At that moment, Christina, Hominkova's twenty-year-old daughter, jumps in between them. Taking her mother by the arm, she says, "Calm down, mother, please; it's bad for your health. After all, it's not the end of the world."

Christina is a tall, lean girl with straight black hair and beautiful almond-shaped eyes. She pats Stefan on the head and smiles warmly at him. She urges him, "Why don't you take your herd over to Vishny's pasture, the grass is high and juicy over there."

Taking potatoes from her basket, Christina quickly fills up the boy's satchel. She says kindly, "You can boil these up for your supper tonight."

The boy is grateful, and strapping the satchel to his shoulders, turns to go. But first, he walks timidly up to Lida Hominkova and apologizes. He sees she is very upset and her eyes are flaming. But she accepts his apology.

With his stick, he chases his cattle into the neighboring field. The sun is hot and beats down upon him and sweat forms on his brow. When a cool breeze sweeps across his face he is instantly revived. Approaching a clump of raspberry bushes, he pops several berries into his mouth and then stoops to peer between the branches. He sees Vishny's pasture. It is spread out before him like a magnificent carpet of yellow-green.

Along the edge of the pasture, he notices a swampy little stream. It meanders gently, and small schools of fish can be seen swimming hurriedly beneath its murky surface. The boy chases his herd into the water and rolling his trousers up to his knees, wades in after them. The cows drink greedily and then turn to the pasture to graze. Stefan sets up camp by a row of linden trees that form a boundary between Vishny's pasture and an adjoining millet field. The sky is a bright blue and flies and mosquitoes buzz nonstop round his head.

After gathering dry leaves and twigs, arranging them in the shape of a pyramid, he strikes up a match. The fire blazes. He carefully pares and quarters each potato with his pocketknife, and then fills up a pot with water from the stream. He throws the potatoes in to boil. Whittling himself a fork from a willow branch, he eats his supper heartily.

As he is about to take a final mouthful, he is startled by a faint trumpeting sound from somewhere in the millet field. He holds his breath and listens. But quiet resumes and he concludes it is only the wind. Taking his last bite and licking the tips of his fingers, he lays down on the ground and watches as the drifting clouds take on different shapes: first a sheep, then a dog, a house, an elephant ... There is silence everywhere, even his herd has settled in the shade of a nearby weeping willow. Then again, the faint trumpeting sound. He strains his ears to listen. Rolling over onto his belly, he places an ear to the ground and to his great surprise hears a distant bugle-like call. It appears to be coming from somewhere in the center of the field.

His eyes light up and his heart begins to race, "Cranes! It must be the crane dance! Grandmother Klimova says that cranes are mystical creatures of the marshlands and that they bring good luck. She says when I see them dance, I'll be happy and my mama will be happy too."

On all fours the boy makes his way into the field, keeping as low to the ground as possible. He pauses frequently to catch the slightest sound, but the heavy millet husks filled with little brown seeds rustle overhead and throw him off track.

The trumpeting sound stops suddenly. Disappointed, the boy rises to his feet and looks round. But there is only emptiness everywhere. Several minutes pass, then half an hour; still nothing but silence. He begins to grow restless.

Spreading apart the millet with his arms, the boy makes his way to the edge of the field. He is exhausted and his hands and feet ache. He wants to stop and rest, but he is determined to see the dance. The sun is lost behind some clouds and he could feel the coolness of the air. He has long since forgotten about his herd, though they could be heard mooing in the not-so-far distance. He trips over what appears to be a gopher hole and falls to the ground, ripping his trousers. Blood trickles from his forehead and there is a pain in his head.

Then unexpectedly from the village comes the loud clanging of church bells. How strange for the bells to be ringing at this hour. Somehow the sounds numb his body and he is gripped by a terrible foreboding.

THEODORE ODRACH

There are blisters on his heels and he finds it difficult to go on. Taking off his shoes, he punctures them with the tip of his pocketknife and then wipes them dry with the cuffs of his shirt. He heaves a deep sigh. At once, he is overcome with fatigue. His throat runs dry, and coughing and gasping for breath, he begins to grow dizzy. He starts to shake as if from fever. His shirt is wet and soiled and his trousers are ripped. He knows his mama will not be pleased. In that instant, thoughts of school enter his mind and he chides himself for his unruly behavior. He regrets neglecting his homework and playing tricks on Madame Sadowska, his teacher. He has caused his mama much grief, and she is so thin and frail. At that moment he vows to reform.

When the church bells again peal across the field, Stefan without thinking makes the sign of the cross. The bells sound so deep and heavy, even mournful, and almost at once he thinks of the widow Prokopa. Who else in the village is old enough to die? Her hollow red eyes appear before him and he pictures her bent, shriveled body hobbling across the road with the support of her cane. Now she is dead and tomorrow will be her funeral.

The boy rolls over onto a clump of grass, and staring up at the sky, imagines the paradise he and his mama will live in once he sees the crane dance. And because Grandmother Klimova says he is destined to see it, everything will soon go his way. Oblivious to the intensifying winds, he immerses himself deeper into his fantasies. As he begins to doze, at once he is wakened by shrill trumpeting. Scrambling to his feet, he rushes along the field's edge, flattening and breaking the millet stalks beneath him.

"It's the crane dance! I can hear it!" he shouts at the top of his voice.

Standing in the middle of the field, he looks first to the left, then to the right. But for some reason, the cranes are nowhere in sight. He rushes to the far corner, then along the edge of the stream, but again nothing. Searching frantically for almost an hour, he comes up empty. He is deeply saddened and disappointed. Horseflies buzz persistently around his head and he shoos them off with his hands. Then a rainbow spreads across the sky – red, green, purple, blue. The colors hypnotize him and, falling to the ground, he enters a deep sleep.

* * *

The boy dreams heavily. He dreams he is in a millet field, the same millet field he has just fallen asleep in. But in the millet field, there is an amphitheater, and he sitting there waiting for the performance to begin. Suddenly dozens of cranes appear. They form a huge ring, bobbing their red-patched heads, jumping, and flapping their wings. They let out deep trumpeting calls. In the center of the ring is the dominant, most vigorous male crane and his heavy blue-gray plumage sparkles in the sunlight. From time to time, on stilt-like legs, he leaps majestically into the air and then bows. The female birds in the ring coo and caw. Pirouetting, accelerating in speed, spreading their broad tails, they move in on the male. Soon the remaining males join in. The boy is mesmerized by the dance and, still dreaming, moves in for a better look.

THEODORE ODRACH

But at that moment a deafening cry erupts from the sky. The cranes are frightened and lift their heads. The cry intensifies. There is a large black bird gliding over them, its wings as if touching the tops of their heads. The cranes remain unmoving. The black bird then lands in the center of the arena and breaks up the dance.

The dominant male spreads his wings wide, and with his long legs pulled out behind him, soars up into the sky; he is followed by the remaining cranes. They form a long, thin line that stretches out as far as the eye can see. At the end flies the black bird.

The boy is devastated and feels as if his whole world has come crashing down upon him. He follows the birds with his gaze until a thick gray cloud appears and hides them from view.

* * *

The boy tosses and turns in his sleep and is finally awakened by the sound of a woman's voice calling for him.

"Stefan, where are you? Answer me!"

Rubbing his eyes, the boy pulls himself up off the ground and makes for his campsite, where his fire is now smoldering. Twilight has set in and the fields have turned into a soft purple haze. As he approaches, he sees Christina standing across the creek by one of the linden trees calling for him. The boy does not notice the sad look on her face and nor does he notice that she'd been crying.

"Come along, Stefan," she says in a hushed tone and takes him by the hand.

But Stefan is too filled with excitement. There is but one thing on his mind.

"I saw a crane dance! It was in my dream!" he shouts at the top of his voice. "It was the most incredible thing! And there was a black bird too."

Then suddenly he becomes gripped by an unexpected fear. Something has gone terribly wrong. Where did that black bird come from? His eyes well up with tears and he begins to tremble all over.

"Sh, Stefan. You must be brave," Christina gives him a hug.

Picking him up in her arms, she carries him across the creek. Once they reach the other side, she holds onto him a little longer before setting him down. She takes him by the hand and together they walk back to the village. As they come to the gates of his front yard, pressing his hand tightly, she whispers.

"Your mama loved you more than life itself. You must never forget that. She's watching over you from Heaven now."

The boy doesn't respond. He doesn't believe what he hears. He tells himself he's still dreaming.

BLOOD

When Zahirsky arrived in a suburb of Prague he turned down a side street and began searching for number 150, a villa in which he had lodged some years before. He had forgotten the name of the street but retained a clear picture of the quaint houses winding up the slope of a hill. For years now he had lived abroad, but being of a sentimental nature, he often found himself thinking of Prague, of Mrs. Yanichek's villa, and of Doctor O who rented a small, damp room in the basement. The street was lined with trees, spring flowers were in full bloom, and rolling green hills obstructed a full view of Prague's old town. Zahirsky wondered whether much had changed within the Yanichek household. And finally, there it was, the memorable two-story house, the same tiled red roof, the same ramose apple trees growing all around.

He turned into the walkway but stopped short. The past was coming back to him and he closed his eyes for a moment and thought of happy, bygone days when he had been a carefree young man in love with the most beautiful girl in the world. And now here he was again, years later, about to knock on the door of Mrs. Yanichek's villa, unannounced.

A nine-year-old boy with big black eyes opened the door and poked out his head. Zahirsky was delighted to note that at one time, Rougenka, the daughter of Mrs. Yanichek had the same lovely eyes. Zahirsky leaned forward and asked him:

"Does Doctor O live here, young man?"

"You mean the fat man who lives in the basement?"

"He was on the stocky side, but not fat," recalled Zahirsky to himself. Then aloud, "How can I describe him to you? The doctor has a round face, thick brows and wears spectacles."

"That's him!" shouted the boy excitedly. "Doctor O, he lives here in the basement. His front teeth are all cracked, kind of rotten, and he wanted to get some gold ones put in. That's him! Even Baba says he ought to but now he's gone and changed his mind again. Baba says he's stubborn."

Zahirsky and the boy descended to the basement and knocked on the doctor's door. There was no answer.

"I'll run up to Baba," yelled the boy and darted up to the first floor. "Baba, Baba, some man is here!"

Zahirsky could hear the boy huffing and puffing at the top of the staircase. He soon joined him in the living room.

An old woman with sunken cheeks and swollen eyes sat by the window on a low divan. Her hair was gray and neatly tied back in a bun. She didn't in the least bit resemble the Mrs. Yanichek he had once known.

"Who are you?" she asked upon seeing him. Her voice was low and uneven.

"I ... I ... if you permit, Zahirsky, Ivan Zahirsky."

"I don't know anyone by that name."

"I lodged here at one time, a few years ago. Don't you remember me? There in that side room. You even brought me breakfast sometimes. I recall your coffee with cream was most delicious."

The old woman narrowed her eyes as she seemed to reflect, "At one time I did have coffee and cream, that's true, but now it's war; everything's changed." She studied Zahirsky a moment, and then shook her head, "But in all honesty, I don't recognize you. You must have made some mistake."

Zahirsky stepped into the light. "That's too bad, Madame. To be quite honest, I don't think I would have recognized you either had we met under different circumstances. You used to look much different."

The old woman clasped her chest and took a deep breath; her face showed considerable fatigue. "That's quite true, young man, about every ten years I change in appearance. When I was a baby, people called me a little angel, I had such pretty blonde braids. Ten years passed and I became a fashionable young lady. Another ten years and I became a handsome, mature woman. And time had no mercy. Now another ten years. Oh, my, my, how time flies, now I'm nothing more than an old baba. My God, if only they knew I still have the heart of a child!"

Grinning sullenly, she shifted slightly and closed her eyes. She seemed to doze off. After a moment, she started again:

"Er ... you have come to see Doctor O, I understand? It's hard to find him at home these days. He drives to Prague every day. Sometimes he just barely steps through the door and the next thing you know, he's up and gone to Jihlava."

The old woman stretched her arm over the back of the divan and looked directly into Zahirsky's face as if scrutinizing him. She said curiously, "You're Ukrainian, the same as Doctor O, I can tell. All of you seem so robust, so tall, and healthy. So, tell me, why can't you chase the Russians out of your country?"

Zahirsky winced; he did not expect such a question. Unable to give her a direct answer, he asked instead, "Why does Doctor O travel to Prague so often?"

"Oh, I don't know. He's always preoccupied with some kind of business. Maybe ... who knows? Times are hard, you know that yourself. Many of us are undernourished. There may be no famine yet but we all feel the rationing. It's war, it's war."

"Yes, times are hard for everyone. Has Doctor O married by any chance?"

The old woman laughed at once, "Hah! That old goat? Are you kidding? He can't see the world for his work. He always has his nose in some book. French, German, Latin. He's mastered linguistics at the expense of his youth. Oh, such a shame! He's never been in love with a woman, but as you see, the world hasn't caved in because of it. Now he's gotten fat and his teeth are falling out. But he's energetic enough: every day he drives to Prague."

A warm sensation seemed to revive inside of Mrs. Yanichek and she released a tender smile. It was as if her mind were somewhere else.

Zahirsky commented, "I suppose he hasn't been very lucky in love."

"Luck has nothing to do with love, young man. Love can capture one's heart anywhere and at any time, providing, of course, there's a desire for it."

"Well, sometimes love captures the old heart too. Who knows, maybe Doctor O's time will yet come."

Mrs. Yanichek shrugged, "One needs a certain level of sensitivity for this to happen. I see you don't know the doctor and since you don't know him, I doubt whether he would want to make your acquaintance. That's the way he is. He's old and set in his ways, and filled with mistrust."

The little boy, who had been playing on the floor building houses out of colored blocks suddenly turned to his grandmother eagerly.

"Baba, will Uncle Pepi really buy a top for me, the big red one I saw in Placek's store window? And it was spinning all by itself, I saw it!"

"Yes, Igichek. He'll buy it. If he promised, then he'll buy it."

Rising from the divan, patting the boy on the head, she said impatiently, "Now why don't you be a good little boy and run out into the garden and play. We don't need you here right now. If I want you, I'll call through the window. Besides, your mother should be home from the city at any minute now. Go on and look out for her."

Reluctantly, the boy rose to his feet and made for the door. When the sound of his little footsteps just barely disappeared down the corridor, Mrs. Yanichek turned directly to Zahirsky. She was in the mood to talk.

"And so, this is life. When the sun shines, that's bliss; when the sun sets, that's sorrow; when the rays break through a cluster of clouds, that, my dear man, is hope."

Zahirsky stepped back and suppressed a yawn. He thought, "What a bore."

She went on, "And year in and year out that ray of hope keeps me going. The father must eventually see his child and the woman he once loved. My heart tells me this day will still come."

Zahirsky looked bewildered, "If you'll excuse me, but I really don't understand."

"Then I don't believe you've ever been in my home before. If you had, you wouldn't talk like that. Something happened here, a tragic love affair."

Her face suddenly clouded and she sat a moment with her head down.

Zahirsky waited for her to go on.

"Rougenka, this is her homeland, but Pepi ... he's tall and broad-shouldered like yourself. One night about five years ago, Pepi roamed the streets with too much drink in him, and then came back home convinced he was not really a Yanichek. That's your blood, I told him. That's your blood. And Pepi knew from that moment on that Alyoza Yanichek was not his biological father."

Taking a handkerchief out of her pocket, the old woman dried her eyes. She continued.

"My husband, Alyoza, was a man like all other men. Sometimes he was happy, sometimes he was sad. He knew how to love and how to hate. Soon after our marriage, he realized fate had passed him by; fate took a turn to the right and he took the opposite road, dragging me along with him. I never really loved Alyoza. I always believed that one day my true love would appear and everything would work out for the best. My God, why are life's mistakes so irrevocable?"

The old woman drew a deep breath, and after a moment's silence, turned and looked full at Zahirsky. A shine came to her eyes.

"And you know, he finally came, he came from the east. He was dressed in rags, hungry, and barely stood on his own two feet, but I recognized him at once. He stole my heart away. But it was too late. Too late. I welcomed him into our home; he even stayed in that back room over there. And my Alyoza, may he rest in peace, never suspected a thing."

"And what happened after that?" Zahirsky raised his brows; she had now completely captured his full attention.

"He had to leave; I paid his way to America. He didn't write for three years, then finally a letter. This was exactly two years after the death of my Alyoza. First, he paid off his debts, and then later began sending money regularly, for Pepi. Now communications have been disrupted; it's war, it's war."

Suddenly the front door creaked open. After a short while, footsteps could be heard going down the stairs.

"That's Doctor O," announced the old woman. "He's just come in."

Zahirsky, thanking her for her hospitality, turned to leave, but she held him a moment longer. "You've traveled a long way; I can see that. You young people are scattering all over the world just as those before you."

As Zahirsky made for the door, a certain unease came over him. He wrung his hands as if there was still something on his mind. Looking Mrs. Yanichek in the face, at last, he came out with it.

"Er, before I leave, I would like to ask you something. Would you please give my regards to Rougenka?"

The old woman narrowed her eyes. She said seriously, "That's really unnecessary, young man. Rougenka's married now and very happy. She's more fortunate than her mother."

A slight embarrassment passed over Zahirsky. He stood a moment not knowing quite what to do. Without anything else to say, bidding her a farewell, he withdrew from the room.

Descending into the basement, as he came to the landing, at once he heard peculiar noises. There was a crash and a bang, then something seemed to hit up against the wall. A man's voice could be heard cursing and complaining from behind a closed door.

"This packing will be the death of me! How am I ever going to manage it all? This is worse than death itself!"

Zahirsky knocked three times.

"Hello, Doctor O, greetings from the motherland. It's Zahirsky, Ivan Zahirsky. It's been quite a while since we last saw each other."

Standing on the threshold, Zahirsky quickly scanned the doctor's room. It was in complete chaos. Stacks of books and journals lay on the floor and piles of newspapers were lined up against the walls. Doctor O stood in the doorway, his shirt sleeves rolled up to the elbows, and there was sweat on his brow.

"All this packing is going to be the death of me! Thirty-five copies of *Novy Shlach*. I was editor, you know. Should

I really take them along, or no? And all these dictionaries; oh, this is too much. What do you think?"

"Why are you packing?"

"Why pack?" the doctor looked incredulously at him. "If you clean out your ears you might hear the bombing. There's a war going on or hadn't you noticed? Any day now and all hell will break loose. There's going to be an invasion, from Dresden – the Bolsheviks. Word has it they're planning to liberate Prague from Nazi occupation. *Liberate*, is the word they use, hah! From one hell to another."

Placing his hands on his hips, he looked round his room as if wondering where to begin. It was then that Zahirsky caught a good look at his face. The doctor noticed him staring at him.

"I look old, is that what you're thinking? Just you wait, young man, you reach my age and the same will happen to you." Then narrowing his eyes suspiciously, "Were you upstairs talking to the old woman? What did she tell you?"

Zahirsky threw back his head, "What does an old woman have to talk about?"

"Old woman, hah! You think she considers herself old? How wrong you are. She's a phenomenon of eternal youth."

The doctor resumed packing but the books kept slipping out of his hands and falling to the floor. He became frustrated.

"I can help you, Doctor."

"Help me? How can you help me?" The doctor showed agitation. "You don't know what's going on, what lies at my feet. You would only disrupt everything. Who are you anyway? What did you say your name was again? Where are you headed?"

"It seems I'm headed in the same direction as you, Doctor."

"You bring salutations from the motherland and you call yourself Zahirsky. Well, I don't recall any such name. And as far as direction is concerned, who knows, it's an open road."

"Then excuse me, I won't trouble you any longer."

"Good. My colleagues should be arriving any minute to help me pack all this stuff up. You'll just be in the way."

"Goodbye." Zahirsky started for the stairs.

"Young man, wait!" the doctor called out after him. "We may meet again somewhere, maybe in the West, maybe even in America. Then we'll have ourselves a good chat. But for now, it must be goodbye."

Out on the sidewalk near the main gates, Zahirsky caught sight of a woman somewhere in her twenties coming in his direction. She was holding hands with a rather good-looking man in a brown checkered shirt and before them little Igichek hopped along.

"Rougenka!" Zahirsky's heart rose and fell. He mouthed her name but no sound came out. Utterly overcome with emotion, he stepped aside and made room for the company to pass. He couldn't believe it was her! Then the woman inadvertently looked at his face, and when she did, he noticed her eyes were still black and still very beautiful. "Rougenka!" he mouthed her name again. But those eyes were now strange and distant, and although they were looking directly at him at the same time it was as if they weren't looking at him at all.

Zahirsky was all torn up inside. He didn't know what to do. He ran across the street and with a swift gait headed in the direction of the Vltava River. There he caught a tram car and from the window looked out at Prague's picturesque skyline. He knew he would never forget Mrs. Yanichek's villa, not the one he had just visited but the one from long ago.

KATRINA

At the confluence of the Vilnia and Vilenka Rivers, Vilno is a beautiful ancient city with its streets stretching upward in a labyrinth of wooded slopes. Often called a baroque city, it is also home to buildings of the gothic and renaissance styles. Bernard, Mihasko and I just happened to be passing by the magnificent Church of Saint Anne in Vilno's Old Town. We were making our way in and around the narrow cobblestone streets, on our way to the suburb of Poplava. This was in the early spring of 1939, just months before the city was seized by Soviet troops. We were students back then, happy-go-lucky, all in our twenties.

Bernard and I were best friends but neither of us was particularly fond of Mihasko (his actual name was Mihailo, but because he was younger than us by a few years, Bernard and I called him by his diminutive). We found him unlikeable for the following reasons: he was pretentious, overbearing, and there was always a certain cockiness about him. As far as his physical appearance was concerned, he was like a thousand other young men, unidentifiable in a crowd. He was not attractive or unattractive, for that matter, but that's not to say he didn't have a certain charisma about him. The one thing that distinguished him from other young men

THEODORE ODRACH

was his full head of curly blond hair. He was very proud of his hair and for some reason women found it of unusual interest.

And it's true, Mihasko had a way with women – they flocked to him like bees to honey. He was very conscious of the advantage he held over us and made no qualms about flaunting his successes. One night, for example, at a dance at the student center just before winter holidays, Mihasko set his eyes on lovely Roksana, who happened to be dancing with Bernard. Roksana was tall and slender, an engineering student in her final year. Walking up to her (still in the arms of Bernard), brazenly, shamelessly, he asked her to dance. It didn't take long for him to steal her away. Bernard was left standing there all alone, fuming. He called out to me, "Did you see what just happened? Mihasko, he did it again!"

Because of situations like this, Bernard and I only came to resent Mihasko all the more. The truth of the matter was, we were deeply jealous of him. When alone Bernard and I made ourselves feel better by stressing his negative qualities: he was vain, he had attitude, he was superficial. Like ourselves, Mihasko studied at the Stefan Batory University, and like ourselves, was very poor, barely able to make ends meet. He went hungry many times and his clothes were threadbare. Poverty was the one thing that tied us all together.

As we approached the outskirts of Poplava, small stuccoed houses with shingled red rooftops began to emerge. We were on our way to Belvederska Street where Bernard kept a studio, which was not really a studio, but, rather, a small, damp room in the basement of some house. Bernard was a devout Marxist and studied fine art and art history. He regarded himself an up-and-coming sculptor and had invited us to view his latest work, which happened to be a bust of Marx. In general, I regarded Bernard's work run-of-the-mill with poor form and lacking in imagination. But because he was of a sensitive nature, I never voiced my opinion for fear of offending him.

Mihasko, on the other hand, was of a different cloth, he had no inhibitions whatsoever and was only too happy to speak his mind. Upon entering Bernard's studio, stepping up to the unfinished bust, examining the beard then the forehead, he burst into a fit of laughter.

"Why, this whole thing is so sorely lopsided, I can't believe it! This is Marx, you say? It looks like the Devil himself! Hah, hah, hah!"

Bernard flushed a deep red. He threw up his arms. "Mihasko, what do you know about art anyway? You're such a boor!"

After leaving Bernard's studio, the three of us decided to head back to Old Town, to a tavern overlooking the Vilja River; it was Bernard's favorite and frequented by local writers, musicians, and fellow artists. The sun was bright and high in the sky, and as we walked, we felt invigorated by the cool patches of shade made by the trees lining the streets.

When we just barely happened upon an intersection, at once we noticed a young woman standing at the curb, looking rather disoriented. Actually, she appeared to be lost. She was of average height, well-proportioned, with very pretty features. With no one else around, she came straight toward us.

"Excuse me," she spoke with a thick, barely intelligible accent and appeared anxious, "could you please tell me what time it is?"

Mihasko was quick to respond. He checked his gold pocket watch, the only thing he had of value, which he got from his late grandfather.

"It's two-thirty."

The woman noticed Mihasko's watch. Nodding as if she understood, she made another attempt to speak.

"Can you please tell me where Pieskova Street is?"

"Why, she's a foreigner!" Bernard whispered to me.

I tried to be of help, "Do you speak German?"

The young woman looked confused and narrowed her eyes.

"Pieskova Street is not too far from here," offered Mihasko, speaking very slowly and distinctly, trying to make sure she understood his every word.

"Pardon my asking," this was Bernard, "but where are you from?"

The woman batted her long lovely lashes and smiled and Bernard completely lost himself. After a moment he began again, "French? Are you perhaps French?"

But the woman merely shrugged and shook her head. Searching for the right words, she attempted to explain her situation. For some reason, she focused her attention on Mihasko, as if singling him out. Breathing tenderly, she edged toward him, she even placed her hand gently on his shoulder. Communicating more with gestures than with words, she began:

"My name is Katrina."

"Why she's English," muttered Bernard, poking me in the arm. "And I bet she's wealthy, too. Look how she's dressed. Her clothes are very expensive, they're of the finest quality." Then back to her: "Are you from England by any chance? Yes, yes, you look very English. Your face, your poise." Bernard emphasized the word English in the hopes that she might better understand him.

"Oh!" She clasped her hands, and then released a deep sigh of relief, "How absolutely wonderful!"

Mihasko stepped forward, "Unfortunately, none of us speaks English."

It appeared Katrina only vaguely grasped what Mihasko had said, but picking up on his warm, very familiar tone, her face flushed and she began to giggle.

"Whatever brought you to Vilno?" Bernard wanted to know. "Are you maybe ..."

But before Bernard had a chance to finish what he wanted to say, Mihasko cut him off and quite rudely, "Are you planning on visiting someone today?"

Blood rushed to Bernard's face; he was furious with Mihasko for having interrupted him. He grumbled into my ear: "That Mihasko! He won't let us get a word in edgewise. Just look how he's all over her, how he's flaunting himself."

"Do you have friends in this part of town?" Mihasko continued, completely ignoring Bernard.

"I don't understand," the young woman tossed her head and shrugged. Her eyes contracted and she looked helpless.

Mihasko repeated his words but slowly and this time she seemed to have understood. With great effort, she proceeded to provide him with an answer. Throwing about her arms, trying to articulate as best she could, she managed to convey she was on her way to Pieskova Street to visit a poor widow she had met in front of the Hotel Bristol, where she was staying with her father. It turned out, the widow was having some kind of financial difficulties and ... But the last sentence came out in a jumble and neither Bernard, Mihasko, nor I could make any sense of it.

"Hotel Bristol," I started, half to myself. "Hm ..."

"Why that's the best hotel in Vilno!" broke in Bernard. "I was right all along. She definitely is well-to-do; you can tell just by the way she carries herself."

Meanwhile, looking the woman over, Mihasko was already weighing his options. Yes, she was definitely worth his while – she was young, she was beautiful, and she was obviously rich. Pointing in the direction of the Vilja River, without any regard for us, he said to her, giving her his arm.

"Come, I will personally escort you to Pieskova Street."

And he began to walk in step with the lovely Katrina, the wealthy Katrina, the aristocratic Katrina. We knew by his smooth and easy gait Mihasko was already celebrating victory over us. We followed close behind.

"And what's your name?" we could hear Katrina ask Mihasko.

But before Mihasko could respond, Bernard called out in an animated way, as if to get back at him, "His name is Mihasko Petrusko Peliusko!"

Katrina laughed and by her gesticulations, it was clear she had never heard such a funny sounding name.

After we walked several minutes, Mihasko turned to us and said with a smile but it was as if he was trying to tell us something.

"No need for you fellows to tag along. I'll take Katrina to Pieskova Street and then we can meet up later on. How about the Nova Tavern around five?"

We watched Mihasko continue on with Katrina down the steep side of a hill. They were talking and laughing as though they had known each other for years.

"Just look at that body," Bernard couldn't stop staring. "Those shoulders, those hips, those legs ... If only I could get her into my studio. I would give anything to have a woman like that model for me."

"Um, Bernard," I said, only half listening. The truth was I was starting to get uncomfortable about what had just happened and reservations were building up inside of me. "Don't you think there's something rather odd about all this? Somehow it doesn't make sense. If Katrina truly has money, then why didn't she take a cab from the hotel instead of walking half way across town? I somehow don't think a well-to-do woman would venture out into the streets alone like that, or, for that matter, go off with a perfect stranger. Something is not quite right here."

Bernard thought a moment, "Yes, maybe you're right; now that you mention it, it does all seem rather peculiar. But on the other hand, it's common knowledge these rich types like a bit of adventure now and then. Yet somehow it doesn't add up. And, did you see how she grabbed hold of Mihasko's hand? A bit on the rough side, I'd say."

THEODORE ODRACH

Three days passed and neither Bernard nor I had heard from Mihasko. He did not even attend classes, which was unusual for him. We believed he was with Katrina. In the morning and during lunch breaks we lingered in front of the Hotel Bristol hoping to catch a glimpse of them. We even looked in on nearby shops and restaurants. But they were nowhere to be found. Finally, we decided to enter the lobby of the hotel. Slipping the desk clerk several *zlotys*, we asked for information regarding a pretty young woman by the name of Katrina, who was staying at the hotel with her father. No sooner had the clerk accepted the money, he began flipping through his registration book. Clearing his throat, he confirmed that two days ago there had been a young woman from England staying there with her father. Yes, yes, he remembered her now. She was very pretty and the father was quite friendly and distinguished-looking. But unfortunately, they had already signed out.

"Did you by any chance notice in their company a young man, quite plain looking, tall, with curly blond hair?" questioned Bernard.

No, the clerk had not seen in their company any such young man. Disappointed, we left the hotel.

"What if Katrina truly was a woman of means," began Bernard. "What if she fell in love with Mihasko and took him back to England with her. But it's strange that he wouldn't come to say goodbye."

Another five days went by and Mihasko still did not appear. We then arranged to head out to his residence but when we arrived, we were informed by his landlady that he had moved out over a week ago and did not leave a forwarding address. For several more days, we searched for Mihasko but did not find a trace of him anywhere. We even went to the Rossa Cemetery, one of his favorite making-out spots, but still no Mihasko. Bernard and I were at the end of our ropes; we were getting very worried. Finally, we agreed this was now a matter for the police.

The next morning after finishing breakfast, I prepared to call on Bernard so together we could go to the police station to file a missing person's report. Along the way to his place, passing a little kiosk, I noticed a stack of newspapers on the counter. The front-page headline caught my eye. It read as follows:

Young Fraud Impersonates Affluent English Tourist. I continued to read, *Sonia Jarabek, a native of Vilno, resident of Kanavariska Street, daughter of a local bricklayer, impersonates an affluent English woman. Assuming the alias Katrina Simpson and working together with her male accomplice, she lures men into her hotel room, offers them drink, and then steals their money and valuables.*

"That's her! That's Katrina!" I shouted excitedly to myself.

Hurrying to Bernard's, quickening my step, I couldn't wait to tell him about this new development. When I arrived, the music of Tchaikovsky filled his studio. He was standing over a table sculpting a woman's head.

"My creation is almost complete," he declared upon seeing me. With his hands on his hips, taking a few steps back to view his work, he went on to say, "I'm sure you recognize her. If I may say so myself, I do believe I have done her justice."

"Yes, um, yes, of course," I was confused. In all honesty, the bust was unrecognizable to me, second-rate, as with all his pieces. I couldn't think of anything to say. Upon closer examination, I finally figured it out. "Why it's Katrina!"

Bernard began touching up the forehead and smoothing over her eyes. "Yes," he said, proudly, "Katrina, lovely Katrina. But you must understand how hard it is to recreate something from memory. If only I could somehow get her to sit for me."

From my inside pocket, I pulled out the newspaper article and waved it in front of Bernard's face. "You've got to read this! You won't believe what's happened!"

But for some reason, Bernard showed no interest in what I had to say. He continued sculpting as if there was nothing out of the ordinary. After a moment, wiping his hands on a damp cloth that lay on the edge of his work table, he said almost mechanically, "You've come with old news, my friend. There's been a rumor going round campus; I guess you haven't heard. About two weeks ago a captain of the secret police signed himself into our university clinic. Sonia Jarabek, otherwise known as Katrina Simpson, not only pocketed 3,000 *zlotys* of his but gave him syph ..."

"Syphilis!" I cut him off before he could finish. "No!"

Bernard raised his brows. "So the story goes."

"Can all this really be true?"

"*Postfactum*."

"What about Mihasko?"

"Mihasko? Poor Mihasko," Bernard smiled vaguely and shook his head, he couldn't help but feel a certain pleasure from it all. "His fate was the same as that of the captain.

Only too bad he couldn't afford the university clinic. Instead, they sent him out to a hospital in Kaunas, the one on Hipodromo Street. Well, if anything, at least the poor fool managed to get his pocket-watch back."

Walking up to a cupboard on the opposite side of the room, Bernard took out two cups with saucers and placed them on a small side table by the window. Filling a kettle with water and setting it on a hot plate to boil, before long he made a pot of tea. Taking a sip, he said.

"We should really get out to Kaunas and pay Mihasko a visit; I'm sure he could use the company."

And so, the first thing next morning, Bernard and I boarded a train for Kaunas.

BATTLE IN THE BLOODLANDS

The small, dismal town of S lies on the southern fringe of the Pinsk Marshes along the banks of the narrow, slow-moving Styr River. It stands on a marshy floodplain and consists of several squat, non-descript wooden buildings, modest whitewashed cottages, and a series of criss-crossing dirt roads. Near an Orthodox church in the center of town is a marketplace, where once a week, peasants from surrounding farmsteads come in horse-drawn wagons to sell their wares. Fruits, vegetables, chickens and eggs fill the stalls and the sound of haggling is heard all around. A main road runs across a wooden bridge from the north end, cuts through the middle of town, and then continues in a straight line to L. Surrounding S is a dense, almost impenetrable forest and is home to a great variety of trees, shrubs, and wildlife.

From 1941 to 1944 of the Second World War S fell under German occupation and it was brutal. For the large Jewish population and the non-Jews married to Jews, atrocities were committed. Jewish people were rounded up, placed into boxcars, and sent to extermination camps. In those boxcars were also Poles, Ukrainians, and gypsies but to a lesser extent.

During this occupation, Soviet troops, determined to keep a presence in the area, set themselves up in small pockets deep in the surrounding woods. They would emerge now and then to raid German supply compounds, disrupt communications, and/or plunder for food. When a large detachment of Russian paratroopers came to land there and set up numerous military bases, they managed to strengthen their position considerably. But still, the Russians remained vastly outnumbered by the Germans.

In the year of 1943, S became a center of sizeable local military activity. In an old run-down schoolhouse on the edge of town, a military training camp was set up, where strong young men from surrounding villages came to enlist. Their mission was twofold: to protect the surrounding towns and villages and to fight the enemies – the Germans, the Russians, and the small bands of Poles looking to protect their interests.

In a nearby cottage in the settlement of M, under the editorship of Julian Lyciuk, an underground Ukrainian press had been established from which newspapers and pamphlets were published and distributed among local inhabitants. Because S was a hub of military activity, the Russians, the Germans, and the Poles watched it fixedly. Though the Russians rarely ventured out of the forest depths, the Germans, with their forces forever strengthening, were already devising ways to obliterate this stronghold of Ukrainian independence.

Sometime at the beginning of November, 1944, the people of S were awakened by the sound of German warplanes. From the open sky came shellfire and bombardment. Balls of light shot up over the horizon – yellow, green, blue – and then exploded. The air was thick with the fumes of gunpowder and aviation fuel. Unfortunately, the people of S were soon to realize they were not only being attacked by the Germans, but also by the Russians and Poles. Small groups of Red Army men could be seen paddling across the Styr in makeshift rafts and Poles were popping up here and there, some already breaking into houses.

Unfortunately for S, the town had been left largely unprotected, as the resistance had been assembled somewhere on the forest's edge for a secret meeting. This is how it happened that the horrible onslaught came to be: a local Russian collaborator had related the news of the unprotected town to the Russians, and this news, in turn, somehow found its way to the Germans and the Poles.

The enemy, or rather the enemies, pounded S and without reservation. From the east, a battalion of Bolsheviks had blown up several buildings; from the west, a German infantry unit leveled outlying houses; from the south, a small band of Polish soldiers, hiding in the Jewish cemetery, struck at townspeople passing by. Each group wanted the same thing: to take control of the small town of S.

Bombs and shellfire continued to fly from all directions and in no time the hospital burst into flames. Soon a stretch of wooden houses caught fire and within no time the streets turned into a raging inferno.

The inhabitants of S, in the meantime, made a run for the outskirts of town and tried to take cover in the brushwood. But German warplanes opened fire. Few managed to escape, most fell to the ground dead.

With much of the local people eliminated, the enemies – the Russians, the Germans, and the Poles – then opened fire on each other. The fighting continued each wanting the town of S for themselves.

When the attack on S first broke out on that fateful November day, editor Julian Lyciuk was not far away in a small cottage in the settlement of M, where he was tending to the presses. He was in the middle of publishing a newsletter updating events on the front. Glancing out the window, upon seeing a thick cloud of smoke over S, running out the door, he called urgently to his colleagues:

"Attention! Attention! Trouble! S is on fire! Hurry, we must pack up our gear at once and get out of here!"

Barely five minutes passed when onto horse-drawn wagons workers loaded up the printing equipment – typewriters, small presses, boxes of paper, sheets of carbon, a shortwave radio, cartons of ink – and as fast as they could, headed in the direction of the resistance camp, stationed somewhere deep in the forest.

As the wagons rolled and lumbered along dirt roadways, Julian couldn't stop thinking about S. His heart filled with despair and he felt horribly pained. He thought about Lida, the pretty young widow with two small daughters living there. She was just over twenty-five, but with her soft, smooth skin appeared much younger. The previous night after finishing dinner, Julian had visited S and had dropped in on her. The resistance had Lida under its protection and supplied her with food and clothing, as it did many single women left to fend for themselves. Her husband had been a commander, and one night, while leaving his post in the forest, had been captured by the Germans. The next day they hanged him from a telegraph pole in the marketplace and left him there three days for all to see.

When the wagons finally turned onto a bumpy forest road, thoughts of Lida began to consume Julian's mind. Had she managed to get out of S? Was she alive? Was she dead? If enemy factions had got hold of her, without a doubt they would have raped her in front of her children and then later murdered her; the girls they would have bashed to death with wooden clubs.

The wagons finally entered a dark and dense part of the forest. The resistance camp was now only a few kilometers away. Everything was so dismal and so silent. As they passed a stand of alders, a rustling sound suddenly erupted, followed by the snapping of twigs. Before long a small group of people emerged, waving white handkerchiefs and shouting. They were survivors from S. The horses neighed and reared themselves and then came to a halt. Among the people was the widow, Lida, and her two daughters. Julian felt indescribable relief upon seeing them. Jumping down from the wagon, embracing all three at once, he cried aloud:

"Thank God you're alive."

Unable to catch her breath, Lida started, "Near Fitinka, in a small settlement, I have an aunt. That's where we're headed. But will things be any safer out there? From one hell to another."

The survivors climbed into the wagons. They came to a tiny clearing surrounded by low-lying shrubs and columns of broad oak trees. It was the camp. A kettle of water boiled on an open fire and men sat in small groups eating kasha and drinking hot peppermint tea. There was a slight frost in the air, and thick winter clouds could be seen rolling across the sky, threatening snow. A few meters away, camouflaged by clumps of raspberry bushes were about twenty carts filled with such things as food items, boxes with medical supplies, and various ammunitions.

The injured were quickly pulled from the wagons and laid up in thick woolen blankets around the fire. The camp doctors and their aides tended to them. One man with his leg bandaged from a bullet wound spoke of the horror.

"When the shooting started everybody ran from their houses. We were all trying to get out of town. The Reds were already swarming the streets; I even saw a few Germans and Poles lying face down in the mud. The Reds were shooting at everyone. As I ran out of my house, I saw Pavlo Revko with his family dead in the gutter. Later I saw Zirka Shumska, the schoolteacher, curled up in the field like a ball and she was splattered with blood."

An elderly man with his arm in a sling shouted angrily.

"Why wasn't the bridge burned down weeks ago? We were no more than sitting ducks! And what were our fighters doing? I'll tell you what they were doing – they were sitting around, drinking vodka!"

At that moment a group of about thirty armed men came storming onto the clearing. The officer in command announced:

"The Germans and Poles are defeated. The Bolsheviks have seized S!"

More armed men appeared and reinforcement units came in from camps to the north. Over two hundred men were lined up, strapping their holsters to their waists, and flinging machine guns over their shoulders. As it turned out, when the sudden raid on S had just barely started, unprepared for such a formidable onslaught, top resistant army officials rushed to meet in an isolated hunter's cabin to plan their counterattack. This was done secretly, as collaborators were everywhere.

It was agreed that the resistance was to cross the Styr approximately six kilometers upriver, where there was a small stretch of muddy grassland separating S from the forest. It was calculated that the Reds would eventually venture out that way with the intention of scouting out the surrounding terrain. In the brushwood to the left and right, the resistance waited for the enemy. When a group of Red Army soldiers finally appeared, fire opened up. Chaos ensued and the Reds began to flee. Most fell dead to the ground, those injured tried to drag themselves to safety. One Bolshevik wearing a drab overcoat and bast-shoes ripped from the feet of some dead peasant, pulled his face up from the mud and snarled.

"You sons of bitches! Stalin will get you for this!"

When the battle was over, the resistance spread out across the grassland and collected weapons such as machine guns, Soviet-made knives, cannons, rifles, and grenades. They then marched into S and using peasant wagons and handcarts, whatever they could find, gathered up the dead, and took them to the cemetery, where they buried them in communal graves.

The next evening back at camp some very bad news arrived by way of a messenger. Large German support units had just been deployed from Lutsk and were forcing their way down the highway toward S. By morning German soldiers would be swarming the area ready to take the town. Such a huge military strength was too much for the meager resistance movement.

Camp was quickly dismantled and the injured were loaded up onto the wagons. Everything, including the supplies and presses, was moved south and a new camp was set up at a concealed location somewhere deep in the forest.

APPARITION

For little Myron, the days became long and unbearable and he lived in constant agony. Some strangers had come and taken his sister, Olga, whom he loved as much as his mother. Now he was alone, and worse yet, abandoned. But his love for his sister was not always reciprocated. At times he was nothing more than a nuisance and would follow her wherever she would go. In spring when the grass along the banks of the Styr River was spotted with forget-me-nots and tender shoots of fern, he would not let her out of his sight, or when she and her girlfriends set out to pick sorrel he would not only stay at close range but try to listen in on their conversation.

But now those happy days were gone. And all because of Matvy Youshka.

One Sunday evening as Olga was preparing to go with her girlfriends and sing songs along the village streets, Myron began to cry.

"I want to go with you!"

"No. It's past your bedtime."

"I want to go!" Myron wouldn't let up.

His father, reading the paper, looking up from under his horned-rimmed glasses, finally settled the matter. "That's enough, young man. Do you intend to cry much longer?"

Myron swallowed back his tears. Reluctantly, he made his way out of the house and walked toward the barn where he slept on a cot. Passing the chicken coop, at once he heard the sound of singing coming from the village; it made him stop, it was sweet and melodious and beckoned him to such an extent he forgot the stern words of his father. He hid behind the shed and waited for his sister to come out. When at last she stepped into the yard, he watched as she slowly made her way toward Grandmother Barbara's house, then run headlong across the wheat field. Myron, in his bare feet, followed after her. The tall stalks of wheat swayed gently in the warm summer breeze and the full moon illuminated the way. When Olga came to the footpath that led into the village, to the boy's great astonishment, rather than continuing on, she turned in the opposite direction and made across the neighboring property toward a field of oats.

"Strange," thought Myron. "Where could she possibly be going?"

As she approached a wall of oak trees, Myron's heart began to pound and sweat came to his brow. He had a terrible feeling. Pressing his back flat against the fence of a small enclosure, he didn't dare breathe. Then suddenly from behind one of the trees, the shadow of a man emerged. He was tall and burly, like a giant, and under the light of the moon, he looked like a monster. The man's arms were outstretched and within seconds he was embracing his sister. To the boy's horror, he heard them kiss.

"I thought you weren't going to come tonight." Myron could hear the man's voice at a whisper. Then, "Oh, Olga, I don't know what I would do without you. I swear I would slit my throat."

"Don't talk like that!" this was his sister. "Palady Turkavka did just that over Marsessa Duba. And now poor Marsessa."

"I love you, Olga."

And suddenly Myron recognized the voice of Matvy Youshka. The leaves began to rustle as his sister and Matvy dropped to the ground. Then more kisses. Giggles, soft breathing, faint cries – one ghastly sound after another. Myron's stomach began to turn. He hated Matvy Youshka and he hated him with all his heart. Tears of pain and anger poured down his cheeks. He was about to let out a cry of protest, but from fear of being discovered, he quickly collected himself and ran home. The lights in the house were still on, and racing into the living room, he shouted as loud as he could.

"Mama! Papa! Olga's kissing with Matvy Youshka!"

*   *   *

The next day the boy noticed his sister's eyes were red and swollen; she had been crying. He had got her into trouble with their parents.

Later, when he slipped into the kitchen to get something to eat, he overheard his father's voice from the living room. He and his mother were talking something over in low whispers, and it was about his sister. Horrifying thoughts flashed through the boy's mind. Perhaps they were planning to throw her out of the house or sell her to the gypsies, or maybe they were devising some sort of dreadful punishment like locking her up in her room and discarding the key. And all because he had to go and open his big mouth! He worried constantly. On the second day when his sister's face went back to normal and she started about her business in her usual way, he was able to relax.

One morning Olga's friend, Marta, came over and together they set out for the garden to pick cucumbers.

"Take me with you!" the boy wanted to go.

"No."

"Please, I won't tell anymore. I promise."

Olga thought it over and then finally agreed.

Olga, Marta, and Myron together set off along the pasture's edge. The girls walked up ahead and talked to each other in such a way that Myron could not hear. From time to time they turned to look at him, laughing and snickering. Myron tried his best to strain his ears but could not make out anything they were saying. When they came to a low wattle fence, they hopped over to the other side, and passing the cucumber patch, walked between rows of pole beans dotted with delicate red flowers.

Myron tried to be of help. He called out to them, "Hey, you just went past the cucumbers!"

Olga and Marta ignored him and walked on.

At the end of the rows of beans, there happened to be an outcrop of nettle, and of the stinging variety. The plants were high and robust-looking, and their deep green leaves were filled with needle-like hairs. Olga took a knife out of her pocket, and examining several plants, found the biggest and broadest and cut them at the base. She turned to her brother.

"This is for you, Myron."

Myron shrugged confusedly. He tried to be of help. "Why don't you take smaller plants, like those over there? They're more tender."

Olga let out a little laugh then instructed him to follow her. Happily, he obeyed. When they came to a narrow slow-moving stream, at once she turned on him and her eyes were on fire.

"Pull down your pants you big blabbermouth!"

It was only then that the boy realized he had fallen into a trap. He began to wail. Marta grabbed him by the scruff of the neck and proceeded to unbutton his trousers; Olga laid him over her knees. He kicked and squealed like a pig off to slaughter. Suddenly he could hear the nettle whistle above his head, and within seconds he felt the needle-like hairs sink into his flesh. After several blows, his bottom was as if on fire.

"You snitch!" yelled his sister, as she struck again. "Let this be a lesson to you!"

The girlfriends kept at the boy, showing no mercy. When his bottom swelled up like a ripe tomato, they let him go. Myron took to his heels and fled home. He was about to run into the kitchen and tell his mother everything, but in the end decided to go into the barn instead. There he filled up a bucket with cold water and relieved his pain privately. For several days thereafter he walked about the fields stiff as a board and he was barely able to sit down.

Changes began to occur. One day Matvy Youshka and his grandfather appeared for a visit. They sat down to the table with his father and drank vodka. Olga disappeared into the kitchen and Myron sat by the door playing with his toys. The men talked cheerfully as the bottle emptied. When Olga emerged, she filled up a glass for herself, and turning to Myron, said tenderly, "Here. Myron, have a sip. It's a celebration."

The boy was confused; he didn't know what to make of it all. He became afraid.

"I don't want any! I don't want any!"

The adults sitting around the table paid little attention to the little boy. They were chatting and toasting and having a good time. It was a most unusual visit. Myron got up and ran to the barn. He was crying. He was certain the guests did not come with good intentions; he was convinced they were evil people and they had come to cause trouble and pain.

Sometime after midnight, Myron heard everyone bid their farewells. Matvy Youshka's deep voice overpowered all the others and further added to his misery. When he noticed Matvy and his grandfather walk toward the gates, half in a frenzy, he ran after them and blocked their way.

"Hey, Myron," said Matvy, startled to see the boy, "you should be in bed."

The boy remained silent.

"Here's some candy." Matvy rummaged through his pocket, then stretched out a hand that was shaped like a shovel.

"I don't want any! I hate you! You can't have Olga!"

Grandfather Youshka smiled and shook his head. Hobbling down the road with the support of his cane, he could be heard muttering to himself, "The heart of a child, as innocent as the morning dew."

They came and took Olga; the house was now sad and empty. The boy moped all day long, he lost interest in everything, he could hardly eat or sleep. He would walk to the gates and for hours on end stare across the field in the direction of Matvy's house. His sister lived there now and she would never again return. He could not understand why she would want to leave home and move in with a complete stranger. The boy could not find a moment's rest.

One sunny afternoon Myron decided to hop the fence into Grandmother Luda's yard. She was sitting on the porch in her old rocking chair, smoking a pipe. Her eyes were red and watery and her cheeks a hollow gray. She called out in a feeble voice, "Myron, why such a long face today? What's wrong?"

"They took Olga away," the boy couldn't stop crying.

"I know, child, I know. Cry, it'll do you good. You will understand soon enough. By the way, have you seen the kittens out in the shed? Go and play with them for a while. That'll cheer you up."

Myron went out back to see the litter.

The nights were the worst. The barn was cold and damp and he would lie on his cot beneath his eiderdown and cry himself to sleep. Finally, he couldn't bear it any longer; he couldn't just sit back and do nothing. Jumping out of bed, slipping on his trousers, buttoning up his shirt, he made for Matvy's house. The night was dark, almost pitch black, but there was light in one of the windows. He tried his best to catch a glimpse of something going on inside, anything, but to his dismay, there came no movement. Suddenly a dog began to growl from somewhere behind the barn, and before long it started to bark and rip at its chain. Myron took to his heels and fled.

The next day when darkness barely fell over the village, the boy once more set out for Matvy's house. This time, he hid behind a rather large willow tree just outside the front yard. He was careful not to disturb the dog. There was a light in the kitchen and he could see Matvy sitting with his back to the window and he appeared to be eating. At that moment a woman appeared with a large mixing bowl. She set it on the counter and then turned to fill a kettle with water. It was Olga! Seeing his sister in this strange house upset him. His eyes welled up with tears. He edged closer to get a better look but then the dog at once fell into a fit of barking. Myron ran back home.

Myron's nocturnal visits became routine. He now set up position away from the fence, in a grove of alder trees. The dog was no longer a problem.

Late one night when the sky was covered by a mass of heavy dark clouds, the boy stood by the alders and watched. The contour of Matvy's large whitewashed house was barely visible, and the tinned rooftop rising upward, was as if lost in the darkness. There was a faint light coming from one of the bedrooms, but Myron was too far away to be able to make anything out. He moved closer with the intention of peering through the window but stopped short for fear of disturbing the dog. He remained motionless and waited, trying to think of what to do next.

Then quite unexpectedly, as if out of nowhere, a strange whistling sound erupted from behind. The boy gave a start. It was as if someone were breathing down his neck. He flung around to see what it was but there was nothing. The breathing stopped. There was silence. Then it started again. He became certain someone was out there, hiding in the trees, trying to scare him or play a trick on him. He suspected it was Matvy Youshka. He held his breath and listened. Then from the open pasture came the cracking sound of a whip, and Myron quickly concluded it was some local shepherd chasing his sheep to pasture. Again, he felt a hot breath on his neck as if someone were directly behind him. About to spin around, suddenly a shrill almost despairing cry went ripping through the night. Frightened and with his muscles all tensed, he made for the neighboring yard. He ran like the wind. Gasping for breath, he sought the quickest way home. He turned toward Grandmother Luda's house, and climbing over the fence, fell head-first into her flowerbed. The lights in her house were turned off but a gentle stream of smoke rose out of her chimney and floated across the sky.

In that instant, the breathing started again. It was louder and more pronounced and he became paralyzed with fear. Suddenly a woman appeared before him. She was very tall and beautiful and dressed in a white gown. She looked like a bride, but to his knowledge, there had not been a wedding in the village for some time. Scrambling to his feet, scared out of his wits, he could feel his own teeth chattering. The woman edged toward him slowly, her gown making fluttering sounds. From her lips came the same shrill whistle-like sound he had heard moments earlier. The boy wiped the sweat from his brow, and though he felt as if on fire, at the same time he was cold and shivering. Had he not been so terrified, he would have noticed the woman's uncanny resemblance to Grandmother Luda. Little Myron let out a heart-rending scream as the woman reached out to grab him. In a wild frenzy, half hysterical, he flung himself around and raced home. He made it as far as the front porch then collapsed.

* * *

The next morning Myron regained consciousness. The color had returned to his face and his big blue eyes were raised. His sister was leaning over his bed gently stroking his head.

"How do you feel today, Myron?" she asked in a comforting voice.

Myron made a slight mumbling sound and then fell silent. His gaze wandered slowly round the room – he came upon the dresser drawer, a vase with freshly cut flowers, a small night table ... And then, by the window, there was a man leaning against the wall. He was broad and tall and was smiling and looking in a kindly way. At first, Myron thought it was his father, but it wasn't his father, rather, it was his number one enemy, Matvy Youshka! What was he doing here? Why wouldn't he just go away?

Then he saw Matvy stepping toward him, slowly, carefully, and he was holding something in his big hand.

Myron watched him closely.

"Here, Myron, I carved you this horse and wagon. I hope you like it."

Myron's eyes lit up. Never had he seen such a beautiful toy. And just for him! He looked up at Matvy in wonderment. For the first time, the two exchanged glances.

Myron's mother walked into the room with several towels folded over her arm; in her left hand, she carried a hot water bottle. She looked at the young couple, and nodding her head worriedly, hastened to explain.

"Myron came tearing home around midnight last night and gave way on the porch. I'd never seen him look so pale; he looked like he'd seen a ghost."

Barely having finished her words, suddenly the bells from the church steeple began to chime. The young couple lowered their heads and made the sign of the cross. Myron's mother clasped her chest and uttered a prayer:

"Grandmother Luda died last night. May her soul rest in peace."

LICKSPITTLES

The author Kopelyuk belonged to a certain breed of lickspittles but his personality deviated from the norm. Though
it was common knowledge lickspittles possessed very little
stamina and suffered from a weakness of character, Kopelyuk's breed took things a step further: they had soft backbones and supple necks. Their soft backbones enabled them
to bow to the ground with great elasticity, while their supple
necks allowed their heads to bob to and fro, wherever the
index finger of a non-lickspittle pointed. Not only did Kopelyuk's breed excel at being lickspittles, but they possessed an
even further flaw: they had an inordinate amount of venom
in their bloodstreams, which in turn not only thoroughly
saturated their tongues but caused them to denounce all
that was familiar to them. But where Kopelyuk was concerned, Mother Nature had turned stingy; she had deprived
him of the many traits in which his peers took immense
pride. Kopelyuk felt cursed. The surplus of iron flowing
through his veins not only reinforced both his backbone
and neck but curbed all desire to spurn his own. As a result,
he became known as a lickspittle outcast.

One evening in a dimly-lit tavern on the edge of town,
a man of a superior breed began to openly ridicule lick-

spittles. He called them all kinds of nasty names. "You're a bunch of subservients," he said to them, "submissives, subordinates." Kopelyuk did not appreciate such brazen name-calling and anger boiled up inside of him. He boldly took it upon himself to defend his peers. Rolling up his sleeves, clenching his fists, he took a swing at the man, but the man somehow managed to duck successfully and escape harm. And if that wasn't enough, moving in from behind, the man then grabbed hold of Kopelyuk's legs in such a way it made him fall flat on his face. Blood trickled from Kopelyuk's skull and it appeared his nose was broken. The lickspittles cheered and clapped for the opponent and even egged him on. As the opponent was about to finish Kopelyuk off by sinking his boot into his stomach, Kopelyuk, to everyone's astonishment, jumped to his feet and punched the man with such force that he fell to the ground, half unconscious. The lickspittles dropped their jaws in disbelief. A lickspittle had just overpowered a man of a superior breed, unbelievable. The police were called in and the two men got arrested. A trial followed and the man of superior breed called upon the lickspittles to act as witnesses on his behalf, to which they readily complied. Trembling and bowing fawningly before the judge, the lickspittles condemned Kopelyuk, who, in the end, was found guilty and sentenced to pay a high fine.

Contrary to what one might think, this incident did not set Kopelyuk against his fellow lickspittles. Deep down he still had faith and believed they would come around. This was why he set out to make a psychological study of his peers throughout the world. Like most writers he was a very poor soul and had it not been for his supernatural powers, this study would never have been conducted. Astral projection was his specialty.

He would lie stretched out in bed on his back with his arms crossed over his chest, breathing steadily, almost inaudibly. With a pink lamp dangling over his head from a cord, its warm penetrating glow would make his skin translucent. Ever so slowly, he would fall into a deep trance. With his lids half-closed, he would then have his spiritual self rise and float up to the ceiling.

His spiritual self was an adventurous, fun-loving young man by the name of Future, who could travel faster than the speed of light; he loved to visit different parts of the world and spy on lickspittles. He visited Argentina, Europe, South Africa to mention a few. After his latest bout of traveling, putting together all his notes of observation, he set out to write his next novel. He had already conceived of a title: *Lickspittles, Come to Your Senses!* He typed day and night and sheets of paper began to pile up. After a year his manuscript was ready for publication. In the city where he lived there were many affluent lickspittles, but unfortunately, he could not depend on them for funding. The whole financial burden fell on his penniless yet creative shoulders. He borrowed money from a questionable source at a very high percentage rate and then started producing his book. When his novel finally appeared in print, like a raging storm it poured into the homes of lickspittles. The frenzy it was about to create was like something never before seen.

One evening in a large, fancy downtown hotel there was to be a business executives' banquet, which Kopelyuk planned to attend. That night when the clock struck ten, he lay on his back and allowed the pink rays to light up his face. His body floated upward, but instead of rising all the way to the ceiling, it made an abrupt turn to the right and traveled straight in the direction of the hotel hosting the party. His body busted through a wall. An orchestra was playing on the podium and the guests sat around marble tables making light conversation, eating and drinking. The most influential lickspittles sat up front: Ticket, Anderson, and two others – Roman Rohalic, a mortician, and Collin Karrick, a lawyer. The four men were huddled around a table, telling anecdotes and releasing loud, hearty laughs. As Future passed them by, they quickly exchanged glances then fell silent.

Anderson was the first to speak. "Well, well, whom do we have here? Why, if it isn't Kopelyuk himself! Thank you for sending your novel. Not too bad, not too bad indeed. Nice and thick, something to grab hold of."

"How wonderful you were able to make it," threw in Ticket. "In fact, I just sent someone to go and fetch you. Can we offer you a glass of wine perhaps?"

"No thank you, I don't drink."

"Tell us, did you make much money with this book of yours?"

Future shook his head, "I don't write for the money."

"You don't write for the money?" Ticket burst into a fit of laughter. "What a waste of time that is!"

At that moment Sofia, Ticket's wife, brushed up to the table. She was a short, plump woman with red lipstick and fingernails to match. Her strapless mauve gown, belted at the waist, accentuated her round form. She had just finished dancing with some young man and was completely out of breath.

"Oh, I'm absolutely exhausted," she fanned her face with a handkerchief from her purse. Then noticing Future, looking him over, she bent over and whispered into her husband's ear, "Wally, dear, how rude of you not to ask this fine-looking gentleman to join us."

"What a treasure you are, darling. You are such a fine dancer." Pecking her on the cheek with a kiss, he put in, "Actually, I've already reserved a table for him in the back, in that far corner by the restroom."

Sofia fluttered her hands, and after casting a warm, flirtatious smile in Future's direction, she turned to address the table of lickspittles.

"The strangest thing happened to me this morning. At about nine o'clock the mailman knocked on my front door and handed me a parcel. It was a book written in the oddest fashion. Who could it possibly be from? I thought to myself."

"Er, Sofia, dear," her husband was quick to interrupt, "please, watch what you say. This young man here happens to be the distinguished author, Kopelyuk."

In that instant, an old hunchback by the name of Gabriel hobbled up to the table. He had small, slanted eyes, a balding head, and crooked legs. He came from the lowest level of lickspittles and was not only in the habit of bowing before his fellow-lickspittles but even before telephone poles when he walked along the street. He had something important to say:

"Pardon me for interrupting, Mr. Ticket, sir, but that fellow you sent me to fetch, well, he's lying on his bed and it looks like he's dead. I said to him: 'Get up Mr. Kopelyuk. You are cordially invited by the local business people to attend their annual banquet. But he didn't move, not even a muscle."

"You say he's dead?"

"He certainly looks dead, sir."

"Excuse me," Roman, the mortician couldn't hold back. "Does anyone know if he has life insurance? Naturally, I wouldn't decline my services."

Anderson shook his head and laughed, "You're just an old fool, Gabriel. You were in Kopelyuk's room and you didn't see a damn thing. It wasn't Kopelyuk, it absolutely couldn't have been. You're as blind as a bat."

"I swear I saw him. I saw him with my own two eyes, as clearly as I see that man over there."

Randomly, he pointed to Future. Then noticing the uncanny resemblance between him and the alleged dead man, he went into shock. The two looked exactly alike.

"That's him! That's the dead man!" he screamed.

Bowing nervously, walking backward, he made for the door and fled outside.

"Hah, to be so scared of a corpse!" Roman shook his head. "I've never seen anything so ridiculous. Why the dead are the best customers one could have, and they never complain."

Ticket turned to Future and examined him closely. "Hm, you seem normal enough to me, you certainly don't look dead. Yet, at the same time, somehow your eyes are rather unusual, they're too round, too shiny. Very strange. You don't drink you say?"

Collin then started, "Anyway, yesterday I received your book, *Little Ladies, Come to Your Senses!* Or something like that anyway. Well, you see, I've even read the title and I consider that a great honor for any writer."

"I'm sorry, but you have all made a very big mistake." Future cleared his throat, "I am not who you think I am. I am not Kopelyuk, I am the novelist Future. It's true my book did appear on the market recently, but I myself didn't mail any out."

"Oh, how absolutely exciting!" Sofia clapped her hands. "I'm so impressed. Your name is Future? Your novels are brilliant, so filled with intrigue and romance. I absolutely adore them."

"That's another mistake. I don't write romances."

"You don't write romances? Oh, I'm so sorry," Sofia flushed with embarrassment. "I must have got you mixed up with someone else. But never mind, you're still a very fine writer, I'm sure."

Anderson raised his glass and belched: "A toast to you, Mr. Future, and to your fabulous new novel! And even if no one agrees, for me it is still fabulous. Why? Because you wrote it, that's why. On behalf of our distinguished guests, I would like to place an order for one hundred copies."

Guzzling glass after glass, the lickspittles only became more and more drunk.

Finally, Collin, leaning toward Future, tried to sound sober, "What is this novel of yours about?"

"Ladies and gentlemen," Future spread his arms out wide, happy to fill them in on the details, "my novel is about lickspittles. If you like I can quickly summarize the story."

The lickspittle executives screwed up their faces; they would never have expected anyone to write a book about lickspittles of all things. All they wanted was to drink and be merry. However, not wanting to be rude, they agreed to sit back and listen.

"It's about a young man called Ivan who roamed the world in search of happiness."

"*Ivan!*" interrupted Roman. "What a horrible name that *Ivan* is, *John* would have been much better. *John* has more of a poetic ring to it."

"Sh, don't interrupt," Sofia waved her hand angrily in front of Roman's face, "It's not every day a writer finds us of interest and is willing to spend time with us, let alone write about us. Let him finish his story."

Future continued, "Ivan searched for happiness around the world. He was a fawning and meek man and no one respected him. He fell in love with the beautiful daughter of a very rich and powerful man. The girl's name was Monica. At first, she returned his love but later, witnessing his weakness of character, became disgusted and left him."

"How terrible," Sofia burst out at the top of her voice. "Who does this Monica think she is anyway? Tampering with the heart of a poor lickspittle, then dropping him like a hot potato!"

The surrounding lickspittles clapped in agreement.

"So, what finally happened to this poor Ivan?" this was Anderson.

"He met a lickspittle, they married, and had lickspittle children. Later he died in an old age home, but just before he died, he was arrested by the police – for a life of questionable lickspittle activity."

"What a terrible ending. How I despise sad endings," Ticket took a drink and looked down.

"Oh no, this is not the end by any means," Future went on. "There is still a trial to come."

"What?" Collin opened his eyes wide.

"Yes, that's correct, and it will be a lickspittle court with a lickspittle judge and lickspittle lawyers."

"Why that's impossible!" Collin objected. "A lickspittle court? That's downright preposterous. And how can a lickspittle judge possibly pass sentence?"

"Very simply. With a hammer. When a lickspittle starts to denounce himself or his own, he will be struck on the side of the head. If he tries it once more, THUMP, on the head again, with mathematical precision. Naturally, many lickspittles will go mad, some will even commit suicide, but there will also be those who will be redeemed."

Anderson decided to take a stand, "So this is the sort of trash you've written. It looks like I'm going to have to cancel my order. Who are you really? Kopelyuk? Future? An imposter? And what's the name of this book of yours?"

It's called "*Lickspittles, Come to Your Senses!*"

At the sound of these words, a thundering noise shot across the reception hall and it shook as if struck by an earthquake. The music came to a sudden stop and dancers on the floor went scrambling in all directions. The lickspittles still at their tables held onto their seats as they watched bottles of champagne go flying in all directions. Ticket was hit in the head with a jar of mustard; a tray of hors-d'oeuvres landed on Roman's lap; and Sofia face got covered with potato salad. Anderson lost it completely and started raving like a madman.

Future was swept up by a fantastic wind and whirled out of the banquet hall.

* * *

Future made his way safely home and bounced back into Kopelyuk's body. He was completely exhausted from the night's activities and slept for four days and four nights. When on the fifth day he finally managed to drag himself out of bed, he made to the other end of the room and opened up the window. The cool breeze revitalized him. Rubbing his eyes and taking a deep breath, he then stepped out into the corridor and went downstairs. Reaching the front door, he peered out into the vestibule. On the floor lay a pile of soiled parcels, and on top of the pile lay an official envelope from the post office. Ripping it open he found a bill for the return of the parcels, and when he read the outstanding sum his head went into a whirl. Almost all his books had been returned. About ten personalized envelopes lay scattered on the floor by the door. Picking them up he started to analyze the crude, barely legible handwriting.

One letter read: *Dear Mr. Kopelyuk or Mr. Future, or whoever you are, from MacChinchoy. You mailed me your book thinking I was a lickspittle. I once was one, that's true, but now I've changed my name to MacChinchoy. A word of advice: find yourself another profession.*

The next letter was filled with round and crooked letters. It was from a Pavlo O'Gronsky who misspelled the author's name: *Dear Mr. Kopelyak,* it began, *I read your book and couldn't make sense of it. Perhaps you wrote it under the influence? In any case, I passed it on to my neighbor who in turn passed it on to his neighbor. The best of luck.*

The remaining letters were written in more or less the same fashion. One woman wrote a pleasant enough note, but neglected to affix a stamp, and ended with *May God help you!*

Back in his room, Kopelyuk dropped his head over his desk and fell deep into thought. The room was still, not even a floorboard creaked. Then slowly the doorknob began to turn from the outside and within seconds a man appeared. It was the old hunchback, Gabriel.

"Hello there, Mr. Kopelyuk. If you don't mind, sir, but I came straight up. Your front door was wide open. I would like to ask you something. Are you alive or are you dead? If you're dead, then I'll be on my way, but if you're alive, I have some news for you."

"I'm neither here nor there; however, I'm always happy to hear news, good or bad."

"It's bad, sir, very bad. They've taken Mr. Anderson to the psychiatric ward. He keeps mumbling about some hammer hitting him on the head, and Mrs. Anderson wants to have you arrested because she says you're dangerous."

"Not a bad beginning," Kopelyuk mused. "You say someone's hitting Anderson on the head? And what about Ticket?"

"Mr. Ticket and his wife Sofia decided to send you this cheque. They ask that you not visit them anymore because you'll only frighten their children. Mr. Ticket wants to know if the amount is sufficient. Sofia sends you her best and hopes to see you write another novel soon, because, despite everything, she really enjoyed the part about the hammer on the head."

Gabriel laid the cheque on the table, and after bowing and bobbing his head several times, shuffled out of the room.

From the top of his desk drawer, Kopelyuk brought out his lickspittle address book and started flipping through the pages. He was feeling a bit rascally. First thing tomorrow he would pay them all a visit.

MOUNTAIN CLIMBER

"What beautiful mountains," thought Tanas Wieter as he gazed up into the sky. "Mountains everywhere. This magnificent Carpathian range doesn't even begin to compare to my native Pinsk Marshlands."

With the palm of his hand, he shaded his eyes from the bright afternoon sun and studied the massive contours. Directly over his head, a steep cliff, lined on either side by thick groves of beech and fir, shot straight up. Then to the left the sound of a rushing stream, its crystal-clear water racing downward, jumping vigorously over rocks and fallen branches. When a spotted salamander slid across his way, Wieter waved his walking stick and frightened the little creature into a tuft of grass growing alongside the path.

Finally, his eye came to rest on a blue-black mountain peak that towered above all the others. It was thickly forested at the base, but its summit, partially shaded by a blue-gray mist, was treeless and sprinkled with snow. Over that mountain was the Slovakian border.

"But what mysteries must lie up there," he thought in fascination.

Pulling the rim of his cap over his eyes, he took a deep breath. It was as if the summit beckoned him.

Wieter was an adventurous young man with broad shoulders and strong muscular legs. His hometown of Pinsk was behind him forever. He stood at the foot of the highest mountain and marveled at its beauty. Something seemed to be pushing him from behind.

"Go quickly, young man, climb that mountain, there you will find your destiny."

In that instant, from behind a small wooden hut an old *Huzul* emerged, smoking a tobacco-filled pipe. His face was long, thin and rugged as the surrounding range.

"How far is it to the top?" Wieter asked, pointing.

The old mountain man rubbed his long white beard and examined the young man closely. Screwing up his eyes, there was contempt in his voice.

"What do you think?"

"Maybe a couple of hours, no more."

The *Huzul* released a loud and sardonic laugh. "A couple of hours? Hah! You lowlanders are all alike. You'd be lucky to get there by nightfall."

Wieter rolled his eyes and threw back his head, "Before nightfall you say? I bet I can get there in half that time. Besides, a little hike will do me good."

When the old man just barely disappeared behind a stand of trees, Wieter went on his way. After about half an hour he paused to rest. Building a fire on the edge of a narrow, fast-moving stream, he boiled up some coffee and then took sandwiches from his knapsack. The cold mountain air increased his appetite and he ate heartily. In the distance he could see a flock of sheep grazing peacefully in a lush pasture and farther down, huddled in the heart of a u-shaped valley, was the outline of a *Huzul* village. For a brief moment he considered visiting it, perhaps even spending the night there, but when he looked up and saw his snowy peak, he quickly threw his knapsack over his back and started to climb.

The path raced upward. At times it was as taut as a string, other times it spiraled precariously around narrow ledges, and sometimes it twisted and turned into dark forested expanses. The sun was high in the sky and the blistering heat beat down upon his back. In no time Wieter was covered in sweat. He took off his cap to fan his face and then gulped water from his wineskin. He considered returning to the creek to refresh himself, but he didn't want to backtrack. The summit drew him onward.

By late afternoon, he came upon a largish hamlet. It was the last Ukrainian settlement before the Slovakian border. As he passed by a row of small wooden cottages with thatched rooftops, an old woman made toward him. For a fee she offered her grandson to guide him over the mountain. But the stubborn young man would hear nothing of it, he was determined to go it alone. He grinned and said:

"No thank you, I like to go my own way."

He climbed another hour. He encountered a spectacular waterfall that thundered down into a broad, shallow pool. Bending down and cupping together his hands, he took several drinks; the water was cold and refreshing and revived him almost at once. Then undressing, he rinsed out his clothes and hung them on a tree to dry. Wading across the pool, he stood under the falling water and with the sediment washed and shaved. He then put on a clean pair of trousers and a fresh shirt, and after packing up his belongings, continued on his way.

He was very pleased to note that from the start of his journey all was going smoothly and according to plan. Then he thought of the old *Huzul*. That arrogant old man, making such a fuss about everything! But no sooner had this thought entered his mind when to his great dismay he came to a fork in the road.

"What should I do? If I go to the left, I will undoubtedly get lost. And who knows where the path to the right leads."

After a short deliberation, thrusting out his chest, he decided against going either left or right. Instead, he chose to go his own way, straight into the thicket. He was confident his way was the way that would get him to where it was he was aiming to go.

At first, the forest was thin and sparse and he felt invigorated by the lacy shadows cast by the trees. But before long the ground beneath him became rocky and irregular. It was hard on his feet and soon sharp pangs started shooting up his legs. He was certain his peak was just beyond the trees, and according to his guess, it could not be more than a kilometer away. By the position of the sun, he determined there was still enough light left to guide him.

But to his surprise, the trees, rather than becoming thinner, thickened. When he gazed upward, only random patches of open sky could be found. Stumbling onto a stretch of tangled hazelwood, his right foot became snagged and he fell to the ground scraping his knees. Cursing and picking himself up with the help of his walking stick, he quickly moved on. He scanned the surrounding area. Dusk seemed to be moving in more rapidly than expected, and he suddenly realized it would soon be dark. He could feel himself grow anxious. At that moment he regretted ever starting up the mountain on his own. Why hadn't he listened to the old *Huzul* or taken the guide up on the woman's offer? He feared that beyond this forest a denser one awaited him, perhaps even one that was impenetrable. Why he could be lost for days or weeks, he might even die of starvation. But he soon shook himself free of these thoughts and, taking a deep breath, tried to get a handle on things. He shouted defiantly out into the craggy terrain:

"Who's to say I can't reach the summit by nightfall? I'll show them!"

The mountain now angled at almost forty-five degrees, and everywhere the rock was heavily covered with slippery lichen. As Wieter ascended, he grabbed onto random shrubs and bushes to keep from falling. When he started to climb over a moss-laden boulder, he lost his balance and fell, banging his head on a sharp ridge. His forehead was cut open and almost instantly blood gushed out, running down his face and onto his shirt. Taking a handkerchief out from his pocket and soaking it with water from his wineskin, he quickly applied it to his head to stop the bleeding.

After pulling himself up, he balanced on the rocks with greater caution. His arms and legs were badly scratched up and he had blisters on his heels. When a sudden waft of cold air swept across his face, he felt encouraged: the summit could not be far off. In the distance he noticed a break in the trees. A circular clearing overgrown with spiked grasses and dwarfed wildflowers appeared before him. As he continued, he was overcome by a feeling that he was not alone. Without making a sound, he kept to the edge of the thicket, stepping carefully over rotting deadwood and uprooted trees.

When he peeked from behind a solitary spruce, to his great surprise, a flock of wild sheep emerged before him. They were grazing on the edge of the grassland, their compact, muscular bodies shimmering brilliantly in the evening light. Swishing their short white tails, from time to time they lifted their heads and made slight grunting noises. When Wieter accidentally stepped on a clump of dried underbrush, the snapping sound reverberated across the plateau and the sheep fled.

Wieter climbed higher and higher up the wooded slope, and when he came to a long, serrated ledge, he took out his binoculars and looked to the west. He was certain the snow-laden summit would finally appear before him. But to his great disappointment, the trees still obstructed his view. He noticed they were now somehow different, stunted and thinly spaced, with the trunks curbed and the bark hard and cracked. The grass was different too, its blades not soft and lush as in the lowlands, but rather, sharp and erect almost like a knife. Taking a deep breath, his lungs filled with the cold, crisp mountain air – he felt exhilarated. At last, he had reached the tree line!

Beneath his feet, the ground became littered with rocks. He prided himself on his physical endurance and boasted of his bold and impulsive spirit. He had walked on the edge of precipices, he had hung from cliffsides, and he had waded across cold mountain streams. And now he was about to set foot on the summit, to conquer nature itself. His legs felt faint and his mouth had long since run dry, the lack of oxygen made him dizzy. When he came upon a steep rock face, on all fours he climbed to the top; a sharp, cold sensation suddenly pricked the tips of his fingers.

"Snow!" he cried aloud. "I've done it! I've reached the unreachable!"

He stood triumphantly on the summit and examined the wild splendor. Mountain peaks covered with drifting snow jutted out endlessly in every direction. The panorama was breathtaking. Looking upward he could see streams of clouds roll across the sky, and then disappear behind steep, rugged contours. Never in his imagination had he envisioned such untamed beauty. He had gone where no man had gone before.

The sun had dropped behind a high mountain wall. Laying his knapsack on the ground, Wieter decided to set up camp. His stomach grumbled from hunger, and by the light of the moon, he collected dry grasses and twigs to start a fire. He would boil up some potatoes. As he was about to strike up a match, in the far-off distance, atop a small ridge, somehow, he caught the flickering of a faint light. At first, he thought it was his mind playing tricks on him, but upon closer examination, he made out the outline of a rooftop, and then a chimney. He was dumbfounded:

"A house? In this tundra? Impossible!"

Setting out in the direction of the light, after about ten minutes, he did indeed come upon a house. It was built from unpeeled logs, had carved wooden shutters, and a

THEODORE ODRACH

red shingled roof. He climbed the steps of the porch and knocked on the door.

*   *   *

The mountain climber had a good night's sleep. When in the morning he awoke, he found himself in a small cabin located behind the main house. He lay in a large wooden bed and was covered by a thick eiderdown. A warm golden sun poured in through the raised windows and in the distance he could hear the bleating of sheep. The door creaked open and a middle-aged *Huzul* woman poked in her head.

"Time to get up," she said in a pleasant singsong. "Your breakfast is ready."

Setting down a tray of food on a small side table, Wieter enjoyed a meal of scrambled eggs, black bread, and coffee. After washing up he quickly put on his clothes and went outside.

In the soft morning light, the summit that had so beckoned him had now somehow lost its luster. It no longer looked magical and forbidding, rather, it was much like all the other peaks. He couldn't help but feel disillusioned. Nonetheless, he set out to explore the rocky terrain. He hiked in and around boulders, made his way to the edge of promontories, and climbed steep rock faces. A slight gurgling sound caught his attention. When he turned to have a look, he found a fountain of water spurting out of the ground.

"A natural spring!" he shouted excitedly.

Stooping down and taking several swallows, he could feel the cold, fresh water prick his tongue, and then make its way down into his throat. The discovery enthralled him.

When he came to the house for lunch, the *Huzul* woman was standing over a hot tile stove stirring a pot of soup. Her hands were broad and chapped and her hair, tied back in a bun, was gray at the temples. Upon seeing him, she smiled and said, "Did you have a good walk?"

"Yes," he replied, "and I'm well rested, the cabin is very comfortable."

He was excited to tell her about his discovery, "During my walk, I came upon the most wonderful natural spring. It's so fresh and clear. It's a few kilometers north of here, behind a clump of ..."

The *Huzul* woman was quick to cut him off.

"Yes, I know exactly what you're talking about. That spring is very popular. People come all the way from Lviv to fill their bottles. They say it heals the lungs. But, of course, now things have slowed down around here, it's war, it's war ..."

"From Lviv? You say they come all the way up here from Lviv?" Wieter felt discouraged.

After a moment another thought came to him. He had a proposition to make, "Would you mind if I stayed in your cabin a few weeks? I could use the rest before moving on. Your mountains are so peaceful."

The *Huzul* woman shook her head apologetically, "No, I'm afraid that would not be possible. Helena, my daughter, is coming up from the city. The cabin belongs to her. She's a student and spends almost every spring break there. But

now that the Bolsheviks are moving in on Lviv, she's returning for good. It's safer up here than down there."

Wieter looked disappointed, "Doesn't she like to stay in
the main house?"

"I wish she would. But she insists she needs her priva-
cy; she says she likes the cabin because it's higher up – the
higher the better. If she had wings, I swear she'd fly to the
moon. Young people today are so restless; they're interested only in making it across the border. But then, again,
it's war, it's war; the Bolsheviks are driving all our young
people away."

Three days passed and to Wieter's great relief Helena
did not appear. He spent his time exploring the mountains,
meditating, and studying the flora and fauna. Closing his
eyes, he listened to the tones of the wind. He was overcome
by a hopeful calm. In the lowlands, a wild war was raging,
but in this far-off range, there was nothing but peace and
tranquility.

Early one morning as he lay in bed, he began to amuse
himself with thoughts of Helena. What was she like? What
did she look like? And before long he found himself answer-
ing his own questions: light brown hair, hazel eyes, sturdy
legs. Independent, obstinate, presumptuous.

No sooner had these thoughts entered his mind when
a loud thump came from outside, and then the door flew
open. A pretty young woman with bright blue eyes and
wavy shoulder-length hair appeared on the threshold. At
the sight of the strange man, she let out a shriek and disappeared. Wieter jumped out of bed, put on his trousers, and
quickly washed his face with water from the little washbasin

on the dresser. There was an abrupt knock on the door. The *Huzul* woman hurried in. It was not hard for Wieter to guess what she was about to say. He said, disappointed:

"Well, it looks like my time is up."

Gathering his belongings, he looked at the woman, as if there were something on his mind. He hesitated several minutes and then finally came out with it, "Would it be possible for me to stay in your barn for another week or so? I'm not quite ready to move on."

When the woman agreed, Wieter threw his knapsack over his back and happily set out for the barn. Clean sheets and a down pillow were laid down on the hay, and two woolen blankets lay side by side. The arrangement pleased Wieter and he continued to spend his days hiking in the mountains and drinking water from the spring. He didn't want to think about the long journey ahead of him.

One afternoon as he roamed about exploring the terrain, he noticed two narrow but well-trodden paths several hundred meters apart spiraling downward. He stood back astonished. The fork in the road he had encountered earlier in his trip came to mind: these were the very two paths he had refused to take. He couldn't help but berate himself.

"And you thought you had reached the unreachable when even a child could have found his way up here, blindfolded, and with two paths to choose from!"

Every evening Wieter appeared at the main house for dinner and sat opposite Helena. He was courteous to her and tried to make conversation by inquiring about her studies, about Lviv, and about the political atmosphere there. But she remained standoffish and answered only

THEODORE ODRACH

in monosyllables. As a result, Wieter came to avoid her as much as possible, but from a distance he couldn't help notice how lovely she was.

After dinner one evening as Wieter started out in the direction of the spring with the intention of filling up his wineskin, he noticed Helena sitting on a rock reading a book. In an attempt to get her attention, he jumped behind a clump of bushes and shouted at the top of his voice:

"A bear! A bear!"

Helena burst into a fit of laughter, "You are too silly. Even my grandfather doesn't remember seeing bears in these parts."

To Wieter's great surprise, he noticed Helena was smiling and she was even quite friendly. But her eyes seemed somehow clouded and when she finally spoke, she did so with a timid curiosity.

"My mother tells me you're leaving tomorrow."

"Yes, I'm heading for the border. I still have a long road after that."

Raising her brows, she felt a little awe of him. She clasped together her hands. "Oh, how I envy you. Someday I'm going to leave and see the world too, maybe when the war ends. There's so much uncertainty everywhere right now and it really frightens me. This horrible war is destroying everything."

Wieter could only but feel compassion for this free-spirited mountain girl.

The next morning with his knapsack on his back, Wieter set out on his journey. Helena and her mother stood by the gates of their front yard and waved.

Helena called out: "If you ever happen to be on our mountain again, come and visit!"

"Just keep that hay warm!" he shouted back.

This time Wieter kept to a well-trodden path and the descent was swift and easy.

THE NIGHT BEFORE CHRISTMAS

The Informer was a wartime underground weekly edited by Julian Lyciuk and compiled in the attic of a small, secluded house on the edge of a forest. In the far-right corner of the attic, on a crude wooden table stood a Telefunken short-wave radio. Beside it from morning till night, with pen and paper in hand, recording the latest news, sat Motria. She was young and very pretty with wavy brown hair, high cheekbones, and large, melancholy blue eyes. The daughter of an Orthodox priest from the Pinsk Marshes, she had married an army commander who had been killed in 1941 by the Bolsheviks in a battle near Sarny. Her five-year-old son, Danilo, whom she missed terribly, lived with her grandmother in a village of prominent size on the banks of the Pripyat River. Along with thousands of Ukrainian women, she possessed a deep desire to fight for the freedom of her country, and as a result had joined an underground movement for independence.

In an adjoining room opposite a large window overlooking a stand of conifers, sat Oksana. She was a tall, gangly teenager, a student from a local gymnasium who rarely spoke. Little was known about her life except she was of peasant stock from a small hamlet somewhere in the Carpathian Mountains. She was a diligent worker and spent her days sitting at her desk typing out edited material given to her by Julian.

While editing *The Informer*, Julian resided in a remote settlement near Svinarin. Each morning at the crack of dawn, after wakening, he would cut across an extensive oat field and follow a thin trail of trampled brushwood to the little house in the forest. There the housekeeper would greet him with a pot of hot tea and a breakfast of rye bread and boiled eggs. Barely having swallowed his food, he would dart upstairs and begin flipping through the large pile of statements recorded throughout the night by Motria. The news came in from three directions: Moscow, Berlin, and London. Because it was often vague and contradictory, Julian came to use only a small portion of the information, the remainder of which was burned in a tile stove in the kitchen downstairs.

One morning when he had just set foot in the attic and begun discarding the unnecessary papers, Motria glanced up at him, her eyes weary and red-rimmed. She was discouraged.

"Is this why I spend all night up here listening to the Telefunken, recording the news, so you can just burn it in the stove?"

"Motria," Julian tried to explain, "not everything ends up in the stove. We need accurate information for our readers and the most reliable, as you know, comes from London. But we still have to be aware of news from other places. Take a close look at the map." He pointed to a large

THEODORE ODRACH

map pinned to the wall behind her. "The black marks give us a good indication of where the front is located."

Rubbing her eyes and suppressing a deep yawn, she lowered her head a moment and then with some reluctance went back to work.

Along with news from the radio, *The Informer* also received information from Ukrainian partisans and a host of anonymous correspondents. All the material received was examined thoroughly by Julian, typed up, and then sent off by courier to a mobile printing outpost somewhere in the forest. Although Julian did not know of the press' precise location, he knew of its troubled history.

On the thirteenth of December, 1942, during the time of German occupation, an acquaintance of his, PT, had one night secretly dismantled his presses in Kovel and taken them into the forest. When still operating in Kovel, the Germans had forced PT to print propaganda material for their soldiers as well as material to be sent out to the Third Reich. However, unbeknownst to the Germans, PT also covertly produced material for the Ukrainian underground movement such as pamphlets, notices, and newsletters. When the Germans caught wind of PT's forbidden activities, they set out to not only quash the operation but place PT and the workers before a firing squad. Before the Germans could get to them, supported by partisans, four horse-drawn sleighs appeared in the middle of the night, loaded up the presses, and drove off with them in the direction of the Svinarinsky Forest. In the heart of the forest, under the protection of the army, the presses now operated freely. Although *The Informer* was published weekly, Julian never came to meet with PT.

One winter morning of the following year as day broke over the horizon Julian looked out his window. A row of icicles overhanging the pane glistened invitingly in the dim light, and in the yard, a high north wind swirled flakes of snow up into the air. He wanted to sit back a moment, to absorb the tranquility and beauty of the surrounding wintry countryside, to forget the war raging all around. But this morning he was running late. With great haste, he pulled on his boots, buttoned up his sheepskin coat, and wrapped a thick woolen scarf around his neck. Stepping outside, the bright snow crunched beneath his feet and the frost collected instantly on his brows and lashes. He kept his lips sealed to prevent the cold from entering his mouth. When he finally reached the little house and opened the attic door, he was startled to find Motria bent over her desk crying. Hearing him enter, she quickly dried her eyes, and said, "Don't be alarmed. There's nothing wrong, really. It's just that today is Christmas Eve and I miss my son terribly."

It had not occurred to Julian that it was the Christmas season, let alone Christmas Eve. Glancing about he noticed the attic had been cleaned and tidied. A small table was covered with a red and black embroidered cloth, in the middle of which stood a plate filled with honey cookies and a bowl of *kutia*. During the night the two women had made preparations for the evening's festivities. When Julian offered to go into the woods and chop down a tree, a look of anguish passed over Motria's face. Resting her arms on the table and lowering her eyes, Julian understood instantly that a decorated tree would only remind her of her son, whom she had not seen for several months. Instead, the three resumed working and continued to do so until the appearance of the first star.

When dusk fell over the forest and a small faint star finally emerged, upon hearing the neighing of horses, Oksana rushed to the window. She yelled excitedly, "We have guests!"

Footsteps could be heard down below and then they rapidly ascended the staircase. Before long four men dressed in heavy gray overcoats and high leather boots stepped over the threshold. Julian immediately recognized his good friend Lieutenant Sidorenko. He was a middle-aged man, tall, with an elongated face and a thick gray mustache. Under his arm he held two parcels tied with red ribbon: one was for Motria, the other for Oksana. Smiling warmly, he extended his arm first to Motria.

"This is for you," he said. "A little something to insulate you from the cold."

He then turned to Oksana, "And this is for you. I noticed yours were getting a bit worn. Merry Christmas to you all!"

Tearing apart the parcels the two women's eyes lit up. Oksana slipped on a pair of black leather boots lined with sheepskin and Motria put on a lovely brown fur-lined jacket.

"And you, my good friend," the lieutenant turned Julian, "I haven't forgotten about you."

From his pocket, he produced a small pouch filled with home-grown tobacco and two packets of rolling papers.

"You couldn't have brought a finer gift. Thank you."

The lieutenant and his men took off their overcoats and sat down on a wooden bench opposite the decked table. From the kitchen, the housekeeper, to honor the Christmas

Eve feast brought up a pot of hot black tea and a pitcher of water. As she poured, a bright smile came to her face.

"It's nice to see we'll be having company for dinner. For three days I labored over the twelve traditional courses. As you know supplies are scarce."

Pausing briefly to comb her hair from her face, she added rather boastfully, "I really don't know how I did it, but I've managed to come up with all the food. We will have a true celebration. The bread just came out of the oven, it's still steaming."

The soldiers shifted uncomfortably. Something was obviously up. The lieutenant looked at the housekeeper sadly, "Unfortunately, we have orders from headquarters to bring Motria, Oksana, and Julian to the camp tonight. It's getting dark outside. Time is running out. We must hurry."

"But my dinner!" The housekeeper threw up her arms and then fell into tears.

Two horse-drawn sleighs were already waiting in the yard. Oksana and the lieutenant sat in the first sleigh and Julian and Motria settled in the second one. The other soldiers followed on foot at a close distance.

Up above the sky extended in a massive stretch of royal blue. Stars sparkled in great profusion and a round silver moon cast an array of shadows all around. The horses labored through the deep snow and the runners of the sleighs floated silently on top, as if in mid air. Motria looked up at the frost-covered trees and muttered as if to herself:

"The night before Christmas makes me think back to when I was a child – my mother in the kitchen preparing borscht, my father singing carols, the sheaf of wheat in the corner. Oh my, how it all vanishes so quickly."

As the sleighs passed by snow-laden shrubs and under broad overhanging branches, Julien could feel the cold air cut at his face. He dropped his head and started to doze. Before long he nodded off and began to dream:

A narrow spiraling path of trampled snow appeared before him and on either side a dark, dense forest. He was in a great hurry and at his waist he wore an ax. He then encountered a broad meandering river that was iced over, its surface like glass, glistening in the darkness. An unexpected wind howled through the trees and then seemed to push him onto the river. Tonight was Christmas Eve and there was magic everywhere. The sound of gunfire had long since stopped – the Bolsheviks had picked up and retreated to the east, the Germans to the west. Again, there was peace on earth. The news excited him, yet he remained wary. The truth he decided was in the river. Undoing his ax, he began hacking at the ice. In a short time, he hit the water but to his great horror in the middle of the ice-hole lay a speckled trout, belly-up, its eyes wide open. Shuddering, he jumped back and then ran along the bank screaming.

"Wake up! Wake up!" Julian could feel someone grab hold of his arm and shake him. "You must have been having a nightmare. You were jumping around so much you almost fell out of the sleigh."

The horses made their way deeper into the forest. Somewhere in the far-off distance bomb explosions shook the earth and projectors set fire to the sky. Motria hung her head between her shoulders, closed her eyes, and plugged her ears with the tips of her fingers; she couldn't bear it anymore. On either side of the path tall, magnificent trees stood proud and unmoving, like candles. The path grew narrower and narrower, and the horses now pulled the sleighs as if by instinct, weaving in and around the odd boulder and rows of fir and aspen. Snow started to fall lightly. Finally, the path disappeared altogether, but the horses, snorting and switching their tails, plodded onward.

Suddenly in the distance came the flickering of a light. The horses kicked up their hooves and released a series of high-pitched, screeching neighs. As the sleighs approached the light, two box-like buildings emerged before them. They were constructed of old wooden planks with broad, heavy doorways and shingled rooftops. The previous summer a group of partisans had by night dismantled these buildings in the village Ozutich and transported them via horse and wagon to this location. Originally, they had been constructed by the German army to house their soldiers, but when Bolshevik troops launched an attack and the German forces fled, these buildings were left abandoned. Now they stood in the heart of the forest used by Ukrainian partisans.

When Julian, Motria, and Oksana entered a large hall in the first building, they were astounded to see long rows of tables neatly covered with white tablecloths and set with colorfully patterned dinnerware. On either side sat fresh-faced young men in uniform, and along the far wall laid out on the floor was an impressive collection of weapons: German machine guns, rifles, Soviet-made knives and so on. From the kitchen out back the aroma of frying mushrooms quickly permeated the room, and then came the smell of baked bread. By the head table next to a lavishly decorated Christmas tree was an icon of the Virgin Mary framed with a hand-stitched cloth and beside it stood a sheaf of wheat. When Lieutenant Sidorenko entered the room, the young men jumped to their feet and saluted. A procession of cooks emerged almost immediately from the kitchen carrying large bowls of compote, followed by steaming borsht, platters of baked stuffed fish, cabbage rolls, and *varenyky*. From a back table an elderly man dressed in civilian attire rose to his feet and began to sing: "Christ is born on Christmas day ..." His deep, penetrating voice flooded the room and he was soon accompanied by the surrounding men. Just before the chorus was sung a second time, Oksana drowned out the male voices with her powerful operatic soprano. Tears welled up in Motria's eyes and she dabbed them dry with a handkerchief.

As dinner was about to begin, Lieutenant Sidorenko stepped next up to the Christmas tree and raised his hands for attention.

"Comrades," he began, "as you know, our enemies have inordinate strengths, and now, according to the latest update, the Reds are beginning to overpower the Germans."

Pausing briefly, he looked round at all the young faces. He went on, as if trying to keep his voice from breaking, "Men, stay strong and keep the faith. No one will defeat us, not the Russians not the Germans because Christ is by our side."

The hall filled with applause.

He then recited a prayer.

Just as the candles were lit and the borscht served, a young messenger in shabby peasant clothes suddenly came barging into the dining hall. There was a sweat on his brow and he panted heavily. Running up to the lieutenant, he handed him a sealed envelope. Tearing it open, the lieutenant's face tensed at once. There was not a minute to lose. He rose and said severely.

"The Reds have just been spotted on the outskirts of Ozutich. Men, take to your weapons!"

The men jumped up from behind the tables, they strapped rifles over their shoulders and loaded their belts with bullets and hand grenades. Those who had been guarding the camp's grounds were already assembling outside. Before long two hundred men stood at attention in several long rows. Lieutenant Sidorenko shouted out to them, "Forward! March!"

And in single file, the young men started in the direction of Ozutich.

Julian, Motria, and Oksana stood in silence and watched as the procession disappeared into the darkness; the clanking of metal could be heard for the longest time. When the bright moon disappeared behind a clump of clouds, the hundreds of footprints made in the snow were left invisible.

Agony and despair came to Motria's face and she trembled all over. She crossed herself three times, and closing her eyes, repeated again and again.

"May God help them!"

THEODORE ODRACH

PANDEMONIUM IN PILSEN, OR BOMBING OF ŠKODA ARMAMENT WORKS

Pilsen, April 25, 1945

The Second World War was rapidly drawing to a close. The Germans were not only coming to be defeated but already tens of thousands of German soldiers had surrendered and more kept surrendering by the minute. But that's not to say German anti-aircraft defenses weren't still dangerously effective. And then there were the Soviets, quickly advancing from the east, positioning themselves to lay political claim to as much of Eastern Europe as possible, including Pilsen. Pilsen was of special interest to the Russians as it was home to the Škoda Armament Works, and they were looking to capture it in order to help them rebuild their military. Roosevelt and Churchill did not want this armament in Russian hands and, as a result, decided to have it bombed.

And so, in 1945 on this early spring day, with the war almost at an end, America's Eighth Air Force roared into Pilsen, the capital of Western Bohemia, on a mission: to bomb the Škoda Armament Works (which had also been a major source of arms for Germany during their occupation). This would be the last bombing mission, and it would come to be called "Hell from Heaven".

Two men, Yuri and Damian, the first older than the other by a good fifteen years, found themselves on the outskirts of this unfortunate city. They were refugees from faraway Ukraine, and they were laboring along a winding dirt road, pushing an old wooden handcart loaded with boxes, loose bundles, and several medium-sized leather valises. When the men came to the slant of a hill, with all the strength they could muster, they forced it upward, working to keep to the ruts in the road. Yuri could not stop from coughing, and he coughed until he was blue in the face. What he needed was a doctor, but the medical aid station was still ten kilometers away, on the other side of Pilsen. A young woman by the name of Natalia, not a relation to either of the men, but traveling with them, trailed a few meters behind. She had two small children, the youngest of whom she carried in her arms. Trying to catch up to the men, she called out.

"Slow down, please! I'm so tired. Oh, how these roads go on and on. And everywhere nothing but rubble."

Taking a handkerchief from her jacket pocket, not much over thirty, she brushed the dust from her face. She went on. "They say the war's in its final hours, but now the Americans are dropping bombs. I can't take it anymore. And Melanka just cries and cries and Christina's always hungry. The Germans might be retreating, but those Russians are forever getting closer, may God help us."

Both Yuri ad Damian ignored her and kept on.

"Oh, how my feet ache. Maybe by some miracle we'll get to Bavaria. Another two or three days and we should reach the border."

Upon hearing her last few words, Yuri suddenly stopped in his tracks. He had had enough. He turned on her with animosity, "Another two or three days, you say? How crazy do you think we are?" Then under his breath, so Natalia couldn't hear, "That woman is insufferable. She has some nerve. Does she really think that for another two or three days we're going to lug her baggage around for her? What does she think we are, a couple of bulls?"

Damian tried to keep the peace. He whispered back, "I'm sorry to say this, but whether you like it or not, we're stuck with her; let's just try and make the best of it."

"The best of it? All these valises, these bundles, and these crates filled with god knows what. It's back-breaking. And those kids of hers, that constant crying grates my nerves. Taking her with us was the biggest mistake."

Damian took a step toward his friend. "Hush, she might overhear you."

"Let her overhear me; in fact, I even want her to. A lone woman is the same as a noose around the neck. Some friend that Viktor Kuprenko was of yours – makes you promise to look after his wife should something happen to him, and the minute he finds the chance, he bolts just to save his own skin. Hah, the joke's on us! He abandons his wife and children because he found a couple of fools to do his dirty work for him. I say, nothing but a coward that Viktor Kuprenko."

Then pausing a moment, as if giving it some thought, "But I can't say that I blame him. She never shuts up!"

A constrained silence followed. Although Damian very well understood Yuri's frustration, there was not much he could do about it. Like it or not, they were stuck with Natalia Kuprenko.

Natalia finally caught up to them. She was out of breath and could hardly articulate.

"My God, what are we going to do? The trains aren't running, the tracks are all ripped up, and there are no cabs anywhere. And to add to it all, some of these Czechs are looking at us so strangely as if we weren't normal. They think something's not right with us because we're heading west and not east, because we're running from their 'Soviet brotherhood'. Don't they know what's happening in the East? Don't they know what the Bolsheviks are capable of?"

Natalia fell into tears. She wanted only to find her husband, whom she believed had been captured by the Germans and was now suffering a fate worse than death. She pattered on.

"My poor, dear Viktor, is he alive, is he dead? Will I ever see him again? Oh, dear Lord, please spare my Viktor and let him come home to me."

At once little Christina began to tug at her mother's sleeve. She needed to relieve herself and couldn't wait a minute longer. Natalia took her by the hand and disappeared behind a bush.

Damian suggested they take a break. "There's no point going on; as you can see, Pilsen's on fire, and it doesn't seem like things are going to let up any time soon. And the children look tired. Let's set up a small camp over there in the coppice; it seems camouflaged well-enough. And while

THEODORE ODRACH

they're resting, why don't you and I head into the city and see if maybe we could find ourselves a horse and wagon, or even some stray dog to help us with this load. Natalia and her girls will be safe here."

As the two men started down the road, fighter planes roared across the sky. Clouds of black smoke wafted over the rooftops of the little cottages they passed, and people everywhere could be heard yelling, cursing, and howling.

After about fifteen minutes they came upon a hillock. A great panorama opened up before them and the entire city came into view – it was nothing short of spectacular. There were broad avenues with buildings of various conglomerations, the Berounka River, winding its way toward the Pilsner Brewery, the magnificent St. Bartholomew's Cathedral, The Great Synagogue.

Yuri took his binoculars out of his satchel to get a better look. But it only made him gloomy. "Such a beautiful city up in smoke. There's almost nothing left of the Škoda Armament; it's been nearly completely leveled. Just imagine, yesterday it employed up to forty thousand workers and now nothing but smoke and ash. And in Old Town Square I can see people running around and there are tanks in the streets."

Then something caught his attention in the synagogue. His voice broke.

"There are people up in the towers! They're Nazi snipers and they're aiming at the Americans in the air!"

Yuri quickly passed Damian the binoculars but Damian didn't care to look. It was all too much for him. He muttered gloomily instead:

"The war's drawing to a close, but Pilsen is being ravaged, and all to stop the Russians from getting hold of the armament. And yes, the Americans are putting the last stops on Hitler and ending Nazi occupation, but the Russians are moving in with unprecedented speed from the other end. And the Reds are unstoppable. Rumor has it they've already encircled Berlin, and now there's talk that several Soviet Army fronts are advancing toward Prague. They will catch up to us before we know it."

As the men turned down some side road, within minutes they came to a rather large clearing densely covered with houses made of wood and brick. Looking in on at least a dozen of them, they hoped to find some sort of horse or oxen or even a wagon in half-decent shape. But luck was not on their side. After about ten minutes they entered a small market square, where there was a gathering of people. There were about twenty of them, massing around a fire, rubbing their chilled hands, jumping up and down to keep warm. They were talking loudly amongst themselves and gesticulating. It soon became apparent they were arguing over who should take control of their city – the Americans or the Russians. Half was for the Americans, the other half, the Russians.

One voice came out over the others. It belonged to a man and it was very serious. "It appears to me the Americans will soon be occupying our city. In my opinion, we stand a better chance with the Americans."

Then there came a woman's voice, "A better chance with the Americans?" She went on at length. "To hell with the Americans! We need the Americans like we need a hole in the head! They say they're liberating Pilsen, but just look what they're doing to our city. There's nothing left but rubble. True, yesterday they were kind enough to drop leaflets from their P-51 Mustangs to warn us of today's bombings, but look what good that's done! And then Eisenhower made a broadcast over the radio early this morning warning us of allied bombers targeting the Škoda Armament, telling people to get out and stay out until this afternoon. But they didn't count on the Germans intercepting. And now what have we got – nothing but pandemonium. This heavy cloud covering isn't helping either. And rumor has it Škoda workers have already been killed."

"Don't be fooled, people." An old man with a bundle under his arm had something to say. "This war is coming to an end, and it will end, but not for us. Pilsen is being liberated by the Americans from the Nazis only to be handed over to the Bolsheviks. Out of the hands of Hitler and into the hands of Stalin! And it's no secret the Bolsheviks are moving in to lay claim to as much of Eastern Europe and Germany as possible."

A young man stepped in, most likely a student. He wore a red armband and a visor cap was pulled down over his eyes. He addressed the old man.

"You obviously don't understand what's going on here. There is change in the air and things are only going to come to a good end. Yes, the Russians are on their way as we speak; all our hope lies with the Russians. The Bolsheviks will free us at last from all oppression and our lives will become filled with peace and joy. There will be plenty of everything for everybody – food, clothing, medicines."

Yuri was getting more and more agitated; he couldn't help but react. He called out to the young man, "If you think the Bolsheviks will save you, you are deceiving yourself. The gulags, the *kolkhozes*, the famines. When the Bolsheviks come, that's when your suffering will begin. Mark my words."

"And who are you? How do you know so much?" Some youngish-looking woman stepped forward. "Don't you realize the Bolsheviks are our only hope. There's nothing to fear from the Bolsheviks." Then looking him over, "Obviously you're not a Czech. Where do you come from?"

The student made it a point to answer. "He's not a German, that's for sure. Maybe he's a Pole or a Ukrainian." Then looking at Yuri directly, "And how is it you're such an authority on the Russians? Are you maybe heading for Prague? The Bolsheviks are moving in, God bless their souls."

Yuri was about to say something back, to put the student in his place but thought it through and held his tongue. He said instead, "We're headed West; Bavaria, to be more precise."

"Bavaria?" the youngish-looking woman cupped her hand to her ear as if she hadn't heard correctly. "Something's pulling you to the Germans, is it? Have you lost your mind?"

Yuri was quick to respond, "We're not being pulled to the Germans, rather, we're running from the Bolsheviks."

"Running from the Bolsheviks?" a man shouted. "My dear sir, you have nothing to fear from the Bolsheviks. Stay with us in Czechoslovakia. Nothing bad will happen to you here. Oh, the Russians, the Russians, what a fine group of people those Russians!"

At once from behind a hill, a fighter plane soared into the sky. Everyone ran for cover. The roaring sound of the engine came in a straight line across the road, and then upon the railroad tracks, which were a few meters away. Lowering itself over a chain of railway cars, it started dropping bombs. Glass went flying every which way and the caboose caught fire. People could be heard screaming and cursing.

Yuri said grimly, "There was a train and now there is nothing. Was there a reason to drop these bombs so randomly and to endanger the lives of hundreds? To the East, the Bolsheviks are quick with the bullet to the neck and here the Americans are bomb crazy. But at least Hitler's retreating. If I had a knife in my hand, I would slit their throats, all of them, one after the other – the Russians, the Germans, the Americans."

The air raid lasted about ten minutes after which the plane flew back behind the hill. Over the city of Pilsen the sun was starting to set. Only the vague outline of the church domes and the broken chimney stacks of the Škoda Armament could be seen. Damian and Yuri picked up at once and hurried to Natalia to see if she and her children were all right.

Natalia was sobbing, hugging her two daughters. She looked at the two men as they approached. "Oh, all this bombing, this gunfire. When will it all stop? Did you maybe find a horse or a wagon of some sort? Please tell me you did. My nerves are to the breaking point."

"Horse and wagon you say and not a limousine?" Yuri couldn't help with the sarcasm. He then gave her a scowling look.

Natalia turned to Damian, "Why does Yuri hate me so much? I'm a burden to you, I know; I'm slowing you down. Oh, if only I could find my husband."

Drying her eyes, she managed to pull herself together. She changed the subject. She looked at Damian directly.

"My Viktor spoke of you quite often; he said you were one of his best colleagues. He was very fond of you and admired your dedication. You taught mathematics I understand? He said there was no one better. But he told me nothing about your personal life. Here we are, covering hundreds of kilometers together and I know nothing about you. Where is your family? Are you married?"

"Family? Married? Yes, or rather I was married. I found the woman I had been looking for, and then I lost her. When war broke out, she was gone, killed. Now I am alone. And I believe I will remain alone."

"Such a pessimist!"

Barely a minute passed when again she became consumed by her troubles.

"Oh, am I ever going to find my Viktor? And these roads go on and on! Dear Lord, it must still be at least fifty kilometers to Bavaria."

Yuri clenched and ground his teeth, "You and that Bavaria of yours. I wish you'd just shut up about Bavaria."

Natalia threw her gaze on him, "Why are you so ill-tempered all the time? Don't tell me you don't want me to find my husband? He told me, should we become separated, we would find each other in Regensburg, in the main square."

and admired at the passing girls. When they came across a large poster nailed to a pole, they stopped. It was a photograph of a young man with deep-set black eyes and disheveled hair. He was wanted by the police. The students studied his face and then looked at one another puzzled.

"That's interesting," said Dudik.

"Interesting, yes, and a very touchy situation," remarked Lonia. "Up until now, we've had peace in our district. To murder the chief-of-police, that's an outright crime. It's the terrorists behind it."

Dudik remained silent a moment, then began to philosophize. It so happened that very year he was studying Hegel.

"You see, Lonia, everything that happens happens for a reason. Imagine, for example, that someone has broken a leg. The reasons for this broken leg can be countless: this someone could have fallen down the stairs, or tripped over a rock, or stumbled into a ditch; all these possible reasons are valid explanations for the broken leg in question. It just proves my point that everything is tied in with reason."

"What are you getting at?"

"It's very simple. The chief-of-police who was found murdered could have been a tyrant; he could have tortured people, kicked in their teeth, or bashed in their heads. He could have been a murderer himself. Who knows for sure? Maybe he deserved to die."

"Well, excuse me, but from the point of the law, your theories don't hold water. What about the courts? Don't you think it's up to them to decide?"

"Just a minute, Lonia. Who says the courts are always right? They can be filled with evil and corruption, and what worth has justice then? Law is written by the elites, it's fair to them, but for others – it's a noose around the neck."

"Now you're talking like an anarchist!" the priest's son was taken aback.

"Lonia, can't you see what's going on!" Dudik was becoming excited and argumentative. "The chief-of-police is the very man for whom I've created my theory."

"You're a long way from graduating," Lonia laughed, "and you're already creating your own theories!"

"Just one second, Lonia. It's common knowledge that people are people, but that's a fallacy. One can walk around on two legs, decipher colors, play an instrument even, and not be a human being. There are two types of human beings: one is an actual person, the other, an animal without a heart or soul. Stop, Lonia, don't interrupt! The animal on two legs feels nothing, he has no conscience or intelligence. He is a pawn on the chess board with a revolver in his hand. When he's told to shoot someone, he shoots; when he's told to scratch someone's eyes out, he scratches."

Dudik's reasoning startled Lonia. He grumbled disapprovingly under his breath and had no desire to further the conversation. But Dudik was insistent.

"As far as I'm concerned, that terrorist Kolody belongs to the first group of humans. Look at the poster, take a close look at his face; obviously, it's been retouched by the authorities to make him look like a ruthless criminal, but it doesn't fool me. His eyes are gentle and dreamy, the eyes of an idealist; or look at that scar on his cheek. I'm telling you, Lonia, this face possesses a profound belief in some political ideal. Think what you want, but he's no criminal."

　　　　　　　THEODORE ODRACH

Lonia listened to Dudik with hostility. At first, he tried to be objective and look at the situation from Dudik's perspective, but the teachings of his father, the Reverend Lawrence Bubensky, overpowered his efforts. Since early childhood, he had been taught to obey and respect the law for the simple reason that law was law. For a brief moment Lonia even wanted to quote his father, to further prove his point of view, but thinking it over, he waved his hand and said instead:

"There is no point in arguing about this, it's not getting us anywhere. How about going hunting? I have a couple of rifles; one belongs to my brother-in-law, the other is mine. If you want, tomorrow night we can go into the Skuminsky Forest. There are a hell of a lot of rabbits out there."

This proposition appealed to Dudik. A cold night, the silver moon beaming down from the sky, creaking snow underfoot, a fleeing rabbit. The two friends continued down the road and talked of tomorrow's hunting expedition. As they turned into a park, again they came across a poster of the wanted terrorist, Kolody.

"There are revolutionaries fighting for this county's freedom and independence!" Dudik could not restrain himself. "There is a movement to resist the Red occupiers!"

"Hush, keep your voice down!" Lonia spoke in a low tone, looking around, fearing some of the passersby might overhear.

The two friends walked on in silence. Lonia took pleasure in the passing women, who were huddled in warm sheepskin coats and whose round cheeks had reddened from the cold.

"Such an ugly provincial town, yet such beautiful women!" Lonia couldn't help but be delighted. "I'll never agree with anyone who says women from the big cities are lovelier than our provincials. Look at that girl in front of us. She walks like an aristocrat; her legs are long and shapely and she moves with such grace. Pity you didn't catch her face, Dudik. She's alluring, appetizing, just like this cold, clear provincial air."

They turned toward the river, and standing along the edge of the bank, looked down. The river was covered with a thick layer of snow, and as a brisk wind swirled the flakes up into the air, patches of ice became exposed. A short distance downriver some people were skating on one of the larger patches. Young women in short dresses and thick woolen socks were shouting and laughing happily, their long hair falling and tangling over their faces.

"Life is worth living if only to admire beautiful women," remarked Lonia. "If they stood before me in a row and I had to choose one, believe me, I'd fall in love with them all. I have an irresistible weakness for the finer things in life. I think I got that from my mother's side of the family. My father isn't much of a romantic."

The students walked onto the river's frozen surface to get a closer look at the girls. Their faces radiated health and joy; they skated gracefully upon the circular patches of ice. Lonia shouted out to them, "Hello, beautiful Olympiads!"

The girls waved back and skated away.

The students continued further along the bank, then turned and entered a broad residential street lined with colorful wooden houses with tin roofs. As they entered the

THEODORE ODRACH

marketplace, Arcen, the servant, was already standing by the cart waiting to go home.

*　*　*

When Dudik had finished talking with his parents and sisters, and the sun had been replaced by a silver moon that gleamed down upon the snow-covered rooftops, there came a knock on the door. It was the servant girl from the Bubensky household with a message.

"The Bubenskys ask that you come for a visit." The girl spoke rapidly and the entire time she kept her eyes fixed on the ground.

"Come in, please," said Dudik, eyeing her in a warm and friendly way. He asked her, "What's your name?"

"Nadia."

"Very well, Nadia, I will be ready in just a moment. Please, have a seat."

Nadia blushed a deep red. It was not customary for the upper class to be so courteous to a servant girl.

"Don't be embarrassed, please," went on Dudik. "Well, I'm ready. I think the temperature is going to drop tonight but that's fine by me. I find the cold weather most invigorating."

He and Nadia went out onto the street and he gently took her by the arm. "How long have you been in the Bubenskys' employ?"

The girl blushed again and then tucked a strand of loose hair behind her ear. Dudik's unassuming tone made her uneasy.

"Oh, just a few months," she replied.

"I see. Nadia, I hope I'm not being too direct, but I think I ought to warn you ... about Lonia. Listen to me carefully, but please, don't take it the wrong way. He's somewhat of a ladies' man and you should stay away from him. If he tries to make a pass at you, smack him across the face. And I know he will try because you're a very pretty girl. Keep in mind what I've said."

"Why are you telling me this?" the girl looked nervously about.

"Because you could find yourself in a rather compromising situation. Where do you sleep?"

"What do you mean?"

"Hey, Nadia, don't say I didn't warn you."

When they arrived at the Bubensky home, a dog chained to a tree out back barked ferociously. The house was all lit up, and soft gray smoke rising out of the chimney spread across the sky. Nadia freed herself of Dudik's grip and hurried to the back door that led into the kitchen. Dudik stepped onto the veranda and knocked. After a moment the door opened wide and he entered a spacious living room, where the Bubenskys liked to relax after dinner. Wood crackled in the fireplace and the sweet smell of pine and birch filled the air. Father Lawrence was sitting in an armchair with his legs stretched out before him smoking a pipe. His thick white beard reached his chest and his oiled hair was combed back from his face. Though he appeared in a pleasant enough mood, upon closer examination, it was evident something was troubling him. His wife, a hefty woman with a big stomach and a full double chin, sat next to him.

She was knitting a shawl and a ball of blue wool lay at her feet. Lonia sat behind a table cleaning rifles and his two sisters, Nastia and Slava, lay sprawled on the sofa, reading.

"You all look so snug," Dudik greeted his hosts. "Warm, quiet, pleasant. What more can one ask?"

"Welcome, Dudik, welcome! Please sit down."

"Thank you."

Settling between the two sisters, he looked at them inquisitively "What are you reading?"

"I'm reading *And Quiet Flows the Don*," said Slava.

"Gorky's *Foma Gordyeeff*," answered Nastia.

They both spoke Russian, though rather badly.

Dudik pressed his lips together.

"Now tell me something, Dudik," the priest's wife placed her knitting in a basket by her side and looked seriously at him. "Why is it that you haven't taken up speaking Russian? Don't Nastia and Slava do a wonderful job of it? Absolutely everybody is doing it, it's the latest fashion. And besides, it's the only way to get ahead these days."

"Oh, Mother, let's not start on that again," Lonia was quick to interject. Then to Dudik, "Did you hear what happened in the village?"

"No, what?"

"A couple of nights ago that red-headed blacksmith, Matvy, hanged himself. He was thrashing wheat in his barn, or so his wife thought, and then he decided to do himself in. As it turned out, he tied a rope to a beam up in the hayloft, slipped in his head, and jumped over the edge."

The story roused Dudik's curiosity. He turned to the reverend, "Did you perform a funeral service, Father?"

Slava cut in, "No, Papasha didn't do anything because it was a suicide and all suicides are buried by the state, without a priest."

"Why did he hang himself?"

"He just went crazy," the wife shook her head with disapproval. "Rumor has it he was deep in debt."

"This is very interesting," this was Dudik. "I wonder why my parents never mentioned anything."

"And that's not all," Nastia put her book aside. "The police searched the whole village for clues. Even our house. It was most unnerving. I can't understand what's going on."

"Everything is coming to no good," Father Lawrence shook his head. "Peace and quiet are coming to an end. The young people have gone mad, that's all."

"You know what I think?" Dudik was quick with his opinion. "I think there is a very good reason why all this is happening. Unrest doesn't just come from nowhere something causes it to happen."

"Oh, no, he's at it again!" laughed Lonia.

"Well, what do you think is the reason then, young man?" Father Lawrence tapped his fingers on the side of his leg with agitation.

"It's really quite simple. Say, for example, you're a wealthy landowner. You have plenty of land, you have servants passed down from your parents, and then one day some stranger appears and chases you off and takes possession of your property. Naturally, you try and defend what's rightfully yours, but the stranger calls that anarchy. So, who is right? And so it goes, the possible reasons for any given thing are countless, and the more reasons one has, the more confusing and obscure everything becomes."

"Well, in our village things are not so bad yet. No landowners have had their property expropriated yet." Growing visibly irritated, loosening his shirt collar, Father Lawrence tried to silence his young visitor. He had no desire to continue with the conversation. He ended, "This is purely a question of law and order."

"Just a minute," Dudik waved his forefinger, a good-natured smile was stretched across his face. "Let us assume, hypothetically speaking, that this stranger *is* the law. Would that automatically make it legal for him to confiscate your property?"

"Dialectics!" shouted Lonia, rolling his eyes. "Papasha, don't start with him, you won't last. He'll only spin your head around."

But Dudik wouldn't let up, "If one were to carefully examine any given thing, it would undoubtedly take on a completely different meaning than one could even begin to imagine. With every given thing, particularly in the case of nations, there are inordinate complexities. Only a thorough observation and a synthesis of this observation will bring us closer to the truth of any given matter."

Father Lawrence raised his brows and looked sternly into Dudik's face; he opened his mouth as if to speak, but wasn't sure what to say. In the end, he employed a safer tactic and tried to end the discussion by patronizing Dudik.

"You talk of reason, reason, hah! I'd like to know the reason for your stubbornness! Why you don't even speak Russian!"

"You say I don't speak Russian. Well, your parishioners speak the same way I do, in Ukrainian. We are not Russians. We are all from the same village and it only follows we should speak the same language. You live in this village too, yet you insist on speaking Russian, the language of our occupiers. They've only just been here a few months and already you've transformed yourself. You're aloof and pretend to be a Muscovite when Moscow's almost eight hundred kilometers away. You don't know who you are anymore!"

"You talk too much for your own good, young man," Father Lawrence threw back his head, now completely unnerved. He got up and walked to the window.

Lonia laughed, "I told you, Papasha, you wouldn't last. He never lets up." Then glancing at his mother and sisters, "It's all nonsense and that's that. Look, the rifles are ready. What do you think, Papasha? Should we go hunting to the Skuminsky Forest or the Dubnitsky Gorge?"

"It's more interesting in the Skuminsky Forest." Father Lawrence found his way back to his chair. "That's where the hot spring is. They say if you swim there it will bring you good luck."

"That's very curious." Dudik contemplated a moment. "But I wonder why it works only on Christmas Eve and not when the weather is more reasonable." Then waving his hand, "Oh, people are always thinking up the craziest things."

"That is exactly why the Skuminsky Forest is so intriguing." Father Lawrence was about to go on to explain, but stopped short, not wanting to provoke his argumentative young visitor.

From this moment on the conversation became light and inconsequential. After midnight Dudik bade his hosts good night and headed for home.

*   *   *

It was dark when the hunters left the village and crossed a vast open field toward the Skuminsky Forest. Lonia's brother-in-law, Zarisky, walked briskly up ahead, carrying his rifle under his arm. He was the husband of Lonia's older sister Nastia and taught school in a neighboring village. Walking side by side, Lonia and Dudik hurried to catch up to him. Dudik did not carry a rifle, as he had not handled one in years. Lonia tried to cheer him up.

"After we kill our first rabbit, you can have a try with my rifle. We'll find you a spot near my ambush."

The snow creaked under their feet and the cold sharp wind cut like a knife across their faces.

As the moon rose above the trees, its silver rays splashed down and painted the snow a scintillating blue. Soft village lights shimmered faintly in the distance and smoke could be seen billowing out of the chimneys. Dudik wore his father's sheepskin with the collar turned up so that his ears wouldn't freeze, and on his head was his student cap looking like a mushroom.

The three men came to the forest's edge. Tall fir trees towered over them and their branches, lined with heavy layers of snow, snapped and crackled from the cold.

"Such magical beauty!" thought Dudik to himself. "The downy snow on the ground and the warm flesh of a furry rabbit: how similar the two were! The rabbit digs a little hole with his front paws, submerges himself, and he's protected from the cold. Then along the track: tap, tap, tap out onto the field, where he rakes the snow and feeds on frozen shoots of wheat and rye, and later in the woods with his sharp teeth he nibbles on young maple bark. How little these rabbits need to survive! And here, on Christmas Eve, the powerful and rational human being, armed with heavy weapons, sits and waits to pounce on these tiny, helpless creatures. How utterly senseless!"

"Why are you so quiet, Dudik?" Lonia poked his friend in the arm.

"Oh, I was just thinking. It seems I always get the strangest thoughts on Christmas Eve. It's a very magical time of year."

"What were you thinking about?"

"About rabbits. Just think, tonight is Christmas Eve, and rather than spending it in peace with our families, we are about to hunt down live, defenseless creatures. What if they're preparing to celebrate Christmas too?"

"Fantasy is a far cry from philosophy," Lonia tossed back his head and laughed.

"Maybe so, but I think fantasy has its reasons too. Anyway, is it at all possible to distinguish fantasy from reality on Christmas Eve? No, Lonia, I'm not going to hunt tonight. Arcen slaughtered a pig yesterday, didn't he? You'll have plenty of meat; you will have a fine celebration without a rabbit."

Lonia thought his friend was joking, but when he saw the serious look on his face, he refrained from saying anything further.

Zarisky called out from up ahead:

"Tracks, look!"

The hunters stepped over the tracks and set up ambushes a fair distance apart: Lonia behind a fir tree, Zarisky behind a clump of rosehip bushes. Dudik studied the string-like trail a brief moment and then jumped behind a thick oak. If a rabbit should appear from the north, Lonia would have the first shot. Dudik felt he had to protect these small creatures from death and resolved to make some sort of warning sound if one should come his way.

Minute after minute passed, but there was silence from all directions. Somewhere a tree crackled. When a branch snapped over Dudik's head, he watched it fall to the ground and pierce the snow. Then again, silence. Dudik fixed his gaze on the trail. Silence from Zarisky's direction, no sound of gunshots. An hour passed, then another. Dudik wrapped his sheepskin tighter around his body and jumped up and down to keep warm. Silence, nothing but silence. The trail showed no activity and the hunters were growing discouraged.

When the moon dropped behind a stand of pine trees, faint silver rays forced themselves through the densely braided branches. Dudik began to daydream. The moonlight always had a pleasant and warming effect on him, and he could not quite understand why so many people feared it.

Suddenly to the left of Dudik on the rabbit trail: tap, tap, tap ... from behind a bush the small shadow of a furry head emerged, then a furry back. "A rabbit!" he cried out to himself. But at that moment, excitement got the better of him and his hunter's instincts took over completely. He could not bring himself to make a sound to scare the creature off. Tap, tap in Lonia's direction. Dudik stood motionless, waiting for gunfire. But there was no shot, only silence. Another moment, then another, and yet another. Silence. Then again: tap, tap along the trail, another rabbit this time in Zarisky's direction. Again, Dudik could not bring himself to scare the creature off. Nothing but silence. Then another rabbit: tap, tap. Again, everything remained still. Dudik held his breath and listened. Pulling down his cap over his ears, he finally decided to make his way to Lonia's ambush to see what was going on. He assumed Lonia had grown tired, laid his rifle up against the tree trunk and nodded off. However, when he reached the ambush, Lonia was not there.

"Lonia!" he called out, looking around. "Lonia, where are you?"

Silence.

Dudik then followed the trail toward Zarisky's ambush. Several times he called out his name, but there was no response.

"They must have got bored and gone home," Dudik had finally convinced himself, and he too set out in the direction of the village.

He turned north, or at least what he thought was north, and started back toward the forest's edge. But the farther he went the denser the trees became. According to his calculations, the trees should have begun to thin out. Coming upon a clump of close-knit linden bushes, he separated the branches with his feet and hands and continued on. He was certain that beyond these bushes lay the open field that led to the village. But to his dismay, the bushes only thickened, and the branches caught his sheepskin coat and snagged at his boots. When he finally reached the edge, he entered a zone of young birch. This baffled him as he did not recall birch growing anywhere in the Skuminsky Forest. But an odd feeling came over him as if he had been there before. A magnificent oak tree suddenly emerged out of the darkness. "How strange for a solitary oak to be growing here." Directly behind the oak was a gentle downward inclination on which grew three gnarled, snow-laden pines. As he made his way to the edge and looked down, he noticed a thick cloud of steam rising out of the ground.

"This must be the hot spring!" he shouted excitedly.

Taking a step closer, he watched bubbles of hot water rise to the surface of the crystal-clear pool and then burst and disappear. When Dudik decided to make his way to the shore and dabble his fingers, unexpectedly he was gripped by a cold, sudden chill: his entire body froze. There was somebody out there. He couldn't believe what he was seeing. A naked man stood on a large rock, looking as if he were preparing to take a dive. He had a strong, athletic build with broad shoulders and a thick neck.

"What is a man doing out here in the middle of nowhere, and in this temperature? How strange. Who could this possibly be?"

The man appeared calm and the cold snow did not seem to bother his bare feet. Stretching his arms above his head, he jumped into the pool. The loud splash reverberated throughout the forest. He tried to swim to the bottom, but the water was too shallow so instead, he floated on his stomach with the pink of his back exposed. Later, he ducked his head, lifted it out, ducked it again. Wading toward the shore, he turned suddenly to face Dudik, as if he were expecting him.

Dudik shuddered and choked with fear. "Impossible! It can't be!"

But it was true. It was the red-headed blacksmith, Matvy, who had recently hanged himself. The two looked each other in the eye. Matvy's square face was heavily marred and there was a gash over his left eyebrow. By the movement of his mouth, it was as if he were trying to relate some sort of message. When no words came out, he started after Dudik, as if intending to strike him. Terror-stricken, Dudik jumped to his heels and fled. Not daring to look back, he ran like the wind, his heart pounding and racing all at once. On his neck, he felt the hot breath of the hanged man, who had been buried without a priest.

As Dudik ran to the edge of the forest, from the corner of his eye he could see the blacksmith's strong, husky form just inches away, ready to pounce on him; any second now and his big fingers would seize him by the throat and everything would be over. When this thought just barely entered his mind, feeling a powerful hand grab hold of his collar, he stumbled and fell flat on his back. "This is the end," he thought to himself. Wildly waving his arms before him, with all his might, he tried to protect himself from his attacker.

"We've finally got you!" yelled a deep, hoarse voice from above. Someone was twisting his right arm and clamping on a pair of handcuffs. It was only then that Dudik made out, not Matvy, but two men in police uniforms standing over him.

THEODORE ODRACH

"What on earth is going on?" Dudik was completely dumbfounded. "One minute a red-headed corpse on my heels and now the police!"

Dudik did not resist the arrest. The sound of a whistle blew. Within minutes, from all sides, about half a dozen policemen emerged with rifles. Dudik heard one of them shout out:

"Commander, we've captured the terrorist Kolody!"

"What?" thought Dudik, gradually collecting himself and wiping the sweat from his brow. He was grateful to be alive.

*   *   *

When Dudik was released from jail and returned to the village, Christmas was over; no more carols could be heard in the streets and the colorful nativity scenes in peasants' yards were gone. Everything had come to pass. Dudik's parents, sisters, and neighbors greeted him with great joy and relief. They buzzed around him like bumblebees and talked with such rapidity and excitement Dudik could hardly make out what they were saying. He was completely baffled.

Then Musy, the village's practical joker, swept up from behind, and baring his big yellow teeth, whispered in his ear.

"Dudik, you sly devil, you! You led them on a wild goose chase. While they were pursuing you, the real Kolody had a chance to escape. They caught you instead. Hah! Hah! Hah!"

"What? Me? Could all this be possible?"

Falling silent a moment as if trying to put it all together, at last, Dudik turned to the crowd and said:

"Someone, go quickly, fetch Father Bubensky. He must perform a funeral service for the deceased blacksmith, Matvy. Tell him we will pay him well."

*　*　*

Before departing for Chernivtsi, Dudik went to visit the Bubenskys. Entering the front yard, he was surprised to find the priest's wife coming out of the barn, carrying a bucket of milk. For some reason she had been milking the cows, carrying out Nadia's chores.

"Servants. They aren't what they used to be," she complained and shook her head. "She didn't even give notice. She just packed up and left."

Dudik bade the priest's wife good-bye, and then turned to take one last look at the Skuminsky Forest. It radiated mystery and was like a soft brush stroke of silver-blue.

THE ICON

Old man Ulianich was an octogenarian. With a sunken face and swollen red eyes, supported by a cane, he walked along the village streets with short, uneven steps. One of his arms was shorter than the other by a few inches, apparently from some defect at birth, and though it occasionally gave him trouble, it never really held him back in any significant way. He wore a black overcoat patched and mended here and there and his trousers were soiled and ripped at the knees. An old fisherman's cap was pulled down over his ears and on his feet he wore bast-shoes.

Burdened by poverty, old man Ulianich never let his misfortunes get the better of him; for the most part, he remained agreeable and friendly and was always up for a good chat. He lived in the small village of Mesiatychy, in the heart of the Pinsk Marshes, one of the largest wetland areas of Europe. Mesiatychy was a few kilometers from the ancient port city of Pinsk. Like his fellow-villagers, old man Ulianich depended on the marsh for life in the same way that his ancestors did before him. Not even now in his senior years was he afraid of the cold, or the rain, or the scorching hot summer sun. Such was old man Ulianich.

But in his younger days, life for him was much different: he was irreverent, wild, took kindly to drink, and his attitude was devil-may-care. Up until the beginning of the twentieth century, like many of his contemporaries, he resettled to Pinsk and made his living working the boats along the Pripyat and Dnieper Rivers. He spent most of his time aboard the *White Stork,* a blue and white tugboat with an elongated nose, well-known for its acceleration of heavy loads.

There was much work to be had during those early years, and the activity up and down the river system was nonstop: day in and day out heavy steamers whistled and roared; stevedores shouted and cursed along the shorelines; and anchor chains smashed and clanged at all hours. This was before the railroad took over, on which higher-valued items such as meats and vegetables requiring greater speeds were already being moved.

But in Ulianich's day, the waterways still ran supreme. Big black slow-moving steamboats in long, endless processions would float along the rivers, pulling behind them barges filled with plywood, boxes of matches, and rough planks of good, strong marsh-wood. Upon their return to Pinsk, these same barges would bring with them wheat flour, watermelon, sugar, and dried Turkish apricots. Ulianich's job on the *White Stork* was to help follow the steamers along the upper and lower courses of the river system and to maneuver them in confined areas.

The captain of the *White Stork* was Greshko Brodsky, an argumentative but good-natured Jew from Pinsk. His long black beard streaked here and there with gray covered much of his face, and his skin, where it could be seen, was cracked and sunburnt. Willful and pugilistic by nature, he was very good at giving orders. Originally, Greshko had been a peddler of trinkets and fake jewelry in the Pinsk marketplace but his dream had always been to take to the free and open waterways. From his stall, day in and day out, he would look out at the Pina River, even though there were so many fishing boats he could hardly see the water. He found it amazing how the Pina was a left tributary of the great Pripyat, and how the Pripyat drained into the even greater Dnieper, only to in the end make a rush for the Black Sea. He saw the river system, forever fed by springs and streams, an incredible source of power and an artery of great commerce. When a tugboat happened to come up for sale at a price he could afford, he purchased it without a second thought. He named it the *White Stork,* the bird of happiness and symbol of the Pinsk Marshes. Greshko had lived in the marsh his entire life and his family history could be traced as far back as the fourteenth century, when Gemidin, the Grand Duke of the Great Duchy of Lithuania, invited Jews to live there. Greshko was proud to be a man of the marsh.

When it came time to load barges at port, Ulianich was the man of the hour. He would impress everyone with his inordinate strength. With his healthy arm, he would lift sheets of plywood weighing as much as thirty kilograms. And in Katerinoslav and Kyiv, he would load sacks of flour and potatoes for the better part of a day. Even when he was hungry and the sweat poured from his brow, there was no stopping Ulianich.

But that's not to say he was one to deprive himself of recreation. When in Kyiv, he would take a night off here and there and visit one of the brothel houses among the shanties beyond the docks. Often Greshko would accompany him and for a reasonable fee the two men would lose themselves in debauchery and drunkenness. A certain Raisa had caught Ulianich's fancy, a tall buxom yellow-haired peasant girl from the Poltava region, and they would spend many a night together until she ran off with one of her customers to live a settled life somewhere in the Carpathians.

Now in his old age, with his wayfaring days long behind him, Ulianich had many stories to tell. Walking the village streets, winter, summer, spring or fall, children especially would follow him around, and pulling at his coattails, beg for him to relate some tale or other about life on the rivers. Sometimes Ulianich would tell a story exactly the way it happened, but sometimes he would exaggerate or even make one up entirely, often adding fantastical spins to the conclusions. The children would sit and hang on his every word. Of course, Ulianich always had two versions for each story, one for the children, which he revised and censored, and the other for the adults, peppered with bawdy details and cuss words.

And so, one day, in front of his house, filling up his pipe with tobacco, the children at his feet, Ulianich began one of his many stories. His tone was low, gruff, and full of animation.

"This all happened in the spring of 1904 when there was growing unrest among the masses, just before the first Revolution. A steamboat hissed and grumbled along the Pripyat ever so quietly, and behind it was a small white tugboat, steering it toward Pinsk. I had been hired out by Greshko for several days to a certain Captain Moor and was sitting on the deck of this very tugboat on a bundle of plywood. I was on the lookout for passing vessels.

"The Pripyat on this particular day was overflowing but quiet, and along the shore I could see reeds, water grasses, and huge willow trees bent over the edge. There was a strong odor everywhere of fish and pitch. Somehow my mind began to drift and all of a sudden, don't ask me why, but I had a terrible foreboding. I thought to myself: what if we get attacked by river pirates, or what if some natural disaster strikes like a storm or a hurricane? Religious people would say there is nothing to fear, just make the sign of the cross and all will be fine. But being the old atheist that I was, I had no patience for any of that. And sure enough, that very night a storm brewed somewhere past the Volinsky Bridge. The winds howled and slashed at the water, and rain came down in a terrible downpour. The tall chimneys of the steamboats whistled and whined and the strong, solid decks became flooded.

"My little tugboat chugged and tugged and tried to fight off the storm and soon it started swinging back and forth. The waves kept smashing against the sides, and I could see part of the stern had been ripped off. Then I realized my boat was sinking! I had no choice but to jump overboard and try and make it to shore.

"Somehow, by a miracle, I found myself on land. Looking round, I noticed an old rundown hut up against a stand of trees. There was a light inside, and through the window I could see a strange shadow moving along the wall. Then right at that moment the door flew open and a big, broad-shouldered peasant emerged, and he was laughing wildly. His teeth were cracked and yellow and he had the largest incisors I'd ever seen, like a monster.

"He shouted to me: 'Be ready, Comrade!'

"I tried to get a better look at him but suddenly right before my very eyes he transformed – it was a like a meta-morphosis. He became as big as a bear and in his hand he carried a rifle! He was no longer a peasant but a Czarist police and his eyes were wild! He tried to grab me by the collar, but just in the nick of time I dodged him and started to run. I could hear gunshots cracking over my head – rat tat tat tat. Somehow, I managed to come to safety. By that time the storm had already blown itself out.

"Later that night I thought of all that had happened. Then I convinced myself it had been nothing more than a bad dream. But when I returned the next day to have a look, what do you think I saw? There by the old rundown hut I found footprints and not just any footprints but footprints as big as a bear's!"

The children sat gasping from fear and disbelief; a girl started to cry and went running to find her mother.

Whether this event actually occurred or was made-up was really hard to say. The fact of the matter was, indeed, in the early 1900s there had been a terrible storm over the Pri-pyat, where much damage was done. Boats and barges sank, the lands were flooded, and over twenty sailors drowned. The people along the river still talk of this event, proclaim-ing it to be one of the worst disasters ever.

But this tale paled in comparison to the one that had turned old man Ulianich into a celebrity of sorts, and he had told this tale many times over. It was a story about an icon that he had one day found in the Dnieper River, and how this icon not only changed his life but came to hang in the village church for many years thereafter.

This happened in the year 1905, the last year he worked the river, an important time in history when the Russian Empire found itself in the midst of revolution, struggling against the rule of the Romanov Empire. There was rebellion everywhere.

And Ulianich, from his travels, saw first-hand the mounting chaos. He was very much pleased by everything he saw. Not only for the first time was the voice of the common man being heard, but the anti-religious sentiments echoed by the revolutionaries were much in line with his way of thinking. Revolution to him was proof that man was truly mightier than God. Impoverished peasants had packed churches, praying to God endlessly for a better life but each time God came back at them with deaf ears. Now, with revolution, the common man was doing for himself what God was unable to do. What was happening in Russia and in the outlying regions was unprecedented, and Ulianich, the old atheist that he was, could not help but feel a part of it all.

In the meantime, Greshko's tugboat continued to work the waterways, keeping the goods moving. Guns cracked nonstop, rockets lit up the sky, and smoke rose over the rooftops of the houses lining the shore.

Then one day, for some reason, everything fell silent, there came a moment of respite. The *White Stork* happened to be floating on the calm, slow-moving waters of the upper Dnieper just outside of Kyiv. Greshko was in the wheelhouse, his towing line pulling a couple of barges full of cargo – melons, sacks of rice, unhulled wheat. Ulianich was sent to stand on the deck of one of the barges and watch for passing vessels.

With the warm sun upon his back, Ulianich's mind began to drift. For some reason, he started to think of his native village, of the people who lived there, and he wondered how they were all doing. And suddenly, for some reason, he became terribly homesick. In his imagination, he could see it all – the small, run-down cottages, the dirt roads, the endless tracts of marsh. He even imagined the little Orthodox church in the heart of the village with its onion shaped-domes, built in the late 1700s. He had not been home in a very long time and he missed his mother with her kindly face and his father with that forever stern look in his eye. He wanted to see his friends, most of whom had long since married and who had children of their own, some even grandchildren.

Life had passed so quickly, and now thinking about it all, it was as if much had been lost to him. He was no longer fulfilled by the waterways or the bordellos in Kyiv and Katerinoslav. He felt increasingly sad and lonely. Never before had he been so sentimental. He couldn't help but say aloud to himself: "What's going on with me? Why am I being taken over with such emotion?"

Even though he still loved the river and all it had to offer, he found himself longing for the peasant life, and no matter how hard he tried, he couldn't get the land out of his mind.

The thick peasant blood running through his veins only made him want to return all the more.

As barges whistled and hissed along the Dnieper, small fishing boats straddled the shoreline with their nets. Ulianich, for some reason, began to carefully examine the water's surface. It was smooth and shiny, almost like a sheet of glass. There was not a sound anywhere except for the soft swirling of the waves beneath him. Then at once the rays of the sun broke from behind a cloud and hit upon something in the water. It shone bright like a candle and flickered. When the sun disappeared behind a clump of clouds, strangely, the light continued to shine, it even intensified.

"What on earth is that?" Ulianich shaded his eyes to have a better look. "How unusual! It must be a reflection of some sort, maybe from a piece of metal or broken glass? But how could it possibly still be shining with the sun gone?"

Ulianich decided to go and have a look. Untying a dinghy fixed to the side of the barge, he climbed down and got in. When the water became shallow enough, rolling up his trousers and shirt sleeves, he jumped in and waded toward the light. It was now brighter than ever, and seemed to be a reflection of an object on the riverbed. Submerging his healthy arm, he pulled it out. It turned out to be a piece of wood, about the size of his palm and rectangular in shape. But wood projecting light? Then he noticed something carved in the middle, an image of some sort. Taking a closer look, he was shocked at what suddenly appeared before his very eyes: it was the Mother Mary herself. And there was a halo around her head and it became all lit up. It was the same light he has seen moments ago. It was unlike anything on earth.

"How absolutely extraordinary!"

And then, for no apparent reason, he started to feel serene throughout his body, as though he were experiencing some kind of spiritual awakening.

"Well, I'll be ..." he rubbed his forehead. "It's an icon. But not just any icon, it's a miraculous icon."

Something definitely blessed was happening to him and stirring his disbelieving heart. Placing the icon in his jacket pocket, he got back into the dinghy and rowed back to the *White Stork*. With the strength of the current against him, he could hardly manage. Luckily, Greshko, who had long since dropped anchor, and who had been all the while watching Ulianich with curiosity, waited for him to moor up to the side.

"What in devil's name were you doing out there? Were you fishing for something?"

Ulianich mumbled barely audibly, "I followed the light."

"The light? What on earth are you talking about? What light? I don't see any light out there."

Climbing onto the tugboat, Ulianich carefully brought out the piece of wood and showed it to Greshko. He said quietly, "A miracle has occurred. Mother Mary has come to me. This piece of wood is a symbol of peace. It's a miraculous icon."

"A miraculous icon?" Greshko laughed and screwed up his eyes. "You're a fool Ulianich. Anybody can see it's just a scrap of wood and someone tried to carve something on it. Throw it back into the river; it's nothing but junk. Besides, what would an old heathen like yourself be doing finding an icon anyway? Hah, hah, hah!"

Greshko's remarks only made Ulianich angry and he started at him with clenched fists. "I'll throw you in the river before I throw in my icon!"

"You haven't a kopeck's worth of brains in that head of yours, Ilya Ulianich!" Greshko continued to laugh. Still laughing, he returned to the wheelhouse.

When the tugboat started on its trek back to Pinsk, Ulianich, returning to the barge, began to look carefully at the icon. He noticed the edges were outlined with a gold stripe and the back had been painted a bright red. Placing it on a sack of flour before him, he stared at it and he couldn't stop staring. Feeling completely overwhelmed, for some reason he began to mutter a prayer that he still remembered from his childhood. He sensed something great and powerful passing over him. The beam of light again emerged from the Blessed Mother's halo but this time it covered the entire deck. Ulianich immediately dropped his head, and making the sign of the cross, repeated several times:

"Our Mother is with us. Our Mother is with us."

And suddenly he felt at total peace within himself. He knew everything must be changed in his life, that he must give up the boats and move back to the land, to the land from which he came. The icon was a sign, he was sure of it.

When the tugboat finally came into Pinsk, Ulianich slipped the icon back into his pocket and went to find Greshko. Looking directly at him, he began:

"I have something important to tell you. I don't know how to put it but I've had an awakening. I've decided to return to the land, and for good. As of today, I'm giving you two weeks' notice."

Greshko remained silent for several minutes not know-ing what to say. The idea of Ulianich leaving his employ took its time to sink in. Though he was not happy to hear the news, he was not surprised by it either; mostly, he was sad to see his best worker go.

And so, Ulianich, packing his bags, said goodbye to Greshko and to life on the water forever. As he set off, Gres-hko called out after him:

"It looks like your ship's finally come in! Farewell and good luck to you, my friend!"

After stopping in the Pinsk marketplace to purchase a few gift items for his family such as a jar of dandelion honey, a small bag of candies, and a kilogram of cheese, passing the large orthodox monastery, Ulianich took the ferry across the Pina River. He set off for Mesiatychy, which was some twenty kilometers away. It was a hot, gray day with heavy clouds and it looked like rain. The road was rough and full of potholes and there was no one in sight to give him a ride. He would have to do the entire trek on foot.

As Ulianich entered the village, he was happy to see it looked much the same as when he had last come to visit, which was several years before. He was met by his elderly mother and his older brother, Marco, and his youngest sis-ter, Anna. His father had passed away several months earlier due to heart failure.

His mother had aged, her face had become thin and pale, and her once vibrant blue eyes were now dull and hollow. Words could not describe the joy she felt upon seeing her son again, and in her old heart she privately hoped to see him settle down and marry. She already had plans for him with the recently widowed Sonia Morovska, and if things moved quickly enough, they could still have children. But of course, all that would have to wait; for the moment, she just wanted to enjoy the return of her son.

Ulianich settled into his shabby old room at the back of his mother's house. After washing and shaving and changing into a clean set of clothes, with his icon in his pocket, he sauntered into the kitchen, where he found his family at the table joined by friends and neighbors. A true peasant feast had been prepared – cabbage rolls, pickled vegetables, and a honey cake. Everyone was eager to learn about his life on the river. But Ulianich didn't know where to begin. Turning at last to his mother and pressing her hand, he began seriously.

"I'd like to thank everyone for coming here today. I have an announcement to make. I've had a revelation."

The people sat with wide open eyes, not knowing what to expect.

"The Blessed Mother has come to me."

Everyone was stunned. This was not exactly what they were expecting to hear, especially from a life-long atheist.

Bringing out his icon, he laid it on the table for everyone to see. He said in a whisper, "I found this miraculous icon in the waters of the Dnieper."

The guests didn't quite understand. Most thought he was joking. What they saw was not an icon, but, rather, a small piece of wood with a crude, barely discernable carving on it. It was good for the garbage, as far as they were concerned.

Anastasia, the plump butcher's wife, couldn't stop laughing. "You say you found an icon? How does an old profligate like yourself go about finding an icon, and a miraculous one at that? You've been on the river too long, Ilya Ulianich. It's gone to your head! Hah, hah, hah!"

Soon everyone joined in the laughter. Ulianich's mother looked down with embarrassment, though at the same time in her old heart she couldn't help but rejoice seeing her impious son finally find God. But the guests continued to laugh at Ulianich and they called his icon a hoax. The priest, who was a relatively young man and new to the region and who sat at the head of the table, shifting uncomfortably, tried to think of a way to deal with the situation. Finally, he came up with a solution.

"Whether it's a miraculous icon or simply a piece of wood with an image on it, I propose we hang it up in the church by the iconostasis. I think it will only but enhance our humble house of worship."

And so, it was there, on the wall behind the iconostasis in Saint Paraskevy Church that Ulianich's small wooden icon found its home. The priest even adorned it with an embroidered cloth along with some cheap jewels he'd bought at the Pinsk marketplace, which was all he could afford. Day in and day out the icon hung quietly in the corner, completely ignored by the Sunday worshippers.

Then one Sunday its time came. This was in the latter part of 1906, sometime in December, just as a raging blizzard was moving in from the north. On that particular Sunday the church was packed with people, so packed there was barely standing room – there were people from neighboring Povhova, from Lozich, even from far away villages such as Vivich and Kalavurovich. But the church was packed not so much out of a willingness to pray, but, rather, because it offered shelter from the cold, as many had little firewood to spare. Even old man Hirsky, who hadn't shown his face in church for over a year, managed to crawl out of his shanty by the river and find a spot for himself by the candelabrum.

As the parishioners started in on the Lord's prayer, it was not long after things started to happen. A strange rustling sound came from behind the iconostasis and the sound intensified. The icon began to shake and swing back and forth, and after several minutes, incredibly, it started to double in size. The people stood stunned and unable to move. Then the image of Mother Mary's face began to get more and more pronounced, and her lips started to move. It was as if she were speaking to the believers and non-believers and rousing in them a profound spirituality. When a light appeared round her halo, it soon covered everything. The parishioners fell to their knees in prayer. Something inexplicable, unearthly was going on and they were all feeling it.

The priest understood at once that what was occurring transcended all natural law and could not be explained. Raising his arms, he cried out: "Dear Mary, Mother of Jesus."

Within a couple of days, the people built a makeshift shrine around the church. The site began to attract pilgrims seeking religious inspiration, miracles, and messages from God. And there were healings reported such as the lame being able to walk, the blind regaining their sight, and the dying coming back to life. The little Orthodox church had become known far and wide.

Of all his stories, Ulianich enjoyed telling the icon story the most and he never tired of telling it. Never did he regret leaving the river life, though he thought back on those days fondly. He went on to fulfill his mother's wishes by marrying Sonia Morovska, and together they had a daughter, Roxanna, and later, a son, Roman. They farmed a small plot of land on the edge of Mesiatychy, kept chickens and geese, and grew hemp, from which they made coarse fabrics and ropes to sell at the Pinsk marketplace. Though the couple forever searched for improvement in their poor conditions in life, somehow, they managed to get by and always found enough to eat. It could be said they were happy together and grateful for what little they had.

Now that Ulianich was an octogenarian and a widower, he didn't have much to do with his days except hobble up and down the village streets or nod off on the divan beside the tile stove in his kitchen.

Over the years not much had changed in Mesiatychy and the people continued to live in grinding poverty, all the while trying to carve a life for themselves whichever way they could. And the forever changing political atmosphere around them didn't much help improve their plight. The Czarists had quashed the revolution of 1905 only to themselves be quashed by the Bolshevik Revolution of 1917. In 1921 the region fell to Polish rule and this rule lasted until 1938. In those years between 1905 and 1938, no matter who came to power in this hopelessly backward region, somehow the icon managed to survive. Believers continued to visit the little Orthodox church and pay homage, hoping to see a miracle.

Then came the eve of Ulianich's eighty-first birthday – September 17th, 1939. On this date, everything changed, and in a way never before seen. The Bolsheviks invaded. Armored cars and lorry trucks poured into the village and Red Army men covered the streets. Life became unbearable. People started to disappear, property got stolen, and anti-religious propaganda appeared everywhere. The little Orthodox church where Ulianich's icon had hung for over two decades, too, fell victim to the new order.

But what exactly became of the little wooden icon no one knew for sure. Rumor had it that on a cold, dark night one of the villagers slipped into the church, snatched it off the wall, and went to hide it somewhere deep in the woods.

As for Ulianich, from September 17, 1939 onward, he no longer told the story about his little icon or of how he found it along the shores of the Dnieper. He kept it all hidden. In his heart, however, he truly believed that it had somehow survived and that it would one day reappear and bless all those who believed in miracles.

THE STRANGER

Two men sat on a bench in B Park and stared silently at a couple of rocks protruding out of the river. The water splashed vigorously against them, forming a stiff foam that was then broken by the current and carried downstream. During periods of drought the K River flowed well below its banks, but when rain poured into its basin it was transformed into a formidable body of water. It filled with turbulent waves that roared to the center of the city, then discharged with an abrupt drop into the depths of the larger V River.

"I notice you sit on this bench every evening," the man wearing the gray overcoat and thick woolen hat pulled over his ears was first to break the silence. "I like to sit and think too, but sometimes I just have to talk to someone. I get lonely." He extended his hand, "If I may introduce myself, my name is Fedko. I believe the more talkative a person is the easier life is for him. Wouldn't you agree?"

At first, the other man did not respond. He submerged his head deep between his shoulders and remained unmoving. After a moment he said, "I'm Dushko. But please, don't confuse the meaning of my name. It doesn't mean *spirit*, but, rather, *to strangle*.

This made Fedko uneasy and loosening his shirt collar as if to catch his breath, he began to tap his fingers on the satchel that lay on his lap. Deep wrinkles scarred his forehead and from under a sparse, scraggly beard appeared a row of yellow teeth. His eyes were shifty.

Dushko watched him closely. With the spring sun in his face, shading his eyes with his palms, he asked, "I noticed you here in the park several times. Do you still practice throwing your rope?"

"Yes, as a matter of fact, I do. The rodeo is going to start up soon and this year I've just got to win. But the problem is I don't have any bulls to practice on. I end up going down into the ravine and hurling my rope around lilac bushes." Then peering suspiciously up from under his brows, "Have you been spying on me?"

"You are a brutal man, Fedko. A very brutal man."

At that moment children's laughter surfaced from behind a grove of linden trees. Fedko sprang nervously to his feet, and grabbing hold of his satchel, hastened in the direction of the park exit gates.

The children raced each other to the bench and settled on either side of Dushko. Lilly, the youngest, a curly-haired blonde took him by the hand and smiled. Her little nose was spotted with freckles and as she spoke her voice dipped up and down, "You promised to tell us the story about David and Anna."

"Tell us, please!" the others joined in.

"All right. But only if you promise not to go into the ravine. Fedko was here a minute ago and in his satchel he had his lariat."

"We saw him leaving," volunteered Michael, a round-faced boy with wide-open eyes.

"You must stay away from him. I'm sure in his pocket he had candies. Has he given you any?"

"He never gave me any," pouted Lilly. "But he gave some to Michael and Daniel because they know how to run fast."

"Did he try and catch you with his lariat?" Dushko looked at the boys with concern.

Michael confessed, "He scratched my chest with the rope and it bled a little. But we won't go there anymore. From now on we're going to play past the bridge out in the fields where there are lots of flowers and grasshoppers."

"You're good children. Fedko wants to practice catching you so he can win the rope throwing competition. But the lariat is evil. At one time it was used to catch people and turn them into slaves."

The children sat pinned to their seats. They wanted to hear more.

"Did they catch that little boy and girl – the ones you're going to tell us about?"

"No, they got lost."

A sweat came to Dushko's brow and he trembled all over. His eyes welled up with tears. As he tried to go on his voice cracked and then broke. He turned a ghost white. The children sat frozen. They did not know whether to feel sad or afraid. Lilly started crying and then ran to find her mother. Her friends followed close behind.

Barely a minute passed when some fashionable young woman in a tailored suit and a blue felt hat came strolling down the pathway. She glanced briefly at the unkempt man sitting by the river talking to himself. Rummaging in her purse, she brought out a coin and tossed it into the palm of his hand. Barely looking at him, she then made a quick turn to the right and hurried off in the direction of the park gates.

Slipping the coin into his pocket, Dushko lifted the sides of his coat collar to keep warm. He then stretched himself out on the bench, closed his eyes, and dozed off.

* * *

The next day Dushko could not find a spot for himself. He was restless. He went to the ravine in the hopes of finding the children. He was certain they had ignored his warning and had continued to let Fedko catch them with his lariat. In a small brown bag, he carried a kilogram of cheap candies he had purchased that morning at the market. Stepping over a fallen tree trunk, he caught sight of Fedko emerging from between two lilac bushes in full bloom. Next to him stood a white short-tailed goat with curved horns, chewing on a tuft of grass.

"Nothing but a waste of money!" Fedko spat on the ground. "I bought this beast to practice on, but he's stupid as hell. I try to chase him off with this stick so I can hurl my rope, but he won't budge. He just snorts and aims his horns. Useless animal!"

"You should have bought yourself a much younger goat, a kid even. They scare easier." Dushko tried to be of help.

"You think so? Are you an authority on goats? Did you raise them from wherever it is you come? We all know you're a stranger here. But don't worry, the citizens of our city are very friendly, and our mayor is a most generous man."

As Fedko spoke his eyes shone and there was a smirk on his face.

Dushko breathed with difficulty. Casting a quick glance about him, he searched for the children but to his great relief, they were nowhere in sight.

Fedko turned on the goat and with his whip struck him across the spine, "Why the hell don't you run when I tell you to? Run, I say, run!"

The goat tensed with anger, and kicking up his hind legs, turned on Fedko and charged after him. Fedko took to his heels and scrambled to safety up the nearest tree.

*　*　*

A few days passed and one afternoon Fedko approached Dushko as he sat by the river. He was clearly annoyed, "Why have you been avoiding me? Why don't you say something? You're a very stubborn man."

Dushko did not respond. He didn't hear Fedko. He stared fixedly at the rushing current as if it were carrying some deep, dark secret.

Fedko went on, "Did you by any chance see the big poster by the city hall? The one with the black bull and the rope thrower on it? You probably noticed my name among the list of competitors."

When Dushko still did not respond, Fedko became irritated, "How can you just sit there and say nothing when I'm talking to you? And another thing, your advice brought me nothing but trouble. I went out and bought a kid, and it turned out to be lazier than the goat. A waste of my precious time, not to mention the money!"

Dushko continued to stare at the water as if hypnotized; he barely moved a muscle.

Fedko lost patience, "And about the children, you deliberately set them against me. You know very well I like children. You think I harm them with my rope. Truth is, they like to play with me and in return I give them candies. Now, thanks to you, all my time's been wasted. I will lose the competition."

Dushko shifted uncomfortably, he muttered half under his breath, "You'll win. I know you'll win."

On the northern horizon, thick black clouds started moving in and the park suddenly fell dark and gloomy.

"There's going to be a storm," said Fedko, turning a little red. "The town square will be flooded and no one will come. The bulls won't be able to run in the mud; they will be as useless as the goat."

Quickly rummaging through his satchel for his umbrella, suddenly he turned to Dushko as if remembering something, "I'm curious to know – the other day you mentioned something about the meaning of your name. You said it meant to strangle. What was that all about?"

Dushko's face went white and a chill rushed up his spine.

"Did you kill someone?" Fedko asked.

Taking a deep breath and wiping his eyes with a handkerchief, a sound came from Dushko's throat that was not his own. He struggled with his words.

"I killed two children."

Fedko couldn't believe what he'd just heard, "Are you saying you're a murderer? Did you go to jail?"

"No, I was acquitted. But my conscience is my punishment. I can't escape."

"Your conscience is your punishment? That sounds very serious. When one's conscience haunts him, why, one can go mad." Peering slyly from the corner of his eye, there was something more on his mind, "Um, about the children, you really ought to be more careful. Their parents don't approve of your friendship with them. There's one woman in particular who is against you. She is very influential and on the social committee."

Dushko breathed heavily and looked down.

Fedko's voice grew loud and disdainful, "Her husband is on the town council and she herself is the daughter of the mayor. And ... and Lilly's her daughter."

"Lilly's her daughter?" Dushko echoed the words and became numb.

"Yes, in fact, she's already gone to the police about you. There's something terrible moving in against you. If you don't mind my saying so, you seem like the type who always has a run-in with bad luck. If I were you, I'd watch my back."

Smiling malignantly, Fedko slipped his satchel over his shoulder and walked away.

Dushko lay down on the bench, and crumpling up his jacket, tucked it under his head to use as a pillow. He pulled an old woolen blanket over himself and began to nod off. Before long he entered a deep sleep. He did not notice a faint drizzle coming down or the bolts of lightning shooting across the sky. He could not have been asleep more than

　　　　THEODORE ODRACH

ten minutes when he felt someone nudge him on the arm. Opening his eyes, he saw a tall, long-faced constable in a blue uniform and a visor cap standing over him. He was tapping his baton against the side of his leg. His tone was very official:

"Are you Dushko Millis?"

"Yes."

"Why haven't you registered your place of residence?"

"I live where I can."

"I see, so you're a vagrant."

The constable took a pen and pad of paper out of his inside pocket and jotted something down. After a moment he handed it to Dushko. "Read the citation carefully."

Dushko gazed at the written lines. The muscles on his face contracted and everything around him became dark and dismal. He could only think one thought: "The end is coming."

Lifting up his coat collar and rubbing his hands together to keep warm, he got up slowly and made to the edge of the park.

Thunder exploded overhead and a mass of thick black clouds covered the sky. A gust of wind picked up and whirled bits of garbage into the air. Rain began to fall and before long it came down in a violent downpour. People quickly gathered their belongings and ran for shelter.

* * *

The next day when the storm had died down, B Park was filled with curious onlookers. There was disaster everywhere. Some trees had been uprooted, others had fallen and lay resting on still-standing trees. Branches dangled from all heights, some snapping and falling to the ground. The K River had overflowed its banks and was very dangerous. Pounding against either side, the water roared madly downstream. The spectators watched in fascination and commented to one another – it was quite the sensation.

On a protected sandy shore where the children had often played, long, snake-like streams began to crisscross, almost touching nearby benches, under which were already large pools of water. The streams soon began to seep toward the linden trees, tempting the children to come and sail their paper boats. The children shouted and laughed excitedly.

Lilly's mother, an elegant young woman, sat on a bench with her friends, gossiping and discussing the sad state of the park. As their talk shifted to the topic of men, they huddled together and lowered their voices, giggling and joking. So engrossed were they in their conversation, they became oblivious to what was going on around them. Lilly's mother did not notice that her daughter had wandered away from the other children.

In her little hand Lilly held a red wooden boat, and looking about, she set her attention on a solitary bench that stood in shallow water. She wanted to reach this bench because it would be easier for her to sail her boat from there. None of the other children had such a splendid boat and made of wood, and she wanted to show it off. The children noticed what Lilly was doing and gathered along the shore to watch. Lilly's new white shoes were already under water and the hemline of her pretty pink dress was wet. She hesitated a moment, then took another step. She was almost there. The water splashed against her knees, but she didn't pay attention. Finally, at the bench, she crawled on top of it and sent her boat sailing. It rocked gently, then made its way slowly back to the bench where it got snagged.

Her friends along the shore hollered with excitement and envy. Lilly liked the attention. When she realized her boat was lost under the bench, she reached down and shoved it back toward the river. She wanted everyone to see her boat in all its splendor. Her little heart filled with pride. Let them know how important she was! But again, the boat returned. With all her strength she shoved it back into the river. This time it was captured by a hostile wave and carried off. Lilly fell into a panic; she mustn't lose her boat. Thrusting herself forward in an attempt to catch it, she didn't notice the water deepening. Another step, another two. The water already reached her chest, and the current only pushed her boat out further and further. Suddenly, realizing she was out too deep, she became frightened and tried to turn back. But a fierce wave splashed up against her shoulders and pushed her further into the river. The muscles in her body tensed and she started screaming for her mother. Some men heard her cries and hastened to the shore.

"Danger! Danger! Someone's drowning!"

Lilly's mother looked up and became hysterical. She ran to the water's edge.

"Save my daughter! Oh my God, she's drowning!"

She then fainted and was carried to a dry spot of grass.

The crowd lined the shore and fixed their attention on the little girl. The violent current had already taken her into its icy grip, and her dress bloated up in the shape of a mushroom. She was being pushed toward the two rocks, only one of which was now visible. The spectators looked on in a helpless frenzy and prayed for a miracle.

Then suddenly from the left bank, a partially naked man appeared and dove into the river. At first, the crowd did not see him. When his thin arms skillfully broke the water, hopeful voices surged throughout the park. Ducking his head in and out, the man was unrecognizable. But the swift current, hitting against his legs, forced him beyond the rocks, toward raging rapids only a few meters away. He fought back by treading water. At all costs, he wanted to reach the little girl. Then unexpectedly a billowing wave thrust her in his direction. Her limp, half-conscious body was hurled back and forth, her small head submerging and then re-emerging. Another second and the man's arm rose out of the water and grabbed hold of her arm. The crowd cried madly:

"To shore! In God's name, to shore!"

But the swimmer did not hear the cries. He knew that the real danger still lay ahead. The girl's limp head fell between her shoulders as he fastened his right arm around her waist. With his free hand he fought the water mass desperately. The current played mercilessly with them until their bodies struck the rocks and they went under. A woman let out a shriek.

"They're drowning!"

At that moment a big, burly man in loose-fitting trousers and a checkered shirt made his way onto a rock ledge overlooking the river. Ever so slowly, he started making his way to the wet, slippery edge, balancing himself by digging his heels deep into the patches of moss and lichen. In his hand he carried a thick, coiled rope. Carefully studying the proximity of the victims, he spun the rope three times over his head and then hurled it into the river. The loop whistled over the surface and looked like a large disc. It fell directly over Lilly's head and secured itself under her left arm.

"He did it! Bravo! He's caught the child!" The crowd cheered.

The swimmer noticed this. He let go of Lilly instantly and tried to save his own life by grabbing hold of the rope above her head. But the wild current overpowered his efforts and, casting his body from side to side, thrust him against a rock. He was dragged downstream toward the rapids where he surfaced a brief moment, then vanished altogether.

The spectators in the park were quick to forget about the man with the thin arms; the attraction of the moment was the little girl. The rope thrower stood on the ledge overlooking the river and proudly reeled in his trophy. When she landed at his feet, he quickly laid her on her back and proceeded to pump the water out of her system. But he couldn't manage. Grabbing hold of her ankles he flipped her upside down and shook her until the water hit her nose and came gushing out of her mouth. She jerked. The man then moved her to the grass and announced:

"She's alive!"

People gathered from all directions. Several teenagers came forward and offered to take the little girl to her parents, but the man with the rope blocked their way and grabbed hold of a rock.

"Get away or I'll bash your heads in! She's mine! I'm the one who saved her!"

A large group of people now stood around Lilly, who was breathing slowly and evenly. Gradually she opened her eyes.

A policeman blew his whistle and called out, "Make way for the mayor!"

The crowd parted, creating a path for a silver-haired man with a gold badge pinned to his chest. On either side of him walked Lilly's parents; Lilly's mother was supported by one of her friends.

The mayor walked up to Fedko, and extending his hand, declared, "You will be handsomely rewarded."

"Long live the rope thrower!" the crowd roared.

The bells of the cathedral began to chime. The mayor and his family got into a black car and a dense throng followed. They were headed for the main square. Two strong, young men balanced Fedko on their shoulders. Fedko smiled and waved. The crowd below felt like gentle waves carrying him to paradise.

As the crowd approached the square, Fedko caught sight of the poster with the black bull and rope thrower on it. The bull had sharp horns and panted viciously as if threatening to charge. Fedik couldn't help but smile. Then an image of the stranger came to mind, but he quickly shook himself free of it.

* * *

Summer had long since passed and a thick layer of leaves lay on the ground. The trees were bare and the branches snapped mournfully. A cold wind swept in from across the river and swirled the leaves up into the air. As usual for this time of year, the park was empty. Some evenings when the sun hovered over the cold western horizon, a woman dressed in black appeared with a little girl. The two sat on a bench in silence and threw small wreaths of chrysanthemums into the river.

The park attendant, an old white-haired man with a thick mustache and watery gray eyes, often watched them from a distance. The sign of life made him happy. He raked the leaves into small piles and whistled under his breath:

"Winter's coming, winter's coming."

One day, as he paused to catch his breath, looking toward the garden, he noticed a rosebush barely clinging to life. He muttered sadly to himself, "They were so full, so red, like in a dream."

Then his old eye caught sight of a piece of paper snagged by a thorn. It was torn and faded. "Garbage," he muttered. Not wanting to bend over, he punctured it with a tooth of his rake and lifted it to eye level. He put on his spectacles to read what was on it:

Police Division 12 charges Dushko Millis of no fixed address to vacate B Park within twenty-four hours. July 23, 1946. By order of the Mayor.

"Winter's coming, winter's coming," crooned the old man, slipping his spectacles back into his pocket.

Crumpling up the paper with his hand, he tossed it onto a pile of leaves. Almost instantly it was picked up by the wind and sent in the direction of the river. It flew upward, circled several times, and then landed on the water's surface. The current took it into its grip and carried it downstream, where it disappeared from sight.

THE SURVIVOR

Commander Scharf was a man of courage and initiative. He was a highly accomplished soldier, who had served six months on the front somewhere beyond Smolensk. He talked proudly of the battles he had fought and of the men he had come to command. While on the front a bullet had ripped apart the ligaments in his left knee and after a series of operations he limped severely. He had recuperated under the care of his wife, Erika, in his home town of Tegel, but now due to his physical disability, he was no longer able to return to the front. One day, however, a letter arrived from headquarters ordering him to take on the position of commander of a small agricultural outpost in western Ukraine. This pleased him immensely.

As he kissed his wife good-bye, she called out after him: "Otto, be careful!"

"Don't worry about me, Erika," he replied, happy to again be part of the war, even if in a small way. "I'll be fine; after all, I'm not going to the front. Ukraine is a wealthy place; it's filled with eggs, butter, bacon ... In a week's time, you'll be eating like a queen!"

"Just be careful," she repeated, her face gray from worry. "And stay away from danger. If there's a battle keep to the bushes, let your men do the fighting for you."

Scharf was moved by his wife's devotion and he loved her more today than when they married ten years ago. Although he was well aware of her occasional indiscretion, he could not find it in him to fault her. If an extra marital affair in his absence gave her comfort in times of war, then so be it.

When he reported to his superiors in Volyna, he was immediately assigned to a small farmstead near the village Bezkupich. Under his command, he had ten soldiers of varying age and rank, whose posts had recently been destroyed by enemy forces. They were stationed in a large wooden farm house, surrounded by a thick stand of willow trees, overlooking a narrow and swift-moving river.

Upon Scharf's arrival, Kunde, a man in his mid-thirties with thick yellow hair and a scar on his forehead, saluted his new superior and stated his rank and position:

"Commander Kunde of the Holub Division and administrator of agricultural supplies. At your service."

Scharf nodded briefly and told him to stand at ease. He proceeded to ask questions about the surrounding area of which Kunde had much to say.

"This country is backward, completely uncivilized, nothing but savages here. My good friend, Fritz, was shot in the head while crossing a pond, and for no good reason. He fell over and sank to the bottom. He barely had enough energy left in him to yell 'Heil Hitler!'"

"It's terrible here," agreed Heige, a corpulent man in his thirties. "These Ukrainians are a wild bunch."

Heige wore a knapsack and a loaf of rye bread stuck out from under the flap; his helmet hanging from his neck was filled with eggs, bacon and cheese. He went on to say:

"As you can see, I'm a practical man; that's why I keep my food close. Food is a soldier's tool for survival. Without food, he can't think or run. I like to be prepared." Then patting his belly, "Well, men, I think we have good reason to celebrate. To Commander Scharf! Here's to his arrival!"

A big oak table was shoved into the middle of the room, someone covered it with a white tablecloth, and within minutes it was filled with peasant food: boiled eggs, sausages, cheese, bread, and cabbage. Kunde banged three bottles of homebrew on the table.

"This drink is deadly, enough to rot the gut."

The men lifted their glasses and made three toasts: "To Hitler! To the Reich! To victory!" They drank until the bottles were empty.

"Men!" Scharf stood up; he lit his pipe, "I am extremely pleased our Führer sent me to this outpost. It is very pleasant to be here with you, drink this strong schnapps, and eat fresh food. First thing tomorrow I am going to write my Erika and tell her all about it."

The soldiers clapped their hands and cheered.

Scharf went on, "I've seen the worst of this war, and I assure you, I don't scare easily. I know the meaning of law and order. Our pure German blood must be stronger than granite! We'll put an end to these *Untermenschen* once and for all. My Erika could tell you a thing or two about me: 'My Otto is an exceptionally organized and disciplined man,' she would say. 'The garden is always tended to and not a single blade of grass is out of place, the windows are sparkling clean, and our veranda has a fresh coat of paint every other year.'" Biting into a hard-boiled egg and washing it down with homebrew, he went on with his speech, "As you are all very well aware, I injured my knee on the front. But I take this injury not as a defeat but as a victory because I am alive today."

When at last the meal was finished, Kunde brought out a tin box filled with tobacco and started rolling cigarettes. Passing them out to his colleagues, he said, "You know men, we really are quite lucky to be stationed in this out-of-the-way place. After being on the front lines this is rather like a holiday." Then as if thinking something over, "But if only the local people here weren't so hostile, life would be better still. It's swarming with partisans. I swear they'll shoot at anything. What we ought to do is contact headquarters and demand more men. If a battle were to break out tomorrow, we would be drastically outnumbered. Allow me to tell you something that happened here and not that long ago.

"It all started with my former Commander Stein, who was shot dead in bed along with his girlfriend, Wanda. Wanda was a beautiful, tall, blonde-haired woman, not much over twenty, with a classic Polish nose and lovely green-gray eyes. Stein was in his early fifties and madly in love with her. Though she was Polish, she spoke Ukrainian fluently and acted as his translator. One day along the road, when the two approached some old peasant from a nearby farmstead, Stein told Wanda to ask the old man for five of his best cows. Wanda did as Stein requested but twisted the old peasant's reply. She told Stein that the old man refused to give up his cows because Germans were a bunch of murdering, stinking bastards. Enraged, Stein grabbed a stick from the ground and beat the old man mercilessly, then he grabbed him by the throat and, well, you can imagine what happened."

"What a story! What a story!" Scharf banged the table with his fist and fell into a fit of laughter.

At that moment, Zweit, a red-headed young man with dark eyes and a sunburnt face, rose from his seat; he appeared deeply troubled by Kunde's story.

"But the woman lied and an innocent man ended up dead." Then to himself, "What's the world coming to? Nothing makes sense anymore."

"Well, go on," Scharf was keen to hear more of the story.

"One night after his band of soldiers looted a small village and burned it to the ground, Stein decided to spend the night with Wanda in some nearby hut. She was truly beautiful and had the most unbelievably formed figure you can imagine. In fact, one evening when I was sorting letters in the office, she walked in, and standing at the edge of my desk, leaned forward and asked if she could be of some help. Her breasts poured out of her sweater right under my nose and her light shiny hair dropped over her shoulders like the finest silk. You can imagine how I felt, not having been with a woman for months. I lost control. I grabbed her and started kissing her on the neck, then on the mouth. And she returned my advances. That's when Stein walked in. He pulled her away, and after shoving her out the door, warned me to stay away from her: 'Shame on you!' he shouted at me. 'You have a wife and children in the Reich!'

"'Yes,' I rose in defense of myself, 'but you have a wife and family too.'

THEODORE ODRACH

"'My children are grown; I already have grandchildren. And besides, my wife gave me permission. She said she would understand. She just cautioned me not to forget to send parcels. If I didn't send her butter and cheese, she would become angry. I kept my word. I send parcels on a regular basis and that keeps her happy.'

"Anyway, back to the story. That night when Stein and Wanda were sound asleep, some partisans crept into the hut and smothered them both to death with a pillow. And so, that's how it ended."

At that moment Heige reached his arm over the table and grabbed hold of a loaf of bread. He stuffed it into his knapsack.

"*Um Himmel!*" exploded Scharf. "Don't you ever take that knapsack off? Do you actually think someone's going to steal your food?"

"What belongs to me stays with me. If the partisans out there were to attack us at this very moment you would all be scrambling about and stumbling over each other. I would be first and ready, and with plenty of food to keep me going."

"You're being ridiculous," Kunde sank back in his seat and stretched out his legs. He laughed out loud, "The partisans are scared to death of our little outpost; they wouldn't dare come near it. Besides, the walls are thick; the bullets would never get through."

"Don't underestimate them," Heige's dark eyes narrowed. "Those bastards love surprise attacks; that's where their strength lies. I'm sure if they could smell out our fancy feast they would be here in no time."

"Not to worry, men," exclaimed Scharf, thrusting his fist in the air. "We'll wipe them out!"

"Attention!" Scharf called out.

The soldiers jumped to their feet.

Scharf: "Victory!"

The soldiers: "Sieg Heil!"

Scharf: "Victory!"

The soldiers: "Sieg Heil!"

* * *

Early one morning Scharf and his men marched in single file along the edge of the wood a few kilometers outside of Bezkupich. The earth was damp beneath their feet and everywhere was a tangle of vegetation. The shadows rose huge and dark into the far-off distance. The men were planning to raid one of the most prosperous villages in the area and stock up on grain, meat and other provisions, whatever they could get their hands on. Each soldier had a rifle strapped over his shoulder, a pistol in his holster, and a belt packed with bullets and hand grenades. The men started upon a long, narrow, winding path that led to a u-shaped valley of pasture lands and fields of wheat. They came upon an outcrop of elderberry and honeysuckle bushes, behind which stood an orchard with fruit not yet ripened. Heige, burdened by the weight of his knapsack, trailed behind. Commander Scharf, with his rifle ready, marched ahead, searching for the enemy in the low-lying shrubs and bushes.

Nearing the edge of the valley, the soldiers came upon a small whitewashed cottage with blue shutters and doors, encircled by a wattle fence. The cottage was deserted, but because it had a spectacular view, Scharf commanded two men remain as lookout. The others pushed forward toward a village down below. Kunde came up to Scharf and said concernedly:

"Commander, your idea of launching an attack on the village is unwise. It's too quiet down there. I don't like it. We will be drastically outnumbered; it's downright suicide. We should have contacted headquarters and demanded more men." Then quickly scanning the fields, "Those bastards didn't run away – that's what they want us to believe. They're watching our every move."

Plowing their way through the tall grasses and even taller weeds, Scharf and Kunde made their way to the edge of a hillock and peered through their binoculars. The little white houses, half hidden by broad, sweeping willows, were as abundant as mushrooms after a rainfall.

Adjusting his helmet, Kunde turned seriously to Scharf and began again, "I know this area inside out. We should advance from that hill, because if the partisans surprise-attack us from the houses, we won't have any cover. From the hill, the trees and shrubs will provide us with enough protection to safely make it back to Bezkupich."

Scharf contemplated a moment, then shook his head, "No, we will advance from the river and if need be, we will take cover in the outlying houses."

"But what if we're forced into the river?"

Scharf turned purple with rage, "I'm in command here, not you! Your problem is you think too much about retreat. You should concentrate on attack. If our Führer thought the way you did, we wouldn't be anywhere near Moscow today!"

Scharf signaled to his soldiers and together they began to descend into the valley. A slight breeze picked up and rustled the treetops, and the sun, now high in the sky, played gently on the thatched rooftops of the houses. Creeping into the yard of an outlying house and keeping to a high wooden fence, the soldiers put their rifles in position.

Heige and Zweit climbed the porch staircase and banged down the door. But the house was empty with only a few dirty rags and rusted pots and pans. Heige pulled open the kitchen cupboards then looked inside the oven – there were mouse droppings but not a trace of food anywhere.

Heige and Zweit then went outside and made for the barn. But it too was empty. Heige called to the men, "Let's check the garden out back!"

Rows upon rows of green and yellow beans dangled from behind broad-leafed vines trailing up high wooden poles. Heige together with Zweit started to pick. Then suddenly from behind the fence a slight rustling sound erupted. Zweit and Heige tensed and aimed their rifles. Straining to listen, they scanned the immediate area. A brief silence followed, then again, the rustling sound. All at once, as if out of no-where, a chicken sprang up into the air and landed in the middle of the garden. Heige tried to grab hold of it while Zweit moved in from the other end.

"Zweit!" shouted Heige. "It's coming toward you! Hurry, grab it!"

"Where? Where?"

"Over there, by the fence!"

THEODORE ODRACH

"I can't see it!"

"Damn, now we've lost it."

Heige, getting down on his hands and knees, began to weave in and around the rows of beans.

"I found it!" suddenly Zweit's voice came ripping from the cucumber patch. "Heige, quick! It's over here!"

Heige ran in Zweit's direction; he could hear him huffing and puffing, trying to corner it against the fence. Sensing danger, the chicken flapped its wings and squawked hysterically. Heige then swooped in from behind, and stretching out his hand, managed to seize the bird by the neck; he then tied a rope around its legs and stuffed it into his knapsack.

"It's a little on the scrawny side," Zweit complained.

Heige patted his belly and laughed, "Better than nothing. Now, if only we could find ourselves a pig, then we would have a true feast."

The next house they came to was also empty; a few dishes and busted up furniture lay on the floor. They went on to the next house, then the next, but they were all deserted.

Becoming more and more frustrated, Scharf and his men decided to give up and go back to Bezkupich. As they were about to head down a footpath, Scharf turned round to take one last look at the village. He shouted in a commanding voice:

"Men, set fire to the houses!"

Almost at once, everything went up in flames. Clouds of thick black smoke formed over the valley and made it dark. Scharf was pleased. He said optimistically, "Tomorrow we will try going north. Maybe there we'll have better luck.

Sooner or later these *Untermenschen* will get tired of hiding in the woods."

When Scharf had barely uttered these words, from the edge of a wheat field gunshots erupted. Zweit was the first to cry out:

"Gunfire! It's an ambush! Men, take cover!"

The soldiers dropped to the ground at once, and dragging themselves through the tall, spindly grass, made toward the river. Fortunately for them, it had a smooth, sandy bottom and was not deep. Heige, despite the weight of his knapsack, was the first to wade over to the other side. Barely setting foot on the bank, signaling with his arms, he cautioned the other men:

"Keep to the right, it's only knee-deep over there!"

Scharf started his way across. When he was barely half way, a bullet went off and landed in the thigh of his unhealthy leg. At once blood spewed out and formed a red circular pool on the water's surface. Zweit ran to help him, and pulling him up by the underarms, proceeded to drag him to shore. But with the current sucking up against them, movement proved difficult. In time, somehow the two men along with the others managed to make it safely to the other side. Just as they were about to dive into the thicket and take cover, to their great horror twenty partisans jumped out of a clump of bushes, aiming their rifles.

"Lay your weapons down!" one of them shouted.

Everything fell silent. Then unexpectedly came the sound of a lone bullet and one of the partisans dropped to the ground, dead; he didn't even let out a scream. Kunde stood waving his rifle, cursing and red in the face. He was proclaiming to get every last one of the *Untermenschen*. As he was about to shoot again, gunfire rang out from behind and got him in the head.

"Lay down your weapons!" a voice came ripping from a nearby bush.

Scharf and his men laid down their arms and surrendered.

"Well, well," laughed one of the partisans sarcastically, looking at Heige and peering into his knapsack. "It looks like you fellows had a bit of bad luck today. All you managed to come up with is one skinny old chicken. Hah, hah, hah!"

Then to his men, "Search the banks!"

Scharf stood leaning his body against Zweit's, trying to keep the weight off his wounded leg. He was cold and shivered as if from fever. The pain in his leg was excruciating.

A partisan walked up to him and asked in a severe tone, "Was it you who ordered the houses burned?"

"That's right," Scharf snarled back. "You bastards killed one of my men and now you've completely crippled me!"

Without a word, the partisan grabbed Scharf by the scruff of the neck and punched him first in the face, then in the stomach. He punched him again and again and he didn't stop.

Scharf fell to the ground. Squirming several minutes, moaning and groaning, he then became perfectly still. He was dead.

While this was going on, Heige, completely unnoticed, managed to slip behind a clump of bushes, and then jump behind a broad oak. When the way was clear, he darted behind another tree, then another. Finally, reaching a grove of dense birch, he swiftly made his way into a deep forest. After crossing a narrow, swampy stream, at last, he found his way back to their small agricultural outpost in Bezkupich.

*   *   *

Already in the little wooden house, he quickly chopped off the chicken's head, plucked it, and shoved it into the oven. He then set the table, poured himself a glass of homebrew, and sliced up a loaf of bread. At once he heard a bustling noise outside the door, then the sound of voices. Springing to his feet and peering through the window, he caught sight of Zweit and two other men, making their way across the yard, holding onto one another for support. They were stark naked and their bodies were bloody and badly bruised. When they came inside, looking them over, Heige couldn't help but laugh.

"You idiots! Well, at least they didn't kill you. First thing tomorrow we'll have to contact headquarters in Lutsk and ask for some new uniforms. Just hope our superiors don't wring your necks the way I did my chicken's. Hah! Hah! Hah!"

Then he remembered Scharf.

"So, the old fool got himself finished off, did he? I'm not surprised, not surprised at all. First thing tomorrow I'll write Erika and tell her the bad news. Poor thing, who's going to send her cheese and sausages now?"

Heige bit into a chicken leg, and when some juice dripped down the side of his mouth, he quickly licked it up.

THE VILLAGE TEACHER

Beyond the schoolyard up against a backdrop of a blue-green forest golden stalks of wheat rose upward and swayed gently in the warm summer breeze. The rosebush beneath the classroom window was in full bloom and it couldn't have been a lovelier day. But there was something ominous, oppressive moving in and whatever it was there was no way of stopping it.

That night the sky, instead of filling with the moon and stars, it was set on fire – orange, red, blue. Somewhere in the forest beyond Skulin came the rattling of machine guns and later the explosion of bombs. On the southern horizon, a stream of light shot from one end to the other, making the landscape pale and barely visible.

Marko, the village teacher, sat with his wife, Sarka, in the dark in their little apartment in back of the school. She looked fearfully at him as she pressed their little daughter, Lara, against her breast. She had come to be here with Marko from her native Czechoslovakia, where they had met and married.

Seeing the distress on his wife's face, Marko couldn't help but feel guilty. "How could I have brought her here, to this hell on earth?"

* * *

At the crack of dawn, soundlessly, so as not to waken his wife and daughter, Marko rose, dressed, and went outside. Looking round, he made sure no one was watching him. The air was cool and damp, and as he passed through the yard and beyond the gates, he started down the dirt laneway that connected with the main road. Hurriedly cutting across the village square, he made for an open field. After walking about five minutes, he came upon a path that led directly into a patch of dense forest. In a line of tangled mixed wood, he went straight for a gnarled oak tree that looked a hundred years old. At its base there was a rounded hollow. Stooping, he slid his hand inside and pulled out a wad of rolled-up newspapers tied with brown jute. Three times a week he stole away to this spot to retrieve several papers that were delivered regularly by an anonymous courier. The newspapers were published at an undisclosed location under the protection of partisans with the purpose of keeping the surrounding inhabitants updated on wartime activities. Deemed illegal by the occupying German army, *The Informer* was the most widely circulated. Stuffing the papers inside the bosom of his jacket, he hastened home.

By the time Marko reached the front door of the school, a round yellow sun was already flooding the schoolyard with its warm golden glow. Inside, he could hear his wife busying herself with morning chores: she had already made the beds, washed Lara, and was now setting the table for breakfast. Upon entering, kissing them both a good morn-

THEODORE ODRACH

ing, Marko settled on the sofa in the living room and started scanning the newspapers. His eyes came to rest on the last page of *The Informer*, which listed people recently killed, of whom he recognized several. It read as follows:

Tereshchuk, Constantin, forester, Pinsk Division, robbed and murdered by Bolsheviks; pregnant wife, Anna, raped and killed.

Oppenheimer, Shmuel, and wife Rebecca, shop owners, shot dead by Gestapo; children's whereabouts unknown.

Sarnetsky, Orest, professor of engineering, tortured to death by Bolsheviks, Sarny; wife and children shot three days later.

Laying the paper down, Marko buried his head in his hands. He could hardly move.

"When will it all end? The Germans are coming at us from the west and the Russians from the east; it's a bloodbath. Our men are dropping dead like flies, they are no match for either. The Germans operate in broad daylight, the Russians in the dead of night. What will become of Sarka, of Lara, of me? Will we meet the same end as the Sarnetskys?"

Marko could hear Sarka and Lara in the kitchen. First came the clinking of plates, then the sound of boiling water, then Sarka's voice, scoldingly:

"Lara, don't go near the stove. How many times do I have to tell you?"

In the kitchen, a waft of cool air poured in through the open window. The aroma of coffee and frying eggs filled the room. The young family settled around the table. There was still an hour left before the children would arrive for school.

Suddenly from outside a car could be heard pulling into the driveway. Then came the opening and closing of doors, then the sound of footsteps. Marko froze. Sarka rushed to Lara. Peering out the window, Marko saw several men, some in Gestapo uniform, making for the porch stairs. Any second now and they would bang open the door.

Marko fell into a panic and his heart stood still – he had left the forbidden newspapers scattered on the sofa! How could he have been so reckless! Not wasting a second's time, in a mad fury he raced into the living room, grabbed hold of the papers, and not knowing what to do with them, hurled them under the china cabinet by the sofa. Straightening himself, he tried to look as normal as possible.

The door flew open. Five men entered: three Germans and two collaborators, one Polish, one Ukrainian. One of the men took position by the kitchen door, and with a machine gun under his arm, fixed his attention on Sarka, who stood frightened and unable to move. The remaining four barged into the classroom and started to search for whatever they could find, banging and thrashing as they went. Coming up empty, they stormed back to the living quarters. The commanding officer said to Marko in a snarl:

"Are you the village teacher?"

"Yes," Marko held his breath.

"Do you have an affiliation with any subversive movement?"

"No, I do not."

"Do you own a firearm?"

"No."

The commander screwed up his mouth. "You son-of-bitch! Why are you so pale all of a sudden? Are you hiding something? You want an independent Ukraine, is that it? You nationalist bastard!"

Pushing Marko up against the wall, rummaging through his pant pockets, he looked inside his jacket and frisked the lining. Not finding anything, along with his collaborators, he started upstairs to the bedroom. The mattresses were turned upside down and slit open with a knife, feathers from the pillows went flying, clothes were thrown out of dresser drawers, closets emptied.

Making back downstairs, the men then stormed the supply room, though for some reason, the commanding officer remained behind. He stood leaning against the china cabinet, jotting something down in his notepad, looking up every few seconds. Marko could scarcely breathe. Everything was dead still.

When one of the collaborators returned from the supply room, stepping up to the commander, he uttered something in a low voice as if there was a problem. The two men became rather involved with one another, waving their arms about, pointing toward the kitchen, and every few seconds turning to look at Marko. A few moments went by and then the commander settled on the sofa, again jotting something down in his notebook. The collaborator, to Marko's horror, took an interest in the china cabinet: he opened up the doors, shuffled dishes around, looked in the drawers, lifted glasses. He then directed his attention to the base, as if intending to look underneath. But instead of bending over, he ran his bayonet along the edges. All he had to do was poke it a little further in and then everything would be over.

Marko stood paralyzed. He had to do something. In an attempt to divert their attention, he uttered in a voice he did not recognize as his own.

"*Herr*, my wife has prepared a fine breakfast! Yesterday peasants came with a basket filled with sausages, eggs, cheese, bread, even coffee."

The commander's face tensed then slackened slightly. The offer pleased him. He shouted to his men: "Into the kitchen! Breakfast awaits."

A great sense of relief came over Marko but he could not bring himself to move. Conflicting thoughts whirled round his head. Would the intruders, after finishing their meal, resume ransacking his home or would they be on their way? What should he do? Should he take the papers and make a run for it? Or should he remain with his wife and child and risk the papers being discovered? If they were to be discovered, that would be certain death for all of them. The seconds passed rapidly and he could feel the sweat build on his brow. And suddenly he became convinced he had but one choice: to take the papers and run.

Brushing up to the side of the cabinet and slipping his hand under, he grabbed hold of the newspapers and stuffed them inside his coat. He then ran headlong out the door. As fast as his legs could carry him, he ran across the yard and over the fence. He ran and ran, not daring to look back.

"If only I can get to the orchard, the trees will give me cover."

THEODORE ODRACH

As he neared the first apple tree, from behind came the sound of gunfire: he was already being pursued! He ran deeper into the orchard. Again, the sound of gunfire. When he came upon an outcrop of low-lying shrubs, keeping to the edge, he jumped across a narrow stream and then plunged into a grove of young maple. His heart pounded and his head spun. Finally, in the not so far distance, a long stretch of forest. If only he could make it there, he would be safe. Feeling as if his legs were about to collapse beneath him, he paused to catch his breath. He was startled by the sudden absolute silence. No one was on his tail!

Turning to look in the direction of the village, he could no longer see the small wooden houses that stood in a row or the school with its stuccoed walls and red tin roof. It was at that moment he was struck by the reality of it all. The most terrifying thought came to him.

"What is happening to my wife and child?"

Keeping to the forest wall, he would go to the farmstead of his good friend, Stephan, an elderly beekeeper. The farmstead was moments away on a tract of land in a small clearing. With his wife and daughter, he often visited the old man and brought him food and supplies from the village. He prayed he was still there and had not been arrested or shot by the Germans. He very well knew this would be the first place his wife would come looking for him.

To his great relief, Marko found Stephan out back of his house tending his beehives. Stephan was a widower his wife having died ten years before. Though the old man was never big on going to church, after his wife's death he did so regularly and started supplying the beeswax for the church's candles. In such a way he put himself into good standing with the priest. He had a host of grandchildren and five of them were part of the resistant movement of which he was very proud.

Spotting Marko at a distance, Stephan waved and called out to him, "Hello, Marko! What news do you bring from the village? If I'm not mistaken my old ears heard the sound of gunfire. What's going on?"

"Trouble, nothing but trouble," Marko shook his head, and then in detail proceeded to explain what had happened.

Disappearing into his house briefly, Stephan returned with a pitcher of water.

"Here, drink this, it will settle your nerves. Thank God I live in the forest. This is the only place the enemy will not venture, at least for now. Our boys have ambushes everywhere."

Downing two glasses, Marko, upon the old man's invitation, followed him inside into the kitchen. Against a far wall, behind a long, crudely constructed table sat several young men; in the corner lay a large pile of German and Russian arms. At the waist, each man had about five hand grenades and their shoulder belts were laden with bullets.

Stephan said to the young men:

"A great misfortune has befallen our teacher and he needs our help."

One young man, who appeared older than the others, looked Marko in the face. "Are your wife and daughter still in the village?"

"Yes."

Staring at the floor as if weighing the situation, finally, he said, "You did the right thing in getting out of there. If the Germans had come across those papers, which sooner or later they would have, you and your family would be dead. Now we have to get your wife and daughter out of there before it's too late."

Swinging round, he signaled to the old man. The old man understood instantly what had to be done. As quickly as his crooked legs could carry him, he made for the pantry, where he filled a basket with honey, bread, and eggs. He would take the items to the school.

"It's not much," he said as he headed out the door. "With the will of God, it just might be enough of a deterrent. One thing those bastards like it's to eat."

With his cane in one hand and the basket in the other, Stephan was already half way across the yard. Starting for the outlying trees, his bent shape grew smaller and smaller until it finally disappeared altogether.

* * *

Time passed slowly. In Stephan's house the clock went tick tock, tick tock and the pendulum swung heavily. Marko's heart raced and his head pounded. What news would the old man bring back with him? Were his wife and child alive? Were they dead? He could find no rest.

An hour passed, then another. Marko sat in an armchair without energy for anything; he couldn't have felt more in pain. Getting up to peer out the window, suddenly from the direction of the village he witnessed two approaching figures. Straining to focus, at once he felt a trembling in his bones. Was it Stephan with his wife and child, or was it two Gestapo men coming to get him? At last the outline of a man bent to one side emerged and there was a woman next to him, carrying something. It was Stephan with his wife, and his wife was carrying Lara!

"They're alive!" Marko shouted with indescribable relief. Throwing himself on the door, he raced to meet them. Lara, free of her mother's grip, came at him, crying: "Papa! Papa!"

"It's unbelievable how lucky we got," Sarka struggled with her words; she brushed the loose strands of hair from her face. "It turns out the Gestapo were not interested so much in us as they were in our belongings. They confiscated everything: your suits and overcoat, my clothes, even Lara's toys. Before they stormed out of the house, they destroyed the furniture, and then hurled the china cabinet upside down. Thank God you got out of there when you did." Then pausing to catch her breath, "But when you disappeared, they became suspicious. Now they're looking for you and they won't stop until they find you."

Picking Lara up in his arms and stroking her soft yellow hair, Marko whispered in her ear.

"Don't cry, Lara. Everything's going to be all right. There's a wagon waiting for us. It's come to take us where we will be safe. But instead of sleeping under the comfort of an eiderdown, your bed will now be patches of moss and lichen. No harm will come to you, I promise."

Within minutes the young family was gone, they disappeared into the depths of the forest.

TUMBLEWEED

Dried prairie grass ripped from its roots. Tumbleweed. A cold autumn wind blows in, lifts it up, and chases it across the steppe. It leaps and trundles over *chernozems*, vast fields of wheat, and pasture lands, spreading its seed everywhere. It passes old dirt roads, abandoned villages, burnt down houses. There comes the sound of shellfire and bombardment. Tumbleweed continues on. Under a bright blue sky, it finds itself in the shadows of a guilder-rose and becomes snagged – finally, respite. Suddenly a heavy breeze sweeps up and pushes the little ball upward, sending it flying in a southward direction. It travels freely and easily, bouncing and rolling over vast terrains.

At once dark gray clouds roll in. A storm is brewing somewhere in the far-off hills. There comes a spattering of rain and soon after a violent downpour. It pours and pours. The soil cannot absorb all that water, and the water starts to run off the land into the rivers and streams that are unable to carry it. Everything becomes flooded. Tumbleweed floats upon the water's surface, now and then submerging and then re-emerging. Lightning strikes followed by a clap of thunder followed by the roar of artillery. The artillery and thunder become one but tumbleweed floats on.

The rain finally stops. Tumbleweed continues along the wet land. Frogs croak here and there and birds chirrup high in the sky.

Days pass, the earth finally dries and tumbleweed lands on a gray sandy beach. A strong wind is blowing and the air is salty. The sea, at last!

Small boats rise and fall along the shoreline, and a large black barge sounds its horn as it heads for the dock.

But the sea is not calm and the waves seethe, foam and rage. The water is brownish and murky from the waves throwing up stones and sand from the sea's bottom. Tumbleweed is hurled upward and then dropped onto a high blustering whitecap.

Suddenly warplanes appear. They swoop down and plow the earth with explosions and create a mass, muddy confusion. Everything along the shore goes on fire.

Tumbleweed, riding the waves is safe in the water. A strong north gale comes in and wheels it straight into the open sea. And suddenly, it becomes lost from view, lost forever.

ACROSS THE SIAN RIVER

December 14, 1940, I was in Turka, a small, ancient town high in the Carpathian Mountains. It had snowed heavily that day and everywhere was covered by a thick blanket of white. With dusk fast approaching, making my way down a winding, narrow street, small wooden houses started to emerge. I was looking for a house painted green, belonging to a certain Misko Semkiv, an old acquaintance of mine. I was hoping he still lived there. Back in 1936, I had come to Turka by train, on my way to Czechoslovakia and had visited with him. He farmed a small plot of land in back of his house and worked in wood production. He had a wife and two young children. As it happened, I was in a most desperate situation. I needed his help and knew he was one of the few people I could trust. Finally, there it was, the small wooden house with the brown door and tin roof. Noticing a light in one of the windows, I knocked on it. A moment later a woman's face appeared but it was barely visible.

"I called out to her, "Hello in there! Does Misko Semkiv live here?"

"Who are you and what do you want?"

"Fedir Sholomitsky, I'm an old friend of Misko's."

Before long the front door squeaked open. A man emerged on the threshold, tall, lanky with a broad pleasant face and high cheekbones, but there was something unhealthy-looking about his complexion. He was maybe thirty, thirty-five but looked much older. It was obvious at once he was poverty-stricken. This was not the same vibrant, energetic Misko I had remembered.

"Fedir!" he exclaimed upon seeing me. "What in devil's name brought you to Turka? Rumor had it you'd moved to Czechoslovakia and for good!" Then with his eyes dropping, "Whatever made you come back here to this hell on earth?"

I asked instead, "How have you been keeping?"

"How have I been keeping? Things are bad, very bad, a hundred times worse than before the war. Now the Bolsheviks are here. Every day they send me off to clear the forest and the work is endless, exhausting, and the amount they pay me isn't enough to even build a dog house."

He went on at length, "I had two goats; the regime confiscated one. This autumn the oats didn't produce and the potatoes were the size of acorns, there was nothing to eat. And then they gave us rations to fill, and if we didn't fill them, there were consequences. How do you fill rations from nothing? Bolsheviks, may the devil take them!"

Poking his head out the door, he looked left then right. "It's a good thing you came in the dark. Informers, they're everywhere, even my neighbors next door. If you had come by day, they would have spotted you easily and ratted you out to the border police."

Inviting me in, he called for his wife, "Stasia, Stasia, come meet my old friend, Fedir. Do you remember he visited us a few years back, just after Valentyn was born? Yes, let's have a little celebration. Get out the eggs, Stasia. Fry them up, our guest has come a long way, he's hungry. A little celebration wouldn't hurt!"

Stasia came into the room in her bare feet, her hair disheveled. She was scowling and had her hands on her hips. "Eggs, you say? And where am I supposed to get these eggs you speak of, maybe under the goat's tail?"

The two went off into an argument that lasted several minutes. Misko flailed his arms about and stamped his feet, while Stasia, with eyes wide open, shouted expletives.

Finally, when all was said and done, Misko turned to me a little embarrassed, "My apologies. I thought we had eggs."

Stasia disappeared into the kitchen and after about fifteen minutes came out with a loaf of hardened black bread and a pot of cabbage soup. She filled up my bowl, which I ate heartily. I was so hungry I could eat a horse. But I felt guilty – even one bowl was too much for this impoverished family.

Finally, I turned to Misko seriously.

"I need your help, brother. They're after me – the NKVD. They say I'm an enemy of the people. I need you to get me across the Sian River."

Misko's face darkened. "The Sian? You want to cross the Sian? Never mind the Sian, there's no one who will take you even close to the Sian. It's dangerous, very dangerous. It's so heavily patrolled these days, even a rabbit would have trouble getting across. Barbed wire runs for miles and miles – these Bolsheviks are crazy for barbed wire. There were many like you that have come around. Most didn't make it. Either they got shot or caught, and those who got caught, they've disappeared without a trace."

Silence fell over the room. Misko, with elbows on the table and face in his hands, seemed to be mulling something over. Finally, he said half under his breath.

"There's a man in Yablinka, his name is Klimsky. He might be able to help you. Are you up for a good hike? But you must understand, this Klimsky loves money, it's said he'd walk on the sharpest of knives to get it. I hope you have something to give him, otherwise it's pointless. But he's really not a bad sort, at least not in the way people make him out to be – he's never betrayed us or become an informer as have so many others. If you're lucky, he might guide you to the village Sokolyk, which sits on the Sian, half in Ukraine, the other half in Poland. I'll take you to him. We should go immediately."

From my bag I took out all my clothes. I put on two pairs of undergarments, two pairs of trousers, two shirts, a sweater, a coat, and on my feet, two pairs of woolen socks. It's a good thing my boots were sturdy, well-lined and relatively new.

As we stepped out into the street, Misko said with a grin, "Let me warn you now, my friend, you are about to learn what winter in our mountains really means. But, not to worry, we'll be taking back roads so no one sees us. In summer the way is straightforward, but in winter, especially in the dark, it's easy to get lost."

And so Misko and I set off for Yablinka, which was about a three-hour hike. After passing a few rows of wooden houses, trying to keep to the shadows, at last we got out of town. Lit up by the light of the moon, the mountain terrain opened up wide before us. The snow stretched without a break, and the trees were as if black specks on a white sheet. Several dachas rose out of the darkness and smoke billowed out of their chimneys. I was overwhelmed by the grandiose beauty.

After about an hour, we came to a line of telegraph poles running up the side of a mountain. I could hear the wires whistling in the wind. Following the poles, half-way up, we turned left and made over a jagged ridge, behind which was another slope for us to climb. To say it was freezing out there would have been an understatement, it felt like thirty below, even more. The bitter cold whipped at our faces, numbed our hands, and frost collected on our brows and lashes. The snow at times reached almost to our waists. We climbed higher and higher, and then we started to descend. From time to time, Misko stopped but only for me to catch up to him. I was much too overdressed and the weight of my clothes was slowing me down. And in such a way, from summit to summit, from ridge to ridge, coppice to coppice, at last we arrived in Yablinka, which was in a broad, long valley surrounded by steep, rocky cliffs.

We found Klimsky's house with little effort. I prayed to God he would help me; he was my last hope. If he declined, I'd have no other choice but to go it alone. I'd have to look for some random opening somewhere and make a run for it. I knew this was a crazy idea on my part, suicidal even but time was running out – the authorities were fast moving in on me.

We knocked on Klimsky's door. A stubby middle-aged man with a fleshy face appeared. Yawning, stretching, it was obvious we'd got him out of bed. He did not seem surprised or irritated by our appearance, and it was clear he was accustomed to these late-night intrusions.

Inviting us in, we sat down to a crudely-made oak table. With his finger to his lips, he asked for us to please keep our voices down as his wife was asleep in the next room. Looking attentively at us, he started in an almost business-like manner.

"So, gentlemen, what can I do for you?"

"I need to get to the Sian," I spurted out. "Can you take me?"

Klimsky sat unmoving. He looked down. Finally, he said very seriously without a smile.

"No, I'm sorry, I can't, the situation here is very bad. Still half a year ago it was possible but not anymore. You should find yourself a better spot, maybe on the Slovakian border. I hear there one can still somehow slip through. But here, you'd be digging your own grave."

Misko said pleadingly, "Surely there must be a spot somewhere near Sokolyk."

Slightly screwing up his eyes, Klimsky was as if thinking. Suddenly, he seemed to have changed his mind. "Well, maybe there is a way. Here's what I can do. I will take you within a kilometer of Sokolyk which sits on the Sian. I will explain everything to you when we get there, and then you'll be on your own. But there are no guarantees. These Bolsheviks are experienced hunters, and they'll hunt you down like an animal. How much will you give me?"

"Six hundred roubles, that's all I've got."

"That's not enough, add the watch."

"The watch is gold. I'll give you the watch but only if you take me right to the Sian."

Klimsky laughed, his teeth were yellow and cracked. "No, not for a hundred watches will I take you to the Sian. I value life too much. A kilometer away – the roubles, the watch – that's my final offer."

I didn't hesitate. "It's a deal. I'll turn it all over to you when we get there."

The promise of payment had a soothing effect on Klimsky. Looking directly at me, he asked but with perfect sincerity, "Do you have a gun?"

"No, I don't."

He shook his head. "That's bad, very bad. You might find trouble out there where only a gun can save you – it's the NKVD dogs. Those dogs are highly trained. They knock you off your feet, sink their teeth into you, and then wait for their NKVD masters to show up to finish you off."

A chill rushed down my spine. Dogs! I'd never considered dogs! May God have mercy on me!

Klimsky's face brightened, "Maybe you'll get lucky, maybe by a miracle the guards will be looking the other way. But it's unfortunate the sky is clear and the moon is bright. At least the wind is still blowing, you can be thankful for that. The dogs are typically to the north, and if that's the case, they will not be able to sniff you out tonight. God be willing, the dogs are to the north."

Getting up, Klimsky excused himself and went into the next room to change his clothes. Returning, he put on his boots, a long woolen overcoat, and a white sheepskin hat that came down over his ears. He signaled with his head for us to follow him. Going outside, walking across the yard, we headed toward a small shed half-buried in snow. From inside we could hear an animal making sounds, as if crunching on tidbits of food. Klimsky disappeared inside and after a few minutes came out with a rather fine-looking mountain horse as white as the snow around us. Excusing himself, he briefly ran into his house and returned wearing a long white cape that covered him from top to bottom. Mounting his horse, the two looked as one. He cleared his throat loudly.

"We're about to play a most dangerous game, it's a matter of life and death. I have myself to consider first and foremost."

I understood instantly what was going on and I felt discouraged. Should we be spotted, on horseback, Klimsky, perfectly camouflaged, would be able to effortlessly disappear into the white landscape, while I, in my dark coat and hat, on foot, would be an easy target. But I was in no position to argue, and I realized it would have been completely unreasonable of me to do so. I could only but thank my lucky stars he was even willing to help me.

Klimsky waved for me to follow.

Bading Misko farewell, thanking him and giving him a hearty embrace, I hurried after Klimsky. Misko called after me, "Take care, my friend, stay strong!"

It didn't take long for the distance between Klimsky and me to become considerable, it was as if any minute now he would vanish completely. All I could do was keep my eyes on the tracks that were more like little black holes, sometimes becoming snow-filled and invisible. The tracks now in a straight line shot all the way up the side of a mountain. I labored after them, falling, straining to get up, falling again. The snow forever deepened. Dear God, how tired I was! And suddenly I'd completely lost sight of Klimsky.

A narrow strip of forest became visible. There was Klimsky again but he was no more than a mere speck. I continued higher and higher, falling again and again. I breathed heavily; I could scarcely catch enough air into my lungs. Finally, I reached the strip of forest, which now looked like an immense black wall. And there was Klimsky on his horse, erect, unmoving, as if a statue. Like a giant snowball I collapsed before him.

Regaining myself, after a few minutes I got up.

Klimsky was quick to announce, "Well, my man, this is as far as I go. Pay me now and I'll explain everything."

I reached into my pocket for the roubles and took off my watch.

Klimsky started, "See that slope over there? It leads to Sokolyk. Stick to the row of spruce trees running alongside that stream. When the trees come to an end, the stream will split in two. Stay on the left arm, it will keep you safely out of the village, which is now occupied by the NKVD. Don't stop for any reason, don't look around, just keep going until you come to a house. Behind that house is the river. God be willing, if you make it across, in the village there is a large log house with a sign on the door, reading Katya's. Go there, she will help you. Goodbye and good luck."

Klimsky gave a tug to his horse, and turning round, started back down into the valley. Within minutes he was as if a ghost.

As instructed, I moved against the row of trees, downward, downward. Though the way now was much easier, still, I felt exhausted. I tried not to think about the NKVD men, the dogs, about getting caught. I just kept moving, fighting the snow all the way. I watched for the parting of the creek and at last there it was. I started out along the left arm. Finally, the house. I could already see the frozen river and the barbed wire fence running along side it.

But what I saw next made the blood in my veins freeze. There, a little to the left, was a hut of some sort and next to it stood an NKVD man. He had on a dark woolen coat belted at the waist, high leather boots, and on his head an *ushanka*. A rifle was strapped over his shoulder.

I had no idea what to do next, I couldn't think. I tried to relax but my muscles only tensed. If I went left, I would most definitely fall into his hands; if I went right, he would undoubtedly see me and shoot me. In all honesty, till this day, I can't say if it was a real NKVD man or just a figment of my imagination. If he was real, there's no way he wouldn't have seen me against the snow-covered surface. But one thing was for certain, real or not, in that instant, I had a sudden feeling of such boundless fear as I'd never before had.

Slowly, quietly I tramped toward the river. I listened for shouting, for the sound of a bullet, for the barking of a dog. Incredibly, nothing. Silence everywhere.

Then, to my dismay, when I got to the barbed wire, I noticed not one but two lines of fence running parallel, set

THEODORE ODRACH

about a meter apart. I was so exhausted in every pore in my being, I was sure I would never manage to get over one of those fences let alone two. At once the reality of it all set in, that my life within minutes could be over.

With both hands on the fence, avoiding the sharp edges as best I could, I started to climb. One foot, then the next, higher and higher. Luckily for me, the wire was of a heavier grade steel, which made it more sturdy and better to support my weight. Finally, I reached the top. Was I really at the top? Putting one foot over to the other side, spreading out my arms not unlike a bird, I threw myself into the air. Falling, falling, I landed in the puffy snow. My left hand was bleeding, I didn't remember it being cut, and I saw the arm of my coat torn. I stayed there between the two fences maybe a second, maybe two.

Getting up, I started for the second set of wires, one foot, then another. Already at the top, everything whirled inside my head and it wouldn't stop. I jumped and landed face down in the snow. I could hardly believe it. Was I really in the neutral zone? I listened but there came only the sound of the wind._

Now all that was left for me to do was to cross the Sian. I started, one step then another. There was still much to be feared – the NKVD man, if indeed he was real, should he spot me, he'd come after me and then drag me back behind Bolshevik lines. My heart was as if jumping out of my chest. Just a few more meters and I'd be safe, I'd be on the bank. Then as if things couldn't get any worse, I heard a loud crack beneath my feet. It was the ice, it was breaking. Dammit! I filled with mortal terror. Before long, I could feel myself dropping into the ice-cold water. But by a miracle of miracles, the water was only knee-deep. Instead of getting out and continuing on foot, to put less pressure on the ice for fear of it breaking further, I laid flat on my belly and pushed myself with my hands and feet. In such a way I slid to shore.

One final obstacle awaited me there – another fence. I felt so utterly broken, I couldn't possibly deal with more barbed wire. To my great relief, there was only one line of fencing not two as on the Soviet side, and it stood rather low with huge gaps in it and with almost no sharp edges. I was able to practically walk right over it.

I was now completely and safely outside of Soviet jurisdiction. Up until the last minute, I never would have believed it. And suddenly I was able to breathe more freely. A great sense of peace and joy came into my soul and I felt immediately calm. I was no longer at the edge of an end, but, rather, at the start of a beginning. I looked one last time to the river, to where the ice had broken. Then I looked to my tracks in the snow and followed them back to the two barbed wire fences. It all seemed so far away, so unreal. I looked for the little hut with the NKVD man standing next to it. But there was no NKVD man, there was no hut. There was nothing there, absolutely nothing.

It was still dark but starting to get light. In the distance I could see a collection of houses – the other half of Sokolyk. I went in search of Katya's house.

ABOUT THE AUTHOR

Theodore Odrach was born Theodore Sholomitsky in 1912 outside of Pinsk, Belarus. At the age of nine, he was arrested for a petty crime by the authorities. Without his parents' knowledge, he was sent to a reform school in Vilnius, Lithuania (then under Polish rule). Released at the age of 18, he entered what is now Vilnius University, studying philosophy and ancient history. With the Soviet invasion in 1939, he fled Vilnius and returned to his native Pinsk, where he secured a job as headmaster of a village school. As with all teachers of the time, his main duties were to transform the school system into a Soviet one and usher in complete russification. Within a year, he fell under suspicion by the Soviet regime and became imprisoned on some trumped-up charge. He managed to escape and flee south to Ukraine (then under German occupation), where he edited underground wartime newspapers. Toward the end of the war, with the return of the Bolshevik regime, he fled over the Carpathian Mountains to the West. Traveling through Europe, in Germany he met and married Klara Nagorski. After living in England for five years, in 1953 he and his wife immigrated to Canada. It was in his home in Toronto that Odrach did most of his writing. He died of a stroke in 1964.

ABOUT THE TRANSLATOR

Erma Odrach is an author and translator living in Canada. Her writing and translations have appeared in literary journals in Canada, the U.S. and UK. *Alaska or Bust and Other Stories* was published by Crimson Cloak Publisher, 2015; *The Bank Street Peeper* was published by Adelaide Books, 2021. Her translation of *Wave of Terror* by her father, Theodore Odrach, was published by Chicago Review Press in 2008.

The Complete
KOBZAR
by Taras Shevchenko

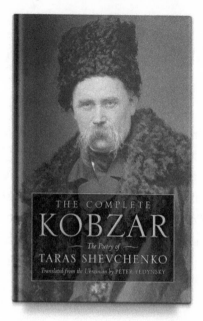

Masterfully fulfilled by Peter Fedynsky, Voice of America journalist and expert on Ukrainian studies, this first ever English translation of the complete *Kobzar* brings out Ukraine's rich cultural heritage.

As a foundational text, The *Kobzar* has played an important role in galvanizing the Ukrainian identity and in the development of Ukraine's written language and Ukrainian literature. The first editions had been censored by the Russian czar, but the book still made an enduring impact on Ukrainian culture. There is no reliable count of how many editions of the book have been published, but an official estimate made in 1976 put the figure in Ukraine at 110 during the Soviet period alone. That figure does not include Kobzars released before and after both in Ukraine and abroad. A multitude of translations of Shevchenko's verse into Slavic, Germanic and Romance languages, as well as Chinese, Japanese, Bengali, and many others attest to his impact on world culture as well.

SEVEN SIGNS OF THE LION

by Michael M. Naydan

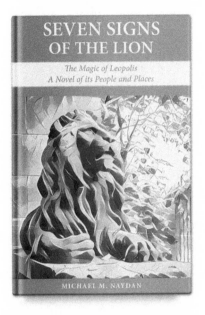

The novel *Seven Signs of the Lion* is a magical journey to the city of Lviv in Western Ukraine. Part magical realism, part travelogue, part adventure novel, and part love story, it is a fragmented, hybrid work about a mysterious and mythical place. The hero of the novel Nicholas Bilanchuk is a gatherer of living souls, the unique individuals he meets over the course of his five-month stay in his ancestral homeland. These include the enigmatic Mr. Viktor, who, with one eye that always glimmers, in a dream summons him across the Atlantic Ocean to the city of lions, becoming his spiritual mentor; the genius mathematician Professor Potojbichny (a man of science with a mystical bent and whose name means "man from the other side"); the exquisite beauty Ada, whose name suggests "woman from Hades" in Ukrainian, whose being emanates irresistible sensuality, but who never lets anyone capture her beauty in a picture; the schizophrenic artist Ivan the Ghostseer, who lives in a bohemian hovel of a basement apartment and in an alcohol-induced trance paints the spirits of the city that torment him; and the curly-haired elfin Raya, whose name suggests "paradise" in Ukrainian and who becomes the primary guide and companion for Nicholas on his journey to self-realization...

Buy it > www.glagoslav.com

HARDLY EVER OTHERWISE

by Maria Matios

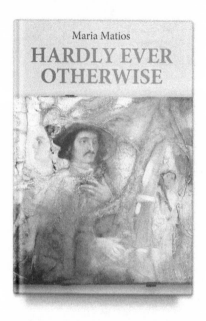

Everything eventually reaches its appointed place in time and space. Maria Matios's dramatic family saga, *Hardly Ever Otherwise*, narrates the story of several western Ukrainian families during the last decades of the Austro-Hungarian Empire, and expands upon the idea that "it isn't time that is important, but the human condition in time."

From the first page, Matios engages her reader with an impeccable style, which she employs to create a rich tapestry of cause and effect, at times depicting a logic that is both bitter and enigmatic. But nothing is ever fully revealed—it is only in the final pages of the novel that the events in the beginning are understood as a necessary part of a larger whole, and the section entitled Seasicknesspresents a compelling argument for why events almost always have to follow a particular course.

Buy it > www.glagoslav.com

THE LAWYER FROM LYCHAKIV STREET

by Andriy Kokotiukha

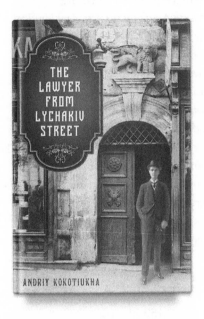

At the beginning of the twentieth century, 1908, a young Kyivan, Klym Koshovy miraculously flies the coop and escapes from persecution by tsarist police to Lviv. However, even here he is arrested – near the corpse of a well-known local lawyer, Yevhen Soyka. The deceased had dubious friends and powerful enemies in the city. Suicide or murder?

The search for truth leads Koshovy through the dark labyrinths of Lviv's streets. On his way – facing daring pickpockets, criminal kingpins and Russian terrorist bombers. And Klym is constantly getting in the way of the police commissioner Marek Wichura. The truth will stun Klym, and his new loyal friend Jozef Shatsky. It will forever change the fate of the enigmatic and influential beauty Magda Bohdanovych.

Buy it > www.glagoslav.com

Glagoslav Publications Catalogue

- *The Time of Women* by Elena Chizhova
- *Andrei Tarkovsky: A Life on the Cross* by Lyudmila Boyadzhieva
- *Sin* by Zakhar Prilepin
- *Hardly Ever Otherwise* by Maria Matios
- *Khatyn* by Ales Adamovich
- *The Lost Button* by Irene Rozdobudko
- *Christened with Crosses* by Eduard Kochergin
- *The Vital Needs of the Dead* by Igor Sakhnovsky
- *The Sarabande of Sara's Band* by Larysa Denysenko
- *A Poet and Bin Laden* by Hamid Ismailov
- *Zo Gaat Dat in Rusland* (Dutch Edition) by Maria Konjoekova
- *Kobzar* by Taras Shevchenko
- *The Stone Bridge* by Alexander Terekhov
- *Moryak* by Lee Mandel
- *King Stakh's Wild Hunt* by Uladzimir Karatkevich
- *The Hawks of Peace* by Dmitry Rogozin
- *Harlequin's Costume* by Leonid Yuzefovich
- *Depeche Mode* by Serhii Zhadan
- *Groot Slem en Andere Verhalen* (Dutch Edition) by Leonid Andrejev
- *METRO 2033* (Dutch Edition) by Dmitry Glukhovsky
- *METRO 2034* (Dutch Edition) by Dmitry Glukhovsky
- *A Russian Story* by Eugenia Kononenko
- *Herstories, An Anthology of New Ukrainian Women Prose Writers*
- *The Battle of the Sexes Russian Style* by Nadezhda Ptushkina
- *A Book Without Photographs* by Sergey Shargunov
- *Down Among The Fishes* by Natalka Babina
- *disUNITY* by Anatoly Kudryavitsky
- *Sankya* by Zakhar Prilepin
- *Wolf Messing* by Tatiana Lungin
- *Good Stalin* by Victor Erofeyev
- *Solar Plexus* by Rustam Ibragimbekov
- *Don't Call me a Victim!* by Dina Yafasova
- *Poetin* (Dutch Edition) by Chris Hutchins and Alexander Korobko

- *A History of Belarus* by Lubov Bazan
- *Children's Fashion of the Russian Empire* by Alexander Vasiliev
- *Empire of Corruption: The Russian National Pastime* by Vladimir Soloviev
- *Heroes of the 90s: People and Money. The Modern History of Russian Capitalism* by Alexander Solovev, Vladislav Dorofeev and Valeria Bashkirova
- *Fifty Highlights from the Russian Literature* (Dutch Edition) by Maarten Tengbergen
- *Bajesvolk* (Dutch Edition) by Michail Chodorkovsky
- *Dagboek van Keizerin Alexandra* (Dutch Edition)
- *Myths about Russia* by Vladimir Medinskiy
- *Boris Yeltsin: The Decade that Shook the World* by Boris Minaev
- *A Man Of Change: A study of the political life of Boris Yeltsin*
- *Sberbank: The Rebirth of Russia's Financial Giant* by Evgeny Karasyuk
- *To Get Ukraine* by Oleksandr Shyshko
- *Asystole* by Oleg Pavlov
- *Gnedich* by Maria Rybakova
- *Marina Tsvetaeva: The Essential Poetry*
- *Multiple Personalities* by Tatyana Shcherbina
- *The Investigator* by Margarita Khemlin
- *The Exile* by Zinaida Tulub
- *Leo Tolstoy: Flight from Paradise* by Pavel Basinsky
- *Moscow in the 1930* by Natalia Gromova
- *Laurus* (Dutch edition) by Evgenij Vodolazkin
- *Prisoner* by Anna Nemzer
- *The Crime of Chernobyl: The Nuclear Goulag* by Wladimir Tchertkoff
- *Alpine Ballad* by Vasil Bykau
- *The Complete Correspondence of Hryhory Skovoroda*
- *The Tale of Aypi* by Ak Welsapar
- *Selected Poems* by Lydia Grigorieva
- *The Fantastic Worlds of Yuri Vynnychuk*
- *The Garden of Divine Songs and Collected Poetry of Hryhory Skovoroda*
- *Adventures in the Slavic Kitchen: A Book of Essays with Recipes* by Igor Klekh
- *Seven Signs of the Lion* by Michael M. Naydan

- *Ravens before Noah* by Susanna Harutyunyan
- *An English Queen and Stalingrad* by Natalia Kulishenko
- *Point Zero* by Narek Malian
- *Absolute Zero* by Artem Chekh
- *Olanda* by Rafał Wojasiński
- *Robinsons* by Aram Pachyan
- *The Monastery* by Zakhar Prilepin
- *The Selected Poetry of Bohdan Rubchak: Songs of Love, Songs of Death, Songs of the Moon*
- *Mebet* by Alexander Grigorenko
- *The Orchestra* by Vladimir Gonik
- *Everyday Stories* by Mima Mihajlović
- *Slavdom* by Ľudovít Štúr
- *The Code of Civilization* by Vyacheslav Nikonov
- *Where Was the Angel Going?* by Jan Balaban
- *De Zwarte Kip* (Dutch Edition) by Antoni Pogorelski
- *Głosy / Voices* by Jan Polkowski
- *Sergei Tretyakov: A Revolutionary Writer in Stalin's Russia* by Robert Leach
- *Opstand* (Dutch Edition) by Władysław Reymont
- *Dramatic Works* by Cyprian Kamil Norwid
- *Children's First Book of Chess* by Natalie Shevando and Matthew McMillion
- *Precursor* by Vasyl Shevchuk
- *The Vow: A Requiem for the Fifties* by Jiří Kratochvil
- *De Bibliothecaris* (Dutch edition) by Mikhail Jelizarov
- *Subterranean Fire* by Natalka Bilotserkivets
- *Vladimir Vysotsky: Selected Works*
- *Behind the Silk Curtain* by Gulistan Khamzayeva
- The *Village Teacher and Other Stories* by Theodore Odrach
- *The Revolt of the Animals* by Wladyslaw Reymont
- *Illegal Parnassus* by Bojan Babić
- *Liza's Waterfall: The hidden story of a Russian feminist* by Pavel Basinsky
- *Duel* by Borys Antonenko-Davydovych
- *Biography of Sergei Prokofiev* by Igor Vishnevetsky
  More coming . . .

GLAGOSLAV PUBLICATIONS

www.glagoslav.com